FORBID

By Ki

INDEX

AUTHORS OTHER WORKS

WHATEVER IT TAKES
EAST END HONOUR
TRAFFICKED
BELL LANE LONDON E1
EAST END LEGACY
EAST END A FAMILY OF STEEL
PHILLIMORE PLACE LONDON
EAST END LOTTERY
FAMILY BUSINESS
A DANGEROUS MIND
FAMILY FIRST
A SCORE TO SETTLE (BOOK ONE)
A SCORE SETTLED
A DANGEROUS MIND (TWO)
BODILY HARM
SINS OF THE FATHER
GREED
EYE FOR AN EYE
CRIME DOESN'T PAY

Web site www.kimhunterauthor.com

QUOTES

"The greatest gift our parents ever gave us was each other."

Unknown

"Brothers and sisters are as close as hands and feet"

Vietnamese Proverb

Main characters

Richard Spires but known to all as Ritchie, is tall, muscular and very handsome. Sadly his personality doesn't match and he is always out for what he can get and cares little for the pain and suffering it causes others. Ritchie uses and discards women with no thought for their feelings until the day he gets caught by a scheming young woman and for him, there is no way out.

Michael Spires, known as Molly, is nothing like his older brother but what he lacks in good looks, he more than makes up for with his kind and caring personality. Whereas Ritchie has a different woman every weekend, Michael is holding out for the one and very rarely asks a girl out. He is even more particular about where he dips his wick and the thought of having sex with the kind of slappers his brother sleeps with appals him. Times were tough and the way the boys lived throughout their childhood was almost Dickensian. Leaving home as soon as they could, Ritchie and Michael found lodgings in a local pub and never looked back. The landlady had taken a shine to the boys, aware of the hardships they had endured she had taken them under her maternal wing.

Mavis McAllister and her husband Burt had run the Lamb public house in Holloway for more years than they cared to mention. Mavis was kind, the sort of woman who always wore an apron and who always had a big pot of stew on the stove out back for anyone she felt needed a hearty meal. A rotund, rosy-cheeked woman, Mavis was also able to hold her own and never needed Burt's assistance when it came to throwing out drunks. Burt was well known for running a good pub and adored his wife, anything Mavis wanted Mavis got, sadly the only thing he hadn't been able to give her was a child.

Sue Nelson was a nasty, greedy and spiteful young woman who took all that she could get without so much as a thank you, especially from her best friend Ellie who was as gentle as a lamb and would do anything not to upset her friend. The two women always went out on either Friday or Saturday nights and had recently started to drink in the pubs and clubs of Camden. Everything was fine until the night they met the Spires brothers, from then on nothing would be the same for any of them!

Ellie Evans was kind, caring and the polar opposite of her best friend Sue. She was also a natural beauty, much to her best friend's disgust. Sweet and kind to others she was liked by everyone but going out at weekends was often a chore. Ellie was on her feet all day at work and sometimes all she wanted was to go home and slob in front of the television but to even suggest such a thing would see her friend fly off the handle. Ellie hated confrontation of any kind so would never say anything to upset Sue just to keep the peace. Not looking for a relationship, Ellie was happy to accompany her friend who was desperate for a man and would go to any lengths to get one. Ellie wouldn't realise until years later just what a bully her so-called friend had been.

PROLOGUE

It was only eleven o'clock but Michael Spires was already propping up the bar in the Lamb public house. Lately, he had started to drink alone and the volume had begun to increase. He knew he had to get a grip or it would end up taking over and in his line of work that would be suicide. He was comfortably off, or at least he was financially but he had started to wonder what it was all for, he was forty-three years of age but felt like he was eighty and it wasn't down to the amount of work he did but the emotional pain he was suffering, without any chance of making things right. Looking at his glass and seeing that it was almost empty, he was about to get another drink when the front door opened and in she walked, the only woman he had ever loved and she was as beautiful now as she'd been on the day they had met over twenty years earlier. Oh, there were a few more lines under her eyes and when she was tired the dark circles would begin to appear but to Michael, she would always be the most beautiful girl in the world.

"Hi love, get everything you needed?"

"No not everything, I swear that place does it on purpose."

Eyeing his drink her brow furrowed and he knew she wasn't happy.

"You're starting early again."

"Don't kick off again babe, I just felt like one okay?"

"Michael I'm not kicking off as you put it but you seem to be spending more time sitting at the bar than you do in the house. I know you miss her; don't you think it's the same for me? If I went down the same road as you we'd be bankrupt in a few months. Some days I struggle to even get out of bed but if I stayed there what good would it do? We have a life darling and with or without her we have to make that life as happy as we can. Now pull yourself together for God's sake. No one knows if they will ever come back but if they do, would you want her to find out that her dad has turned into a pisshead?"

She could see the pool of tears in his eyes and the hurt her words had caused and suddenly she embraced him and clung on as if she was never going to let go. He didn't know what he'd done to deserve her but he was one lucky man.

"Changing the subject, can you go and pick me mum up later from the bingo only her old legs are playing her up and I don't want her trying to get the bus at her age."

"Will do, I'll make this my last."

Draining his glass he stepped from the stool and picked up her shopping bags.

"Come on, let's get this lot put away."

"Thanks. Oh, by the way, I'm thinking of booking a holiday, we haven't been away since,bloody hell Michael we haven't been on holiday since our honeymoon. If the hotel is still there do you fancy seeing if we can go back to the same place? Try and rekindle a bit of the old romance?"

Smiling he leaned in and planted a big kiss on her cheek.

"I like the sound of that sweetheart and yes, I would love to."

CHAPTER ONE
20 Years earlier

Yet to be modernised the Victoria Tavern or the Vic
as all the locals referred to it and who would when
asked, describe it as a spit and sawdust kind of place,
was a rough pub and one you didn't venture into
unless you were a regular. A Public house since 1856,
Marty Stone had been the landlord for the past five
years but he hadn't done much to the pub by way of
decoration in that time. His only interest was making
money and often the bar wouldn't get cleaned for
several days in a row and at times even weeks. The
beer pipes weren't regularly flushed making the ale
taste off more than it tasted good. The urinals stank to
high heavens with dry excrement visible in all three
toilet pans so unless you were desperate, you avoided
them like the plague. The pub was so bad that it put
off anyone who wasn't a hardened drinker and even if
they had dared to cross the threshold, an act that
without knowing anyone or being invited inside, you
took your life in your hands to do so.
Albie and Rita Spires belonged to the group of
hardened drinkers and though they were in the pub
every night, Saturdays were known as bender days.
After being on the lash from lunchtime opening on
Saturday, by early evenings the couple were like a
tinder box waiting to go up. It was a turbulent
marriage at the best of times but when heavy drinking
and weekly domestic fights that no one dared to
intervene in were added to the mix, Saturdays were
by far the worst. For work, Albie held a dock job at

1

Gainsborough Wharf where he unloaded any cargo that came into port as well as helping himself to anything that would fit into his overcoat pockets. For beer and pin money, Rita did two days a week on a fruit and veg stall in Chapel Market. As with most marriages of that era, he paid the bills and she paid for some of the alcohol but there was very little left over for luxuries and food was thin on the ground, to say the least. Albie would regularly set about his wife with his fists and it was usually Saturdays when the beatings occurred or were at their worst. Normally he would wait until they got home but if she really riled him he was known to give her a swift backhander in front of everyone. Rita would retaliate as best she could and had been known to throw a glass at her husband on occasion which always resulted in them being evicted from the premises where the fighting would happily continue on the road outside. Marty Stone never barred them permanently; they spent too much money for that but at times it even got too much for him. The following lunchtime the couple would reappear as if nothing had happened and the drinking would begin all over again.

With little more than two years between them and born in 1975 and 77, Richie and Michael Spires were as close as any two humans could be. Raised in a two-bedroom flat on the third floor of a converted Victorian terrace on Holloway Road, the brothers had sadly been born to Rita and Albie Spires. Neither of the adults was remotely interested in being a parent but both times Rita had been too far along in her pregnancy before she attempted to seek out medical intervention and was instantly refused an abortion. Albie had even beaten his wife while she was pregnant with Ritchie, in his sick mind it had been his idea to force a miscarriage but sadly for all concerned, it hadn't worked. On one occasion when Ritchie was around six years old, his father, in a drunken stupor, had lashed out at Rita, Richie had naïvely tried to protect his mother but he only ever tried that once as he ended up with a black eye and his mother did nothing to protect him, in fact, Ritchie thought he saw her smiling. Rita's eyes were bruised so often that none of the stallholders even bothered to inquire or even comment any more. For the boys, it wouldn't have been so bad if their father was nice to them but in truth, he was a horrible man who they quickly came to despise. Rita wasn't much better, she didn't care about her kids and their clothes were often dirty when they went to school. Left to their own devices each night while their parents went to the Victoria the boys would watch television when there was enough money in the meter or read the second-hand comics that Albie picked up from only God knew where. The only thing their father had ever given them without complaint was his looks as both boys were handsome even as small children, though over the years Michael seemed to have somewhat lost his compared to his brother. When Albie kicked off at his kids it was legendary and all Michael could do was stare at his father. The look of disgust from a small child would wind Albie up even more and he would slap Michael hard around the face in an attempt to wipe away the look. It never worked and over the years Michael knew and accepted what was coming but somehow he couldn't stop giving that look of disgust. There was no parental guidance whatsoever and in all honesty, it was Ritchie who raised his little brother and from birth had called him Molly as he'd struggled to pronounce Michael. Before he had even started school Ritchie knew how to change a nappy and make up a bottle of formula. Social Service were never involved as no one had reported their neglect, everyone turned a blind eye, in the East End you didn't get involved in other people's business and it was something neither boy would ever forget. Hunger was a constant and often Molly would cry only to be consoled by his big brother who told him that one day things would be better, one day they would be out of this shithole and would never be hungry again.

By the time Ritchie reached eighteen things in the flat were almost at boiling point. Ritchie was working as a pot man at the Lamb public house situated at the other end of Holloway Road. The shifts were long and tiring but getting any real sleep was almost impossible when his parents started one of their usual fights. The Lamb was run by Mavis and Burt McAllister. It was old school like the Vic but that's where any similarity ended. Mavis was house proud and everything, from the bottles to the glasses, shone like a new pin. Burt's beer was known to be some of the best in the area and although frequented by many locals, the couple wouldn't stand for any shenanigans and would regularly bar anyone who got too rowdy and unlike the Victoria, it was a permanent barring. The landlord and landlady had never been blessed with children and Mavis in particular had taken an instant liking to Ritchie. She always provided him with a hot meal on shift and would turn a blind eye when he placed any leftovers into a plastic container as she knew he was taking them home. Ritchie had shared his story with the woman early on in his employment and knowing there was another hungry mouth to feed at home, she often overloaded Ritchie's plate on purpose.

Molly was still in school but he hardly ever attended. It concerned his brother but when the truancy officer had called at the flat he'd been sent away with the threat of violence from Albie. The authorities never followed up on the absences, there was no point as issuing a fine would just be ignored and these kids almost always reverted to a life of crime so there was little reason to waste time or resources. Albie and Rita had only dared to show up at the Lamb once in the hope of getting free drinks from their eldest. The embarrassment was evident on Ritchie's face and Mavis was heartbroken for him. Telling him to fetch a box from the cellar so that he wouldn't hear what she was about to say, she served the pair with a drink on the house and then told them they were not welcome and if they ever darkened her doorstep again she wouldn't be responsible for her actions, well, that was the polite version. After finishing their drinks there were a few choice words from Rita but Albie just shrugged his shoulders and pulling on his wife's coat sleeve led her out of the front door.

Six months later Molly finally completed his time in education. Unlike his brother, Michael didn't have a temper unless pushed to the extreme. A bright boy he could have achieved a lot but school had bored him senseless and even though he was hard-working when he bothered to attend, there were no exams taken or diplomas to show for the last eleven years. Eventually, Ritchie managed to get his younger brother a job running errands for one of the illegal bookmakers and loan sharks in the area, a bloke everyone called Porky Smith. The man regularly drank in the Lamb and was only too happy to help out but it wasn't long before Molly began to loathe the work even though both brothers were bringing in a decent wage. They were now able to contribute to the home and to start with their parents took the majority of their son's earnings and began drinking down the Vic even more, if that was at all possible. Four months on the situation on Holloway Road changed overnight. It had been the usual Saturday bender day and after closing, Albie and Rita had managed to stagger home. For the entire length of the road, they shouted and laughed loudly so as to wake and piss off as many of the other tenants in the buildings as possible. People could be heard calling out from the flats below and above to 'Keep the noise down' but it didn't make a difference. As soon as the front door was closed, Rita started moaning about the state of the place and Albie turned on her with such brutality that the punch he landed saw her feet lift off of the ground and she ended up on the other side of the small kitchen. Having only been home for a short while and now hauling himself out of bed, Ritchie winked at Michael who had the sheet pulled up tightly around his neck, he had a temper but loathed violence. There was just one problem, as it was happening in his own home, he couldn't do anything to get away from it. As much as Michael couldn't bear conflict and would never retaliate unless pushed to his limits, his brother was a different kettle of fish and would go in all guns blazing at the drop of a hat.

"I've had enough of those fuckers! Stay here Molly; I'm going to sort them out once and for all."

Now Michael pulled the bedclothes over his head in an attempt to block out the heightened noise that he knew would begin at any second. Walking along the hallway Ritchie stopped in the doorway of the kitchen just in time to see Albi standing over his wife with a knife in his hand. He was foaming at the mouth like a madman and was only seconds away from ending his wife's life but it only took a couple of strides before Ritchie was beside his father and had knocked the knife out of his hand.

"Leave her alone you old cunt!"

"Why you little bastard!"

Albie lunged forward but he was so drunk that when Ritchie quickly moved to one side, the old man fell flat on his face.

"Touch any of us again and I'll break your fucking skull you cunt!"

Offering Rita his hand to help her to her feet it was instantly slapped away as she moved over to her husband and began sobbing as she stroked his brow.

"What did you do that for you little bastard, you've hurt him. Come on Albie darlin' get up now."

"You'll never learn Mum, will you? Both of you have been shit parents, all you've ever cared about is how much piss you could both get down your necks!"

7

With that, Ritchie marched back to the bedroom and told his brother to pack which didn't take but a few minutes as neither of them had much in the way of clothing or possessions. It was raining heavily but it didn't bother either of them and fifteen minutes later they were standing outside the back door of the Lamb. After knocking heavily on the door the two lads waited for someone to come downstairs.

Expecting to see Burt McAllister they were shocked when Mavis opened up.

"Lord above! What are you two doing out this late at night and in this weather? Don't answer that as I can hazard a good guess. Look at the state of you both; you're soaked to the skin. Well, don't let all the hot air out, come on inside."

Mavis led the boys through to the kitchen and placed the kettle on to boil. Sitting at the large scrubbed pine table Ritchie and Michael sat in silence but both hoping with all they had that Mavis would at least give them a bed for the night.

"Here you go. A nice mug of cocoa will soon warm you up."

Joining them at the table, Mavis didn't engage again until the mugs were drained dry.

"You'll have to share as I only have one spare bed but at least it's a double and if I do say so myself, with its feather mattress it's far more comfy than my bed. In this trade, you don't get many visitors so I suppose you're lucky I even have a spare. Come on then, let's get you both tucked in."

Just as they had been told, the bed was sumptuous and the brothers had never had such comfort or slept so well. When they woke to the smell of bacon frying

8

they were out of bed in seconds and scrambled to get dressed. Taking the stairs two at a time as they entered the kitchen they came face to face with Burt sitting at the table reading his newspaper. Mavis was at the stove and she turned and smiled warmly at her visitors.

"Take a seat you two; it'll be ready in a minute."
She must have already had a conversation about them with her husband as Burt McAllister never said a word and they would soon learn that he loved her so deeply that he granted Mavis everything she asked for. Fresh bread had been sliced into thick doorstops, butter was in a dish and when Mavis put a massive plate of crispy bacon onto the table, both boys were salivating and didn't need to be told twice to tuck in.

"Now, Burt and I have been talking and as you work here Ritchie and you have now left school Michael, well, if you want to stay here you are more than welcome. I will expect you to both pay a nominal rent, let's say twenty pounds a week each but for that you will get two hot meals a day, a bed and your laundry will be done for you. So, what do you think?"
The boys beamed from ear to ear and nodded so hard she thought their heads would roll off at any moment. Little did they know that Mavis would save their rent money and come the day that they eventually moved on, she would hand it all back. If the truth was told, they needed the youngsters as much as Ritchie and Michael needed them but it wasn't anything to do with finances. Being childless was lonely, especially for Mavis and having two strapping lads to take care of was like a dream come true for the woman.
Back in their room as they dressed for work Molly

suddenly stopped and turned towards his brother.
"You was right Ritchie,"
"About what?"
"You said one day things would be better and we wouldn't ever be hungry again and you were right."
"Yeah, I suppose I was. Come on or you'll be late and you know how Porky hates that."

By the time Ritchie reached twenty-two and Michael twenty, they had been living at the Lamb for the past four years and it was now well and truly home. Although they didn't call the McAlister's mum and dad, for all intent and purpose that's exactly what they were. Burt would always be Burt but the boys now called Mavis, Aunty and it made her heart swell every time she heard it. It was a miracle but Albie and Rita were still alive and still drinking and fighting. Their paths rarely crossed with those of their son's but when it did happen, Ritchie and Michael would walk to the other side of the road rather than have to come face to face with their mother and father. It wasn't anything to do with fear, nothing could have been further from the truth, the boys were embarrassed and ashamed that anyone should know that the sad pair was their parents. Rita only called again at the Lamb once in all the time that the boys had been living there. She wasn't missing the love of her children but simply their rent money but she was swiftly sent away with a flea in her ear by Mavis and never dared to go back again. Knowing that she had to tell Ritchie and Michael about the meeting, Mavis was worried about how her boys would react and if they would be upset with her but all they did was laugh and then hold her close.

"Good on you Aunty, hopefully the old bitch has finally got the message."

CHAPTER TWO

Ritchie worked the bar at lunchtime and in the evening for five days a week but he was given every Saturday and Sunday off. Mavis knew that young people liked to socialise at the weekend and as she and Burt were past any real socialising outside of the pub, the setup worked well. The regulars all liked Ritchie, he was polite, funny and good at his job but after being a barman for over four years he had started to get bored. Sharing his woes one lunchtime with a regular called Bunter Dennis, a man who was renowned for being hard and also a local gangster, Ritchie was shocked when out of the blue Bunter offered him a job. Luckily Mavis wasn't within earshot or she would have been devastated.

"I was thinking of branching out on me own, so what would working for you entail Mr Dennis?"

"Well, you start at the bottom running errands and if you're any good, promotion will swiftly follow. I'm sixty-six this year Ritchie and to be honest, I'm fucked! Me health ain't the best and I ain't got anyone to take over after I'm gone, or at least no fucker of any worth. I've been watching you son and you're bright and steady and if you're interested I think you might have what it takes."

"Can I think about it?"

For a second Bunter didn't reply but the frown on his face spoke volumes.

"Certainly but don't take too long kid, a lot of the local wide boys would give their fuckin' back teeth for an opportunity like this."

"Just twenty-four hours Mr Dennis, I need to have a word with Burt and Mavis. They have treated me and my brother like sons and I don't want to upset them or leave them in the lurch."

"Loyalty, that's another trait I like. Okay, I'll pop in again tomorrow for a pint."

With that, Bunter downed the last of his drink and then left. For the rest of his shift, Ritchie couldn't stop smiling but at the same time, he was worried about what Mavis and Burt would say. After closing up for a few hours, Ritchie went for a lay down in his room after deciding to discuss the offer with Molly before speaking to the McAlister's.

At around three that afternoon, Michael returned home and just as always, he went straight up to the bedroom he and Ritchie shared. Opening the door he was taken aback when he saw his brother lying on the bed.

"You okay bro, ain't ill are you?"

Ritchie sat up and swung his legs over the side of the mattress.

"No, but I do need to have a talk with you. Bunter Dennis has offered me a job but I don't want to let Mavis and Burt down."

"No worries, I can take your place. To be honest I'm getting fed up with working for Porky. I do the same thing day in and day out and there ain't any chance of a promotion. I quite fancy being a barman and talking to people. So, what do you say?"

Standing up, Ritchie walked over to his brother and hugged him.

"I say yes, come on let's go and tell Aunty."

Just about to call her boys to the table, she smiled

warmly as they both entered the kitchen. Burt was already seated and was puffing away on his pipe as he read the last few pages of his newspaper.

"You two look like the cats that got the cream, what have you been up to?"

Taking their places, Mavis put down two large plates of mutton stew in front of them but Ritchie didn't start as he wanted to break the news first.

"What's up boy, you not hungry?"

"I have something to share with you but hear me out before you both hit the roof. Bunter Dennis has offered me a job and I want to take it but at the same time, I don't want to let you two down. Anyway, I've talked it over with Molly and he would like to take my place behind the bar instead of working for Porky. So, what do you say?"

Mavis and Burt looked at each other and for a few seconds they didn't speak. She was hurt but wouldn't show it and when she shrugged her shoulders her husband knew what she meant. Strangely it was Burt who spoke.

"I think you should take Bunter up on his offer and welcome aboard Michael."

Smiles filled the room and then everyone began to tuck into the delicious meal.

A month later everything was going well. Michael had taken to working the bar like a duck to water, he loved the banter with customers and the fact that most days he was left to his own devices made him feel important as if he was in charge. Mavis and Burt were pleased and now took more and more time off from serving and it suited Michael to be his own boss.

Ritchie was enjoying the work with Bunter and within three months would become Bunter's right-hand man. To begin with, he was tasked with just errands but was soon beside his boss during negotiations. Bunter was planning a robbery on the Wine House, a wholesale alcohol warehouse and it excited Ritchie more than frightened him. Up until now, he hadn't shared any of his work details, not even with Molly but Michael wasn't too bothered when his questions were met with a blank stare. The boys went out most weekends but were respectful of their home and if one of them got lucky and picked up a girl, sex was back at her place or down some side alley. It soon became a competition and due to Molly being shy and very choosey, Ritchie was winning hands down. The job Bunter was planning was arranged to take place the following Saturday so there would be no socialising that weekend.

D day arrived and when Ritchie told Molly that he wouldn't be going out that night Molly knew something was in the pipeline.

"So, what's going down?"

Ritchie knew he shouldn't share any information but Molly was the only person in the entire world he trusted, would trust him with his life if it came to it.

"Bunters men are turning over the Wine House, so expect Mavis to be getting some cheap bottles pretty soon."

"What's your part?"

"I'm just the driver being it's my first real job but I can't wait to get started Molly, I'm going to take over that business one day."

"Course you are and pigs will fucking fly."

15

"No, seriously, it came straight from Bunter's mouth. Seeing as he ain't got any kids he said it might as well be me. We're going places, little bro, you mark my words."

"Well I'll wait and see but a driver? You ain't exactly got much experience have you?"

"I passed my test."

"That was four years ago and you ain't been behind a wheel since."

Ritchie raised his eyebrows but didn't add anything further. Soon after, the boys entered the kitchen ready for their evening meal and as usual, they were both starving. With the food consumed, Ritchie pulled on his coat and headed out. Mavis frowned, this was out of the ordinary and she turned to face Michael.

"Are you not going with him, son?"

"Not tonight Mavis, I think he's on a promise so he doesn't want me tagging along. You want me to do the bar tonight?"

"That's kind of you Michael but a deal is a deal and Saturday is your day off. Besides, Boysie Marsh is coming in later with some women's knock-off undies and I don't think you're the best one to judge if they're any good or not."

Michael laughed, his landlady was right; he was only interested in getting knickers off not what the quality was. After Ritchie set off, Michael switched on the television in the kitchen but there wasn't anything that held his interest. Something in the back of his mind was nagging away but he couldn't work out what it was. Feeling frustrated and a little anxious he decided to call it a day and have an early night but sleep wouldn't come easily.

Ritchie arrived at Bunter's lockup at the end of Biddeston Road and was greeted by Bezel and Dickie, two locals who carried out most of Bunter's jobs plus they did the odd freelance blag for any other firms who were willing to pay.

"Hi there Ritchie boy, how they hanging?"

"All good thanks Bezel. Are we all ready to go?"

"Sure are. Dickie, stop fucking about and get in the van will you."

Dickie Mason was a ditherer but he was also a fighter and definitely someone you wanted by your side if things kicked off. Dickie gave Bezel a look of contempt but didn't say anything, the two had come to blows on more than one occasion in the past and tonight would go better if they weren't at each other's throats. A few minutes later and with Ritchie in the driver's seat, Bezel beside him and Dickie sitting in the rear on an old uncomfortable cushion, the trio set off. The Wine House was situated on Biggerstaff Street in Finsbury Park and at just under a mile away the journey would only take a few minutes. The van was getting on in years, hadn't been well maintained and as it chugged along threw out billowing black smoke not to mention that Dickie was being thrown from one side to the other in the rear.

"Fuck me! You sure you can drive?"

"Of course, I can but this is a piece of crap, I thought Bunter would have provided something fucking newer. The Old Bill could pull us over just for the fumes that this piece of shit is spewing out!"

There was no reply to the sarcasm but Bezel was staring directly at Ritchie making him feel uncomfortable and a tad embarrassed. Biggerstaff had properties on both sides and the street crossed Fonthill Road and then ran into Pooles Park. In the centre was Clifton Court, a nineteen-storey block of flats and not the most private place to carry out a robbery. At the rear of the flats surrounded by a wire fence was a small brick unit. The building was unassuming and with no name to indicate what trade was carried out inside so it was mostly forgotten about by the locals. As the van came around the corner kangarooing and with gears crunching it couldn't be said that the robbers were quiet. As soon as it came to a stop, Bezel jumped out with a pair of bolt croppers in his hand and began to snip away at the fence, the plan was for Ritchie to drive inside once there was enough space. A single door sat beside a roller shutter and with the promise of what was inside, they needed to be as close as possible to load up. In a ground floor flat opposite the building, Gertrude Long was looking out of her front window. In her eighties, Gertie lived alone and would often spend her days just standing behind the net curtain looking for any life that wasn't as boring or as lonely as her own. At night she could be even more nosey as she didn't turn the lights on so couldn't be seen. Hearing the van first, she watched and soon became suspicious but as the vehicle was blocking her view and she couldn't see what Bezel was up to, Gertrude decided to call the police just in case the men were up to no good. Within a few minutes a patrol car came screeching to a halt and blocking any hope of the van's escape, Ritchie froze and just placed his hands on the steering wheel as he slowly began to shake his head from side to side. Dickie was screaming for

Ritchie to let him out but Ritchie didn't dare move and was frozen to his seat in fear. Bezel tried to run but as he barged past the first policeman he was tasered by the second and immediately dropped to the floor groaning out in pain. The first officer, PC Dermot removed his own taser and baton before walking over to the van. He didn't give any order for Ritchie to get out in case the culprit was armed and instead waited for the transport vehicle to arrive. When it did, Dickie and Ritchie were searched and then swiftly placed inside but Bezel was taken separately to the station in the back of the patrol car. Dickie bent forwards and began to whisper.
"Ritchie, when we get to the nick, keep your fucking trap shut! Bunter will know that the job has gone bad and he'll get his brief down to the station as soon as he can."
"Okay, okay, I ain't a fucking idiot you know."
"I know you ain't son but you'd be surprised when they start questioning you how easy it is to fucking cave in."

When Michael woke up he turned over expecting to come face to face with his brother but the bed was empty. Moving the palm of his hand across the surface, he could feel the cold and knew that Ritchie hadn't come home last night. Fear began to build in the pit of his stomach and getting out of bed he quickly dressed and headed downstairs in the hope that Mavis or Burt would have some news.
Mavis was in her usual place in front of the cooker frying up bacon and turned when she heard the door open.

"Morning sunshine! Why darlin', you're as white as a ghost, whatever's the matter?"

"Ritchie didn't come home last night."

"Oh you know him; he's probably getting his leg over somewhere. Don't worry; I'm sure he'll be back soon."

"You don't understand Aunty; he was doing a job last night for Bunter."

Now it was Mavis's turn to worry and carrying the plate of bacon over to the table, she took a seat and poured out three mugs of tea and as if on cue, Burt who had been in the lavatory, walked in holding his stomach.

"That's better! Let some out so I can get some in."

He laughed at his joke but stopped abruptly when he saw the look on his wife and Michael's faces.

"What's up?"

"Ritchie didn't come home last night Burt and before you say it, I already have. He was on a job for Bunter. Oh Burt, whatever's going on?"

"Now calm down the pair of you. Let me have me breakfast and I'll go and see Bunter."

"Can't you get him on the blower?"

"You know better than that darlin', you never know whose listening."

Even Burt McAllister knew that you didn't discuss jobs like Bunter carried out over the phone. True to his word after filling his ever-expanding belly he donned his trilby hat and set off for Bunters warehouse on Biddestone Road. Lorraine Estate Community Centre was right next door and the local youths would congregate outside but no one dared to go anywhere near Bunter's place of business.

Knocking on the wooden door Burt waited to be

invited inside. A few seconds later a small wooden hatch slid open and a pair of eyes stared back at him. It was Skinny Lane and he'd been Bunter's right-hand henchman for as long as Burt could remember.
"Yeah?"
"It's Burt from the Lamb, I need to see Bunter."
The hatch slammed shut and a few seconds later the door opened just enough for Burt to pass through. Skinny looked menacing and Burt knew his name was obviously a joke as the man stood over six feet tall and was at least three feet wide. No words were spoken and as Skinny walked away Burt took it upon himself to follow. Led through the building that was full of crates and boxes in all manner of sizes, the two stopped when they reached a small office situated at the back. Skinny knocked on the door and after pushing it open slightly, turned and walked away.
"Hello Burt my old son. Bit of a change for you to be on my premises but unlike you, I ain't earning any money from your visit."
Bunter Dennis started to laugh, a deep belly laugh that Burt didn't find in the least bit amusing.
"So what can I do for you?"
"I've come to see if you know where Ritchie is. Mavis is worried sick and Molly isn't much better."
Suddenly Bunter's face was solemn and getting up from his chair he walked around the desk and stopped when he was directly in front of Burt McAllister.
"Ain't you heard? The lads were doing a job for me last night and it went tits up. The silly fuckers took the oldest van I have and they all got nabbed by the Old Bill but I wouldn't worry too much, it's Ritchie's first offence so even though he's been remanded, I

21

reckon he'll get off with some kind of work in the community. Go and calm down your old lady and as soon as I have any news I'll drop by the boozer and update you."

Burt thanked the man though he didn't know what he was saying thank you for. Heading back to the Lamb he felt a bundle of nerves, Mavis would do her nut when she found out what had occurred.

CHAPTER THREE
1999

It took three months for the case to come to court and in that time Michael visited his brother every week in prison. Ritchie tried to assure Molly that he was fine and it wasn't as bad inside as people made out but Molly wasn't convinced. Ritchie looked gaunt and he seemed to be on edge every time Michael visited. Finally, it was time for Ritchie to receive his punishment and standing in the dock along with Bezel and Dickie he assumed, as he'd been told by Bunter's brief, that it was just a formality. Doing as he'd been advised, Michael pleaded guilty and was expecting a community service order of some kind. Both Bezel and Dickie each received five-year sentences as they had several previous convictions and after they were led away pleading that they had been set up, the judge turned to Ritchie.

"Mr Spires, I am aware of your previous good character and that this is your first offence. However, that said I need to send a message to any other young men thinking of taking the same path that you have chosen. A life of crime will only lead to heartache and many more years incarcerated at Her Majesty's pleasure which you will soon find out if you continue down this path. Therefore, I sentence you to three years, take him down officers."

Ritchie couldn't speak he was too stunned but he could hear Michael shouting out from the gallery that it wasn't fair, that his brother shouldn't be going to jail and with each word, it felt like a knot grew in the pit of Ritchie's stomach. He had always promised his little brother he would take care of him and would never leave him but now he was doing just that and his heart ached Taken straight outside to the prison van, he was placed into a small caged area and could just make out Bezel and Dickie who were in two separate cages at the far end of the van.

"You okay Ritchie boy?"

Ritchie exhaled deeply and at the same time, he could feel the stinging tears as they dropped onto his cheeks. Wiping his nose with the cuff of his jacket he sniffed loudly.

"Yeah I'm okay Bezel; we'll be out before you know it, mate."

"You will at any rate but me and old Dickie are season ticket holders, it ain't the first and no doubt it won't be the last time we'll be on our way to the pokey. Keep your chin up mate and take all the advice you can get from the seasoned veterans if it's offered."

After a short drive, Ritchie was taken out of the van and as the doors closed behind him he began to panic. Still reeling from the shock of his sentence, he was now feeling scared at the thought of not having the others as backup. After being handed his uniform of a t-shirt, sweat pants and top, along with a pair of socks, the door to Ritchie's cell slammed shut. By three that afternoon, Ritchie was alone in a first-night single-holding cell in Wormwood Scrubs. Bezel and Dickie had been sent over to HMP Pentonville but at least they were together. Thankful at least that he was allowed to wear his trainers, Ritchie changed and then lay down on the small bed. The noise was horrific with men screaming and shouting which continued long into the night. It was also cold and the prison-issue blanket was rough and offered little comfort so he stayed fully clothed. Eventually after imagining being in the feather bed back at the Lamb, he finally drifted off. Woken at six by the sound of keys clanking in the locks and cell doors banging open Ritchie stood up when his door opened. A burley officer who he would come to know as Banksy and who took no prisoners when it came to inmates, told Ritchie in a booming voice to go and take a shower. Nervously making his way along the landing all kinds of horrific images were flashing through his mind as he stepped into the tiled area. A row of eight units that were at the moment mostly empty, were situated along the back wall. There was no privacy and a row of hooks to hang his towel on along with a bench to place his clothes, were the only furnishings in the block. Right up until he was again dressed he was on his guard but he needn't have worried as the shower passed without event. Next, he tried out the canteen and in all honesty, the food wasn't that bad but in no way was it a patch on the crispy bacon that Mavis served but at least it was edible.

Mid-morning, when Ritchie was just lying on his bed staring up at the ceiling wondering how he came to be in this mess, his door opened. It was Officer Banksy who informed him to get his possessions together as he was being moved to a shared cell on B Wing. As Ritchie walked down the steel staircase he felt all eyes were on him and he had never felt so small or intimidated in his life. It seemed to take forever to reach B Wing as they passed through gate after locked gate. Finally, Banksy stopped and opened a door. Ritchie stepped inside and the grim reality of what his life was now going to be, hit home like a bolt of lightning. A middle-aged man who lay on the bottom bunk and soon introduced himself as Wilko Lemon, freely gave the information that he was doing a two-stretch for street robbery. He seemed friendly enough but Ritchie had been warned by Bunter to trust no one. The cell door had to remain open until lock up so prisoners were passing by throughout the day but when a man stepped inside Wilko was on his feet in seconds.

"What the fuck do you want?"

The man who was around sixty years of age and who Ritchie would soon come to learn was the gofer for the wing ruler, one Archie Culver, held up his hands in a sign of surrender.

"Easy pal! I'm only here with a message."

Wilko gave a look that said 'Well then?'

"Not for you Lemon, for him."

He pointed at Ritchie and suddenly Ritchie's guts were in knots again. He hadn't been here long enough to piss anyone off so who on earth wanted to speak to him?

"Guvnor wants a word. Top landing, cell six, ten minutes."

With that, the messenger turned and left and Wilko stood with his mouth open for several seconds.

"What the fuck have you done!?"

"Done? I ain't done anything. Who's in cell six?"

"Only fucking Archie Culver. He rules this wing, can get anything you want for a price and will take out a bloke just for looking at him the wrong way. That

26

little wanker is so far up Archie's arse and will sell you out in a second so never let him hear you say anything, good or bad about Culver."

"What if I don't go?"

"You ain't got a fucking option kid unless you want your face rearranged. When you get there, knock and wait, never go into a man's pad without an invite okay?"

A few minutes later and after sighing heavily, Ritchie left the cell and went up to the top landing. Doing as he was advised he tapped on the door and waited until he heard a voice say 'Enter!' Archie Culver was nothing like Ritchie had expected and he did his best to hide his surprise. Standing only five feet six tall and not overly muscular it was hard to see how he was such a hard man.

"Pleased to meet you, Ritchie. Bunter is a long-time friend and associate and he's asked me to keep an eye out for you, make your time here a little easier if you know what I mean. You won't get taxed on your canteen and the wing fags won't bother you unless you want them to."

With wide eyes, Ritchie vigorously shook his head much to Archie's amusement.

"Is there anything you need son?"

"No, I'm fine and thank you, Mister Culver."

Ritchie returned to his cell wearing a broad grin and couldn't wait to tell Wilko all that had occurred.

"You're still in one piece so I take it that it wasn't bad news?"

"No, not at all. Seems my boss is a friend of his and Mr Culver will be looking out for me. Wilko? I couldn't see why everyone is so scared of the man; I mean it isn't as if he's built like a mountain or anything?"

"Size means nothing in here or on the outside Ritchie. Archie Culver is a psychopath, you know he once boiled a rival alive, he's sick in the head and as much as he said he will look out for you, my advice for what it's worth is to stay well clear of him."

Ritchie sagely nodded his head and decided that if he didn't mix with the others then hopefully he couldn't get into much bother, a wise idea to begin with but the boredom soon set in.

The following Saturday afternoon he finally decided to venture out. The communal room was showing Tottenham V Arsenal in the premier league on the television and being a lifelong supporter of the Gunners, Richie was desperate to see the match. Wilko wasn't into footie so he declined the offer to go along. The room was crammed and every seat was full so it was standing room only at the back. It made for a good atmosphere, almost like being at the match in person. Half time and it was one nil to Tottenham. The Spurs supporters were feeling smug after Allan Nielsen had scored in the twenty-eighth minute and the Gunners were all on the edge of their seats. When Ray Parlour scored in the sixty-second minute there was uproar. The Spurs supporters began throwing their chairs against the wall and seconds later a mass brawl erupted. The sirens went off signalling a riot and as quickly as he could Ritchie slipped out of the door before it was locked. Running back to his cell he slammed the door behind him and woke Wilko who had been having an afternoon nap.

"What the fuck!"

"Sorry mate but it's like a bleedin' war zone in the communal and I only just escaped from being locked inside."

Ritchie wasn't a coward by any means but nor was he an idiot and to get mixed up in a fight that could result in him serving extra time was a no-brainer.

"Good match I take it!?"

As Ritchie sat down on his bed they both began to laugh. Out on the landings, the noise was horrendous and officers wearing riot gear could be heard running up and down. Suddenly all the doors were locked and sighing with relief, Ritchie Spires was just glad he made it out in time.

On Holloway Road, Michael was still pulling pints at the Lamb and after he'd taken over from his brother the customers had instantly taken to him which was helpful. Since Ritchie's incarceration, he'd been down in the dumps and Mavis tried anything she could to cheer him up but nothing seemed to be working. On a quiet lunchtime six months into his new job, the door opened and Bunter Dennis entered.

"Hi Molly my old son, how's tricks?"

"Can't complain but I ain't half missing me brother."

"It's only to be expected sunshine. How do you feel about coming to work at my firm? Since Ritchie got slammed up, not to mention Dickie and Bezel, I'm a fair few bodies down."

As he poured the man a pint of Guinness, Michael took a few moments to mull over the offer. He quite fancied being a bit of a gangster, although it had to be one with no violence attached if that even existed. He was sure Ritchie wouldn't mind but Mavis and Burt might be a bit harder to convince.

"What happens when me bother gets out? I mean will I be out on me ear?"

"No problem, I'd be happy to have you both on board."

Michael accepted there and then but he didn't have an easy ride when it came to telling Mavis and it wasn't because she was losing her barman.

"Oh Molly, I don't think that's a good idea love. What if things go wrong and you end up inside like your brother? I couldn't bear it if both of my boys were banged up."

"Aunty, I'm not Ritchie and I promise I won't take any unnecessary risks. This is my chance to make something of myself and for Ritchie when he comes home. I think Bunter will use me for my brains rather than my brawn, after all, you know I couldn't fight my way out of a paper bag on a good day."

"Well I know that's not true but thank you for trying to make me feel better."

Reluctantly Mavis gave her blessing and a week later after someone to help behind the bar had been found Michael started his new job but he didn't share the news with Ritchie straight away as he wanted to see how things went. Unlike Ritchie, Molly wasn't interested in violence but he did have a good aptitude for business. Within a few months, he had made changes, Bunter was pleased and things were running smoother than they ever had. Loan payments were chased up weekly so that debts didn't escalate, new bodies were brought on board and any jobs were planned down to the last detail so that silly mistakes like the one his brother had been caught up in, didn't happen again.

On his next prison visit when he informed Ritchie of his career change, he was expecting a pat on the back and not the hostile reaction he received.

"Fuck me! Would you jump in my grave as quickly? I expected more from you Molly. That's my job and now you've wormed your way in and I'm out on me fucking ear!"

"Do be fucking soppy. When you get out we will work the firm together. Bunter now wants to retire and I'm going to save as much as I can to buy him out, the rest he said we could pay on tick but I reckon the cheeky cunt will add on a hefty interest. Can you imagine it, the Spires brothers running their own firm?"

Michael went on to explain all that he had done to improve revenue and that as soon as Ritchie got released, together they would do even more but whether his brother believed him was a different matter. Michael was worried; Ritchie had changed since getting locked up. He was now aggressive and cold and Michael could only assume that his sibling was having a hard time on the inside, far harder than he was letting on. In truth it was nothing of the sort, Ritchie's sentence was plain sailing but he was frustrated, He had quickly come to understand that your liberty was everything and he hated being told what to do twenty-four-seven. He had begun to get into fights, all started by him and for no reason that he was able to explain. It got so bad that the other inmates gave him a wide birth; even Wilko was quiet most of the time for fear of setting off his cellmate. It came to a head one evening when Ritchie kicked off in association. A new inmate was taking too long with his shot at pool so taking one of the balls, Ritchie launched in across the table hitting the poor kind straight in the mouth. Blood spurted out along with a tooth and Ritchie was only saved from being brought up in front of the Governor by a screw that was on Archie Culver's payroll. It didn't go down well and finally, he was called up to see Archie and asked what the hell was going on but Ritchie couldn't explain himself other than to say that he was frustrated. "Well, fuckin' sort yourself out sunshine or me and you will be having more than a few words. I take care of this wing and keep it fucking harmonious; I don't need you going off like a bottle of pop for no reason and half the geezers walking around with shiners did nothing to deserve it. Do I make myself clear?" Ritchie nodded his head and then left. Kicking off at others was one thing but protection via Bunter or not, he didn't fancy his chances against Archie or his henchmen if he upset the bloke further. The remainder of his sentence might as well have been in solitary as Ritchie didn't socialise with anyone and the only other person he spoke to was Wilko and even that wouldn't have been on the agenda if they weren't sharing a cell.

Nine months later on a Thursday morning and after bidding farewell to Wilko, Ritchie walked out of the prison. With good behaviour and time served on remand, Ritchie had at last been released. He hadn't expected anyone to meet him so when he heard his voice being called he looked to see where it was coming from. Business had been good and Michael now had a car and had been waiting outside the main gates of the Scrubs when his brother emerged. Closing the window and then getting out of the vehicle he ran over and flung his arms around Ritchie. "Fuck I ain't half missed you, bro."

The embrace made Ritchie feel uncomfortable and he gently pushed his brother away. He had spent so long without any physical contact that it now seemed odd to him.

"Likewise Molly, now get me the fuck away from this shit hole as fast as you can."

Mavis had cooked up a storm for her boy's return and they were both back at the Lamb at just before ten. Tears were shed and Mavis didn't want to ever let go of her eldest. Burt stood there and awkwardly held out his hand while continually puffing away on his pipe.

"Get out of it you daft old sod."

With a change of heart, Ritchie then took the man in a bear hug and the embrace was reciprocated. If he couldn't show those he loved his feelings, then he might as well be back inside. He tucked into the cooked breakfast and as usual, Mavis had prepared far too much but Ritchie couldn't stop stuffing his face. It felt like forever since he'd eaten anything so tasty and by the time he placed his knife and fork onto the plate he was starting to feel bloated.

"If you all don't mind, I think I need to go and have a laydown, my gut feels like it's about to explode."

Once in the bedroom he sat on the side of the feather bed and broke down. For all these months he had kept his emotions buried deep inside and now the relief he felt at being free suddenly emerged. Laying down for what he thought would only be a half hour, Ritchie couldn't believe it when he woke and it was dark outside. Glancing at the bedside clock and with help from a chink of light shining from under the door, he could just make out that it was after seven, he had slept for a full eight hours. The bed was just as he remembered and it was like sleeping on a cloud. Deciding to get up and have a couple of pints down in the bar, he knew he wouldn't need much for it to take effect as he hadn't had any alcohol for such a long time. The hooch inside was gut rot and he had avoided it at all costs so the pints of larger were going to slip down like silk. Sitting at one of the corner tables with Molly, the pair discussed business and Molly explained what had been happening. Now unable to keep his eyes open and continually yawning, he finally conceded to what his body was telling him. Apologising, he told Molly that he was going upstairs to hit the hay, he had so much sleep to catch up on and he couldn't wait. God, it felt so good to be home.

CHAPTER FOUR

Due to the amount of sleep he'd had, Ritchie was up early and was sitting having a chat with Mavis when Michael entered the kitchen.

"What time do you call this you muppet?"

"Fuck me; it's only just after eight."

"Early bird catches the worm me old son. Now don't fuck about with breakfast, we need to get going."

"Fuck you Ritchie, I ain't missing one of Auntie's fry-ups for anything."

Twenty minutes later they were finally on their way to the unit. Bunter hugged Ritchie when he saw him and over the next few weeks, they both settled into the firm well and worked together without a crossword. Bunter had stayed for a further six months until he was sure the partnership would be okay and his firm was in safe hands and then out of the blue, he announced that this Friday would be his last day. The week seemed to drag, Ritchie couldn't wait to be in charge, he'd decided that he would lead and Michael could ride shotgun, after all, he was the oldest and it didn't bode well to have two cooks in the kitchen. Friday at last arrived and just before five, Bunter gathered all the men together and addressing them, he looked at each one in turn.

"Now I don't know if you are aware but I know there have been plenty of fucking Chinese whispers floating about so it's time to set the record straight. Today is my last and from now on Ritchie and Michael will be running things. Anyone that isn't happy can fucking walk away now with no hard feelings. If you stay, from now on you will take your orders from the brothers without question and there will be no running to me telling fucking tales. Do I make myself clear?"

There were a few muffled comments but finally, they all nodded their heads.

"Good! Now, me and the boys have some business to discuss so you can all get off for the weekend but keep your mobiles close in case there's any aggro."

As the men filtered out and headed in the direction of the Lamb for their Friday night skinful, Ritchie, Michael and Bunter made their way to the back office.

"Right lads, just one thing left to do."

Holding his hand out, palm upwards was an indication that he wanted his money. Michael walked over to the filing cabinet and lifting out a briefcase, proceeded to remove a large manila envelope. Since Ritchie's release, the brothers had been able to pool their earnings and were now only ten grand short. They both knew that if they weren't careful the remaining balance could soon increase to twenty but with luck on their side that would be as bad as it got as hopefully, they would soon be able to clear the debt once and for all.

"You'll find a bit more in there than we agreed Bunter for good luck. That just leaves ten left to pay."

Bunter Dennis grinned, they knew the score and that he would be receiving far more than that but for now he was happy. The fifty grand he wanted for the firm was steep to say the least, after all, the unit was rented so they were only buying the goodwill and the debtors from the loansharking, all of whom had paid their loans over and again and still owed more than they had originally borrowed.

"Well, it's been nice knowing you boys and if you need any advice just call me, it's free! Never thought you'd hear me say that did you? Right, I'm off to enjoy my retirement."

Bunter exited the office still laughing at the joke he'd made and Ritchie and Molly just slowly shook their heads. When they heard the front door slam they hugged each other, this was really happening and the Spires brothers were on the up. Ritchie hadn't thought his dream would come true so soon and he scanned the room with a smile on his face.

"Right, the first thing we need to do is get another desk."

By the end of the following week, a new desk was installed along with plastic name plates with Mr R Spires and Mr M Spires. It made the boys feel important but no one in the firm ever referred to them as Mister and Michael was grateful for that as it would have made him feel uncomfortable. As well as Ritchie and Michael, there were eight other employees, though that word was used very loosely as no one paid any tax or national insurance. Things were moving along nicely and there was no falling out or arguing, in all honesty, the men liked how things had changed. True, there was a bit more bother at times but they were happy to flex their muscles as it gave their street cred a boost. For the first few weeks business went without a hitch but suddenly out of the blue they started to have a few late payers, people who had heard that Bunter was no longer on the scene and had decided to chance their arm by not paying their dues. When he found out Ritchie was up in arms and Molly struggled to rein him in.

"Those cunts! If they think they can get one over on us then they are going to find out what's fucking what."

"Okay, okay Bro calm down."

"Don't fucking tell me to calm down Molly. You can't have the tail wagging the fucking dog and we need to lay the law down. If we don't all the other slags will follow suit and before long we won't have a business left."

Calling out, Ritchie shouted for Teddy Edwards and the man appeared in the doorway in a matter of seconds.

"Boss?"

"Pick a couple of names from the list and get Joey and Graham, we're going on a little debt-collecting mission."

"I'll come as well."

It wasn't usually Michael's thing, he preferred to remain at the base and plan the business but he was afraid that his brother might go too far and if he tagged along, then he just might be able to defuse the situation if things got out of hand.

The first name on the list was Reg Colby. A pensioner of seventy-eight, Reg had gotten in a muddle with his electricity bill and when they had threatened to cut off his supply he had panicked and instead of contacting the electricity board had asked Bunter for help. Reg had lived on the manor long enough to know that you only went to a loan shark as a last resort but he was old and in bad health so he just wanted it all sorted out as quickly as possible. The original two hundred pound loan was taken out a year earlier and at forty pounds per week should have been settled in a little over five weeks but he was now more in debt than ever and forty out of his pension meant he was getting further and further into debt with other companies. In the last few weeks, he had received threatening letters from the gas and the club book that he used when he needed anything new and didn't have the funds to pay for it. He knew it was a bad idea but he missed a few of the Spire's payments. Reg had been around a long time and knew the score, knew that any day the sharks would be calling so he had taken to sitting in the dark with the curtains closed. He had turned off the heating and covered with two blankets, was surviving on cans of soup and bread but he still hadn't been able to make any headway with the debt.

The flat in Arlington House was high rise, on the twelfth floor and with the lift permanently out of action, the men were forced to use the stairs. By the time they reached the landing where Reg's flat was situated they were all out of breath so had to take a moment to gather themselves.

"Fuck me! How can people live in these shit holes?" Ritchie laughed and then stopped as he realised that apart from the years with Albie and Rita, they had been lucky and had a warm, welcoming home.

Michael knocked on the door and about to knock a second time he was stopped when Ritchie grabbed his arm. Fast losing his patience he nodded signalling for Graham to smash his way in. They found Reg in his armchair and in the middle of having a heart attack brought on by fear. Ritchie scanned the room but there wasn't anything of any value. Walking over to an old dresser he pulled at one of the drawers and instantly spied a small leather box. It contained the medals that had been awarded to Reg's father in the First World War. Snapping the box shut Ritchie took a step over to the old timer who was now sweating profusely, staring wide-eyed and clutching his chest. "Right, you old cunt! I'm taking these and if you pop your clogs it will settle the debt, if you don't then it's payment as usual next week and believe me, you really don't want us back here again."

Michael couldn't believe what he was hearing but knew better than to challenge Ritchie in front of the men. In the past his brother never would have done something like this, he had changed and Michael didn't like the person he was becoming, had become in fact. Storming out, Ritchie didn't tell any of the men to see if the old man was okay and as Michael went to leave, he momentarily stopped in front of Reg. Grabbing the handset of an old seventies trim phone that sat on a table next to Reg's chair and which thankfully hadn't yet been disconnected, he taped in nine, nine, nine and laid the receiver down on the table. Someone would come, they had to and at least Michael knew he had done something to help.

The second person on the list was Carol Humphries. Carol had been left holding the baby after her boyfriend had walked out of the squat they shared when she was six months pregnant. Rehomed by the council in a flat on Coopers Lane in Camden with just the barest of necessities, Carol had sought out a short-term loan to buy the essentials her baby would need

It was all second-hand stuff and didn't total more than one hundred and fifty pounds so she was confident it wouldn't take her too long to pay off the debt, how wrong she was. Months rolled past and by the time her little boy Ashley was six months old, Carol owed three times more than she had initially borrowed. Ritchie rapped hard on the glass pane of the front door and for a moment, Carol thought about ignoring the caller but deep down she knew who it was and that she would have to face the music sooner or later so it might as well be now. Thankfully Ashley was asleep in his pram and she prayed whoever was at the door wouldn't wake him. Slowly she moved into the small hallway and her silhouette could be seen by the men outside.

"Who is it?"

"You know who it fucking is."

Then for good measure in case any other residents were listening, Ritchie added.

"It's the Spires brothers, open up Carol."

Her heart sank in her chest but Carol knew she had no option. Slowly turning the Yale, she hadn't opened the door more than an inch when Ritchie slammed on the side and it flew back and into her face. Ritchie marched inside followed by Michael and the others and none of them took any notice of the blood that was now streaming from the woman's nose. Tears stung her eyes but reluctantly she followed the men into her sparse front room. Out of nowhere, Joey Harris hit her hard in the chest and Carol fell backwards onto the only chair in the room. The tears were now falling thick and fast and she was scared beyond belief but not for her own wellbeing, Carol didn't care what they did to her as long as they didn't hurt her baby.

"I'm sorry Mr Spires really I am. I know I'm behind with my payments but it was pay you or buy milk and nappies for the baby. I know you will understand, he's so small and I have to take care of him but I'll catch up as soon as I can I promise and…."

Carol was instantly silenced when Ritchie swooped down into the pram and grabbing the baby by one ankle, held him up high in the air. Ashley screamed out in pain and Carol started to plead with Ritchie not to hurt her baby. With the front door wide open, the neighbour's and people passing could hear the commotion and the baby's screams but no one came to help. They all knew what was happening, it was a regular occurrence but you didn't poke your nose into the business of others no matter how pitiful the cries were and neither did you call the Old Bill or an ambulance, a rule Michael had just broken but luckily one his brother would never find out about.

"I'm sorry, I'm sorry but I don't know what more I can do Mr Spires. Please, pleeeease don't hurt him!"

Laying the baby back in the pram, Ritchie walked over to Carol and towered over her like a giant.

"You thought that as Bunter was no longer on the scene you could take fucking liberties didn't you!?"

"No Mr Spires, I didn't, really I didn't."

This time Michael couldn't stand by and watch this horrific bullying any longer.

"Ritchie, leave it out. We don't….."

Without uttering a single word Ritchie shot his brother a look so menacing that it was enough to stop Michel dead in his tracks. The others weren't happy with the situation either but they accepted it went with the job and if you showed any weakness to the scum you dealt with it would be the end of business. "My men will be back next week and I don't give a flying fuck how you find it but you'd better have two weeks money waiting. Get on your back and open your legs like the other sluts on my books. I'm sure there's some sad fuck out there willing to pay you for emptying his load. I ain't a fucking charity sweetheart and you knew that when you came looking for money. Baby or not, if I have to come back, you will both fucking suffer and that's a promise."

Again he turned and marched out swiftly followed by his men. Molly quickly removed his wallet and pulling out five crisp fifty-pound notes he handed it to Carol and at the same time put his index finger to his lips. It wasn't much and although it would help the woman out this time, he couldn't continue clearing her debts. He had to talk to his brother as a matter of urgency, this had to stop and stop now.

Back at the unit, with some of the men taking a breather on the old sofa that sat in the waiting area and the others outside having a smoke, it appeared that things had calmed down a bit. Ritchie and Michael were alone in the office and Ritchie, standing at the filing cabinet, was just about to open up the new laptop to find out the value of the medals he had taken from Reg when Michael turned on his brother like never before.

"What the fuck was all that!"

Treating the question with contempt, Ritchie carried on flicking through the posts which further enraged Michael. Walking over he grabbed his brother by the arm.

"I said, what the fuck was all that!?"

"I heard you and if you can't stand the heat, get out of the fucking kitchen bro. You know as well as I do that if we show weakness of any kind, we'll be bankrupt and a fucking laughing stock within a matter of weeks. Then there's the added fact that the men would probably walk, I mean who wants to work for a couple of pussies. Are you a pussy Michael, not got the balls for it?"

The question was rhetorical but Michael replied all the same.

"I'm well aware of that you cunt! But, holding a baby up by his leg is bang out of order, not to mention the fact that the old bloke looked like he was about to pop his clogs, probably has by now for all we know."

Richie slowly nodded his head.

"I'll give you the girl, I probably went a tad over the top but that old bastard knows the score and was taking fucking liberties and no one treats me like a mug Molly."

"What's happened to you Ritch, you were always a decent bloke but now, well now it's as if I don't know you. You've turned into a complete cunt and a sadistic one at that."

Ritchie took a seat behind his desk and palms together he placed both index fingers under his chin as he spoke.

"You want to know what changed me, little brother? Life, that's what fucking changed me. The shitty upbringing we had, then getting banged up with people you only see in your nightmares. Bunter made sure I was protected and I didn't get bullied but

44

neither did I take any chances. Do you know what it's like having to watch your back every fucking time you take a shower in case some faggot wants your arse or the fat cunts who think nothing of robbing your grub if they fancy what's on your plate? No one will ever treat me like that again and if you don't like my methods then stay here, do the paperwork and let me take care of business out on the streets."

Michael could only stare at the person who had raised him, the person he loved above all others but now didn't know at all. The rest of the afternoon was taken in silence and when they reached the Lamb Mavis instantly knew that there was something wrong, that her boys had fallen out. When the evening meal was over and when Burt had disappeared to the lavatory with the Evening Standard, she sat at the table and took one of their hands in her own.

"I don't know what's gone on between the two of you and I don't want to know but I will tell you both one thing, in this life we only have family, be it blood-related or just through love like our little family is. All that matters is we never forget that fact and whatever we fall out over is never as important as making up and holding on to that bond. I'm going to open up the bar and you two can stay in here until you sort yourselves out! Do you hear me?"

There was no reply from either of them and Mavis left them to think over what she had said. Suddenly Ritchie stood up and walking over to the dresser, removed a bottle of scotch that was kept for emergencies along with two glass tumblers.

"Drink?"

Michael only nodded his head but it was a sign to his

brother that he was open to conversation. Ritchie
wasn't about to apologise, in his mind he'd done
nothing wrong but he had taken on board all that
Aunty had just said.

"I know what happened today bothered you Molly but
you have to understand that in our line of work, it's a
necessary evil. Fuck me, if we could go around being
all sweetness and fucking light to people and still coin
in what we do then don't you think I'd prefer that? Of
course I would but it ain't the way of the world bro, at
least not the world we live in. Can you handle it,
cause if you can't then maybe it's for the best if you
leave the firm and find a job more suited to you?"

"I can handle it, Ritchie, at least I can if I'm not
forced to witness it. I think it's for the best if I stay
office-bound, you know do the books and planning."

Ritchie thought for a moment and then smiling,
nodded his head.

"You know what we need? A good night out, a few
jars and maybe a leg over if we're lucky. How do you
feel about this Friday?"

Michael clinked his glass against his brother's and
grinned.

"Sounds good to me."

"Then Friday it is and all those Camden sluts had
better hold onto their knickers because the Spires
boys will be up for anything."

Michael laughed, this was the Ritchie he knew and
loved and Michael was thankful that he hadn't
disappeared completely and was in there somewhere,
he just had to find a way to get his brother back on
track, permanently.

CHAPTER FIVE

Sue Nelson hummed Billy Ocean's newest hit 'When the going gets tough' as she pulled on her coat ready for the weekend to begin.

"You off?"

Gloria Watson the manager, always seemed to ask stupid questions, as if seeing Sue putting her coat on wasn't enough of a hint.

"Sure am, night out tonight and no work tomorrow. Yippee!"

Gloria was well into her fifties, had lived a sheltered life and if she was honest, was a little envious of the lifestyle her junior lived and one that had always seemed to pass Gloria by. She had never married and had only ever had one boyfriend who did a swift disappearing act as soon as he got his leg over. Now Gloria resided in her one-bed council flat alone and with her ginger tom Sherman, as her only source of comfort.

"Well, have a nice time dear and just remember if you can't be good, be careful."

Sue had no intention of being good and to hell with being careful. If she got up the duff and bagged a man in the process then at least she wouldn't have to work at Walk Easy anymore. It was March and the weather was unusually good, the glorious sunshine made her even more excited about going out that night. Sue had worked at Walk Easy on Barnet High Street since leaving school three years earlier and hated every minute of it. People's feet tended to be ugly and smelly and getting pair after pair of shoes from the storeroom wasn't exactly rocket science. Did she want a career? Not at all, she wanted a nice house, a car, money and a man who loved her, work wasn't even on her radar. If she was honest, she had never wanted a career and men were constantly on her mind but not just any man. Sue thought she was the bee's knees and he would have to have plenty of money and status to catch her. She wasn't bad looking and her figure was neat so she hadn't had much difficulty getting a boyfriend in the past but they never seemed to cut the mustard. As she waited to catch the bus home she sighed heavily and then pulled out her mobile and tapped in her friend's number.

"Hi babe, you all set for tonight?"

Sue's best friend Ellie Evans had also just finished work for the day. Employed at Madam G's hair salon on Wood Street since leaving school, Ellie, unlike her bestie, loved her job and only had a year left until she qualified. She had a ten-year plan and wanted to open her own salon by the end of it. Ellie liked boys but unlike her bestie, she wasn't in any great hurry to settle down.

"Yes Sue but I'm warning you, I ain't staying out late as I have work in the morning."

Tomorrow was Sue's first Saturday off in over a month so she had no intention of going home early tonight and she would make sure that her friend didn't either, even if that meant Ellie hanging all day with a massive hangover at work.

"Okay moaning Minnie. I'll meet you outside the station at seven and don't be late."

With that, Sue ended the call before her friend could

change her mind. Heading home would only take a few minutes as she lived on Moxon Street with her parents and two younger brothers. The house was a three-bedroom terrace but it was still small and Sue's room was little more than a box room. It was decorated nicely as her mother Karen looked on her oldest child as a princess. Unlike her younger brothers, Sue got nearly everything she asked for and Karen was always buying her daughter new gear down the market. Slamming the front door behind her made the glass panel rattle and her father Joe was about to read her the riot act but was stopped when his wife placed her hand on his arm and frowned.

"Leave it darling. Hello there love, had a good day?"

"If you call touching sweaty feet all day as good, then yes I suppose so."

Karen had disappeared into the tiny kitchen before Sue had finished complaining and quickly reappeared with two steaming hot plates of stew and dumplings. Proud of her culinary creation Karen waited for a 'Thank you or that looks good' but there was nothing as her daughter screwed up her face.

"Oh, Mum! You know I wanted something light. I'm going out tonight and if I eat that lot my gut will stick out like a bleeding balloon. Make me a sandwich instead."

Dutifully Karen did as she was asked and as soon as she had left the room Joe leaned over the table and picking up his daughter's plate, proceeded to pour her meal on top of his own.

"Don't know what you're missing. The old girl ain't no Gordon Ramsey but she sure makes a bloody good stew. Put hairs on your chest this will."

49

"Don't be ridiculous Dad, why on earth would I want hairs on my chest."

Joe rolled his eyes, their daughter certainly hadn't inherited his brains. The boys were sitting at the other end of the room engrossed in some silly game show on the telly and when Karen handed her daughter a tea plate containing a sandwich, Sue took one bite and then turned up her nose again.

"Ham?! Ain't we got anything better and it ain't bleedin' good ham either it's that cheap shit in a packet."

"Oh, I'm sorry love. When I do the big shop tomorrow I'll pop in the butchers and get you a few slices of the nice stuff."

Now it was Joe's turn to kick off and he slammed his fork down as he spoke.

"You bleeding well won't! If Miss High and Mighty here wants expensive ham she can bloody well pay for it herself! Oh, and while we're on the subject of paying, you need to up your rent now you're on adult pay. Me and your mother can't support you forever."

Just as Sue was about to argue back, her mother stepped in and cut her off before a word had the chance to escape from her mouth.

"Don't Joe, she works hard and it's good that she can buy herself nice things and…"

As a row began between her parents, Sue stood up from the table and after giving them both a look of disgust, stomped off up to her room. It was just past six so it was time to start getting ready. At work, she had meticulously planned her outfit in her head but when she went into her room a new dress hung on the wardrobe door. Her mother had been down the market again but the offering looked cheap and there was no way she was wearing it even if it did upset her mum. Tonight she was on a mission to get a man and she had to look her best. The dress she chose was from Top Shop but she hadn't bought it new not that she would ever share that snippet of information with anyone. The charity shops up West were pretty good and every month when she got paid Sue would make the trip. She always returned home with several items and best of all no one from her manor ever saw her trawling charity shops so she could brag about spending a fortune on her gear. Sue didn't even share her secret with Ellie for fear it would get out to others. When she reappeared in the front room her mother smiled and then her face fell.

"I got you a new dress love and thought you'd be wearing that tonight?"

"I know Mum but the quality just isn't there. Poor people shop down the market and you don't want people thinking I'm poor do you?"

"Why you ungrateful little mare, we ain't got....."

As her father kicked off again and her mother tried to defend her daughter, Sue walked from the house and slammed the door as she went, she wouldn't let anyone dampen her excitement tonight.

Ellie Evans lived further away than her friend so by the time she got home to Old Fold View it was almost six fifteen. The journey had taken half an hour and she knew that to be on time for her friend meant having less than a quarter of an hour to get ready. After splashing her face with water and cleaning her teeth, Ellie freshened up her mascara and then pulled on a pair of high-waisted wide-legged jeans and a tight-fitting white t-shirt. Topping off the outfit with a denim jacket, Ellie took a moment to look in the mirror. A natural beauty with a thick mane of long blonde curly hair, she never had to try very hard and it was something that really pissed off her friend. Whereas Sue was spoilt and selfish, Ellie would help anyone; give you her last pound if you needed it. The corporation flat she shared with her mother was tired and needed to be refurbished but there was nothing in the council coffers so it would remain the same as it had been since the day they'd moved in ten years earlier. Ellie and her mother Eileen were like ships passing in the night as Ellie worked days and Eileen worked nights down the Mecca Bingo and early morning shifts at the local corner shop so the only chance they got to spend time together was on Sundays. Ellie loved her mum dearly and as much as she could, would help out with the rent and bills every month. Eileen originated from Scotland so locally there was no other family and Eileen had raised her daughter single-handedly with no help from anyone. John Evans had disappeared a few days after his daughter had been born so life had been tough at times. When Ellie was small, Eileen had even gone without food so that her child had a full belly. Just in case Eileen popped home for anything, Ellie scribbled a quick note to let her mother know that she was going out but wouldn't be late back and propped it up against the fruit bowl before dashing out of the flat in the hope of not being late. Sue hated it when people were late and she would go on and on about it all night. Luck was on her side and she reached New Barnet Station with five minutes to go.

Sue was already there and studying her watch as her friend approached.

"Okay, Okay, I ain't late."

"More by luck that fuckin' judgement. Come on the train's in."

"So, where are we going?"

"I've heard the Worlds End in Camden is good and it's got a dancefloor as well."

"Camden!?"

"Oh it ain't far, and the train goes straight there so hardly any walking at the other end."

The girls boarded and just under twenty-five minutes later they were exiting the station. Sue led the way and she was in such a hurry that Ellie had difficulty keeping up. She was beginning to get hot and had a vision of stinking of sweat for the rest of the evening.

"For fucks sake, Sue! I'm sweating like a pig, just slowdown will you."

Sue had already crossed the road and was heading towards the main door to the pub and Ellie was now pissed off with her friend and they weren't even inside yet. Pushing open the bright pink door revealed lots of ironwork and wood but there wasn't any music and for a second Sue thought she'd got it wrong until a group of girls emerged from the rear and music could be heard thumping from inside. Walking up to the bar Sue and Ellie ordered drinks, making sure to pay for their own. Money was hard earned and both of them were careful when it came to splashing the cash. As the barman placed the drinks down Sue smiled and asked the question.

"Excuse me sweetheart but me and my friend ain't been here before and I heard there's a dance floor?"

"You mean the Underworld. See those doors at the end? Go through and it's down in the basement. Ain't no bands on tonight though, just a DJ but he plays some good tunes. You're a bit early so not a lot down there but come about ten and the place will be heaving."

Hearing this, Ellie was shocked. She didn't like this, what if they went down there and it was some kind of satanic club and they couldn't get out again, or there could be a fire or a bomb and they would be stuck underneath some grotty pub? No, it wasn't for her and besides, she had hoped to be on her way home by ten.

"The Underworld? This sounds a bit suspect to me Sue; I think I'm going to give it a miss."

Sue turned on her friend with vengeance, she had waited all week for this and it was her day off tomorrow.

"Fuck that for a game of soldiers. You can get off if you want but I'm staying. You always piss on the matches and try and spoil things, Ellie, I thought you were a better friend than that."

There was no way Ellie would leave her pal alone in a strange place and nor did she fancy travelling home alone on the train so she knew she would stay. Sue's last words had upset her but if she said anything they were liable to get into an argument and then the night would be ruined, so just like she always did, Ellie didn't challenge the accusation.

"Okay but if we don't like it we come straight out. Okay?"

"Okay, okay! You really are yellow Ellie; you never want to take a chance. Don't you want to live a little, you know be a bit dangerous? Actually, don't answer that because you'll only end up spoiling things before we've even gone in and given it a try?"

Ellie hung her head; she hated it when her friend got arsey with her and if it turned out not to be a good night Sue would make her suffer as if it was all her fault. Sue pushed open the doors and the music rose loudly from the room below. Playing at full volume, Ricky Martin was singing 'Livin' La Vida Loca' and as they descended the stairs Sue began to sing along making her friend laugh. The animosity of a few minutes ago was now forgotten and as soon as the girls reached the bottom of the stairs they placed their drinks onto a table and then hit the dancefloor. Dropping their bags to the floor they started to dance with Sue immediately trying to outdo her friend. It was always the same but sadly Sue had little rhythm whereas to Ellie it came naturally.

"You should have been born a nigger."

"Sue! You can't say that, it's racial."

"No, it ain't, it's a compliment. They always have the moves unlike most of us whites. You sure your old mum didn't go for a coloured and get a bit of black inside her?"

"Sue!"

Within the next hour, the room started to fill. It was mostly girls as the blokes tended to drink with their mates in other pubs and then come in an hour before closing in the hope of picking up a girl and getting their end away. It never happened to Ellie, she wasn't about to give herself away to any Jack the lad. Even Sue was starting to get a bit more choosy after she heard a whisper going around that she was a slag and that she put it about a bit. No decent boy would ever decent boy would ever settle with someone like that so she decided she had to be a bit more discreet. By eleven the Underworld was full, it was hot and sweaty and the men now almost numbered the women. Sue had started to study the stairs looking for anyone suitable, as yet it had been slim pickings.

"Shall we start thinking about going home Sue only I have work tomorrow and Saturdays are always the busiest."

"Leave it out Ellie, ain't you havin' a good time?"

"Of course I am but I need my bed, don't you?"

"No, I don't. I've got to wait another month until I get a Saturday off so I'm making the most of it."

"Don't you think that's a bit selfish, I mean you ain't considering me are you?"

The girls were about to have a full-scale row when Sue suddenly held her palm up silencing her friend.

"Fuckin' hell, I've just died and gone to heaven. Have a butchers at the two blokes who have just walked in. Now that's the kind of geezer I'm after. See, I said we needed to wait."

"Where, who do you mean?"

Ellie looked around in all directions but she couldn't see who her friend was referring to.

"Not now Ellie or they'll know we're talking about 'em."

"Well I ain't getting off with anyone, I'm too tired and they will only chat you up so they can have a feel or even worse when the lights go up."

Sue wasn't listening, she was drawn to one of the two men like a magnet to metal and she couldn't take her eyes off of him. By the end of the night, he would be hers, she would make damn sure of that.

CHAPTER SIX
Earlier that evening

Business had concluded for the week, and unless there was an emergency, the Spires firm would always have the weekend off. It kept the men happy and a happy workforce led to trust and loyalty. Ritchie had gone up West to get some new gear and Michael had taken a nap as his brother always turned a night out into a marathon and Molly didn't want to start flagging before midnight. Mavis was about to call Michael down for his evening meal as they needed to line their stomachs before going out on the lash when Ritchie walked in laden down with high-end store bags.

"Did you leave anything in the shop?"

Ritchie laughed as he placed the bags onto the floor. "Where's Molly?"

"Having a kip I was about to call him down, I've made a nice steak pie, mash and veg, it will set you both up for tonight. Burt always says you have to line your stomachs if you're having a night on the piss."

Ritchie hugged the plump woman to him, a woman he looked upon as a mother and one he would have willingly killed for.

"We don't know what we'd do without you Aunty, no one could care for us more."

"You're right there; I love you both like you're my own. That said, have you seen or heard from your mum since you got out?"

"No, and I don't want to, Molly told me the old man had a heart attack and then popped his clogs but I ain't interested and that old cow don't want to come around here sniffing for a fucking handout either!"

Mavis wasn't a vindictive person but the words still made her heart swell, she loved the boys so much and the thought of another woman, even if it was their mother, trying to come between them scared the life out of her. Molly walked into the kitchen rubbing his eyes with the palms of his hands.

"I only planned on having a half hour but I went out like a bleedin' light."

"Well you must have needed it boy, sit down I'm about to dish up dinner."

Just then Burt reappeared looking flushed. No one said anything but they all grinned; the poor old sod was a martyr to his piles and would often sit in the lavatory for over an hour as he strained his guts out trying to have a shit.

"You all sorted?"

"Yes my love but it took a bit of doing I can tell you, thought I was going to start digging for England."

"Burt!"

"Well, you asked my sweet."

Suddenly Ritchie and Michael couldn't contain their laughter and Burt narrowed his eyes at the pair of them, about to scold them he was stopped when Mavis placed the food on the table. Food was Burt McAllister's weakness and not a thing could keep him from it, not even a telling off so for the moment the piss-taking was forgotten about as they all tucked in. It was strange, during the day the two men were hardened criminals well at least Ritchie was but when they walked through the backdoor of the pub they were respectful and acted like any other family. After the boys had helped to clear away the dishes they went up to their bedroom and just like a couple of girls, Ritchie proceeded to unpack the bags and show his brother all the gear he had purchased.

"Fuck me, Ritchie, you got enough clobber?"

"I'm going to get me leg over tonight I can feel it in me bones so looking me best means I won't end up with some ugly munter, at least I hope I won't but my sacks are so full that if push comes to shove I'll take anything I can get."

As Ritchie headed for the bathroom, Michael smiled and slowly shook his head. His brother didn't care where he dipped his wick but Michael was far choosier. Some of the girls they had paired up with in the past looked like they had been around the block more than once which had put Michael off. By the time Ritchie had showered, dressed and soaked himself in aftershave it was just gone eight. They both walked into the bar for Mavis to inspect them and give them the thumbs up. Michael had chosen a pair of smart black trousers and a pale blue jumper, he looked nice but nothing compared to his brother. Ritchie wore a pair of stonewashed jeans and a brilliant white t-shirt that hugged his well-toned torso. On his feet, he wore a pair of beige suede loafers and had topped the outfit off with an obligatory thick gold chain.

"Well, don't you both look handsome! You got everything you need?"

About to say yes, they were shocked when she handed Molly a couple of condoms.

"You can't be too careful nowadays and I don't want one of my boys catching anything nasty. Have a good

59

time and keep the noise down when you come in I need me beauty sleep."

Ritchie blew her a kiss and at last, they headed out. "So, where are we going?"

"I thought we could start at the Hawley Arms, then have a few in the Elephants Head and finish up at the Worlds End. It's usually a bit heavy for me but Joey said there's a DJ on tonight and there should be plenty of skirt about.

"Sounds good to me."

Michael placed his arm out into the road and hailed a passing cab.

"Where to guvnor?"

"Hawley Arms on Castlehaven Road please."

They both sat back in their seat but didn't engage in conversation with the driver. He had recognised Ritchie Spires as soon as he got in the cab and Ronnie South liked his pearly's too much to risk pissing off this villain. Just over ten minutes later the journey came to an end and after Michael had tipped the driver well, they both entered the pub and ordered their first pints of the night. After about an hour Ritchie started to get bored, there wasn't much going on in the Hawley and none of their usual crew that they drank with was there. Having spent the entire day in his brother's company there wasn't much left to say to each other and when Michael loudly yawned Ritchie was straight on the case for fear that his brother would call it a night.

"Fancy moving on to the Elephant's Head?"

"Anything's better than this, it's as dull as fucking dishwater in here."

Once outside Richie hailed another cab. It was only

just over half a mile but the rain that had been forecast had just started and there was no way he was risking getting his new loafers wet. When they gave their destination the cabbie gave a look of being pissed off at such a short journey but when they pulled up outside the pub and Ritchie tipped him a tenner, he was soon smiling and wished the boys a blinding evening. Stepping inside, the music was blaring out and the long narrow bar was rammed with Friday night drinkers. Michael heard his name called and when he turned around he saw Monty Withers waving his hand in the air at the far end. Monty and Michael had been schoolboy mates and it had been a few years since they had seen each other.

"Follow me, Ritch, one of my old muckers is down there, he's a top geezer and a right good laugh."

Ritchie sighed which wasn't heard by Michael due to the music. He wasn't relishing just standing there like a nob while those two talked about old times but he needn't have worried. As it turned out Michael was right and this Monty bloke was a scream. He told joke after joke and within a few minutes, the boys were crying with laughter. Just before eleven Ritchie decided that it was time they went to the Worlds End, if they left it much later the best-looking birds would be spoken for.

"You coming with us Monty?"

"Thanks for the offer but the little woman is waiting at home and I'm on a promise."

"I didn't know you were shacked up with anyone Mont?"

"I ain't just shacked up Molly, I got hitched last year and it's the best fucking move I ever made. You

61

remember Wendy Flanagan from Roden Street?"
Michael started to laugh but the other two remained
stony-faced, Ritchie because he didn't know who they
were referring to and Monty because he knew what
was coming next.
"You never fucking married Bendy Wendy did you?"
"Careful you cunt! That's me missus you're talking
about. We've all got a past Michael, even you, so
don't fucking judge, alright?"
Suddenly the atmosphere became icy and Michael
couldn't wait to get outside. After apologising to his
old friend he motioned to Ritchie with his eyes as if
to say 'Fuck me, let's get out of here pronto'. This time
they didn't need to hail a cab as the Worlds End was
only at the other end of the High Street.
"Come on then."
"What?"
"Bendy Wendy, spill your guts."
"It ain't anything really but Wendy would shag
anyone. It was said, though I never went there myself,
that she liked it from behind and would bend over
almost double, hence the nickname but I think I
touched a nerve back there."
"You think so?"
The sarcasm didn't go over Michael's head but he
hated offending anyone and now it would bother him
for the rest of the night.
"Don't suppose I should have said that considering
they are married now."
Ritchie slapped his brother on the back and laughed.
"Don't let it bother you, kid, if the cunt married a
slapper then he should be ready to take the flack.
Come on, let's go get us both a bird and the dirtier the

62

better as my balls are starting to ache."

Just as Sue and Ellie had done, the boys got their drinks at the bar before pushing open the rear doors and heading down to the Underworld. Tragedy by steps was blearing out and it was a song Ritchie liked, though he'd never admit it and as he took the last step he moved his head in time to the music, unaware that Sue had clocked them and was nudging her friend.

The boys made their way to the back bar, they didn't need a drink but it was commonplace for the men to stand at the back and watch the girls dancing. Sue pulled Ellie onto the dancefloor as soon as the DJ started to play 'One More Time' by Britney Spears.

"Come on, I fucking love this one."

As they both started to dance, Sue exaggerated her movements which became more and more provocative and she continually laughed even though there was nothing remotely funny happening. Ellie took no notice, she had seen the same scenario many times and knew that her friend was trying to get the attention of the bloke who had just walked in. If she pulled then it would cause Ellie a problem getting home but there was no point in saying anything.

"Is he watching me?"

"Who?"

"The geezer I said looked nice when he came down the stairs, don't look now but he's at the bar in the white T-shirt."

Ellie glanced over and when her eyes met Ritchie's he smiled.

"I think so but do you really want to go there Sue, I mean he looks like a right player."

"Don't matter if he is, once he's had a taste of me I'm

sure I can tame him."

When the song finished Sue grabbed her friend's arm again and pulled her over to where the Spires brothers stood. Ritchie was smiling but it wasn't at Sue and Ellie knew it but she just looked away. All she could think about was her bed and getting up for work in the morning.

"Can we get you two ladies a drink?"

"Vodka and coke for me and she'll have half a larger."

Ellie shot her friend a glaring look. Once you accepted a drink from a bloke they always expected more. Declining the drink she whispered to Sue that she'd had enough and was going home but her friend didn't care. As loud as the music was, Michael could still make out what was being said.

"You want me to walk you to the tube?"

"Look mate, I ain't being funny but I'm not interested in anyone."

"I'm not trying to pick you up sweetheart but it's late and the pubs are starting to empty. Camden's nice but not a place a young woman should be alone in at night."

As soon as Ritchie realised he didn't stand a chance he turned his attention to Sue, she wasn't bad and he was desperate to get his end away. As Ellie headed towards the staircase she felt Michael's hand on her arm.

"Come on I'll walk you."

Outside in the cool air, it had started to rain again and by the time they reached the underground station they were both soaked to the skin but it didn't seem to matter. Conversation came easily and Ellie was beginning to warm to the stranger.

"So where do you live?"

"Old Ford Way, Barnet and you?"

"Holloway Road. Me and me brother live at the Lamb pub. Fuck me, you've got a bit of a journey ahead of you girl?"

Ellie raised her eyebrows in a pissed-off kind of way. "Tell me about it and I've got work first thing, Sue can be a real piece of work at times. I don't mind coming out but when I've got work I like to get home before midnight but sadly my so-called friend only thinks about herself. Sorry, I must sound like a right two-faced bitch."

"Not at all and if I'm honest my brother is exactly the same. I learnt a long while ago that in this life there are givers and there are takers, my brother unfortunately, is the latter."

Ellie didn't comment but his words now had her worried for her friend and she silently prayed that everything would be okay. They continued talking, Ellie told him that she was about to qualify as a hairdresser and wanted her own shop one day and Michael shared that he was in business with his brother although he was economical with the truth regarding what they actually did as he didn't want to scare her off. Before they knew it they were standing outside Ellie's block of flats, the time had flown by and she thanked her companion for getting her home safe. Michael told her she was welcome and then turned and headed to catch the train home. Ellie was disappointed that he hadn't tried to kiss her or asked to see her again but then she smiled to herself, he knew where she lived and worked and if it was meant to be it would happen.

As the night came to a close at the World's End, Ritchie led Sue outside. They both knew what was about to happen but it wasn't discussed. A covered alleyway ran down the side of the pub. It only led to a locked gate but at least they would have shelter and a bit of privacy. Ritchie roughly pushed Sue up against the wall and in a matter of second's his hand was under her dress and inside her knickers, as his fingers slid inside her she moaned with pleasure. That was the sum total of any foreplay and releasing his erect penis, he lifted her up and spread open Sue's legs. Ritchie didn't bother with the condom supplied by Mavis and as he entered her Sue could feel every inch of his large thick penis as he moved in and out. Ritchie began to grunt loudly and he was so sexually pent up that it didn't take more than a few thrusts before he ejaculated. While Sue removed a tissue from her handbag to wipe herself, Ritchie leaned up against the wall and lit a post-coital cigarette.
"Fuck I needed that!"
Sue had been left wanting but she didn't say anything. Why did blokes always think they were great lovers when in fact they only ever cared about their own satisfaction? When the cigarette was finished and the butt ground into the concrete, the pair headed back to the main road.
"You going to see me home?"
"Where do you live sweetheart?"
"Barnet."
"Fuck that for a game of soldier's darling, I ain't going all that way. Here, take this."
Ritchie pulled a fifty-pound note out of his pocket, stuffed it into her hand and at the same time put his

arm out and hailed the next passing cab. When she was seated in the back he slammed the cab door and walked off. It suddenly dawned on Sue that she'd behaved no better than a Tom and the shame was almost too much to bear. No wonder people had started to talk about her and now she felt dirty. Well, there was nothing for it, they would have to come back next week and hope the blokes were there again. Sue liked Ritchie Spires and she had to show him that she wasn't a prostitute. Not once on her journey home did she give Ellie a second thought or wonder if her supposedly best friend had gotten home safely. She didn't respond when the cabbie tried to make conversation and tears streamed down her face for the entire journey. The night shouldn't have ended like this it wasn't what she'd planned and Sue Nelson planned everything. Well, there was nothing for it, she would just have to keep trying until she got her man and she had well and truly set her heart on Ritchie Spires.

CHAPTER SEVEN

By the time Michael got home, Ritchie was already in bed but he wasn't asleep. Michael crept in so as not to wake his brother and almost jumped out of his skin when Ritchie spoke.

"Fuck me, you took your time. I hope you got a shag or were you a lily-livid cunt and acted the perfect gentleman as usual?"

As Molly got undressed in the dark he rolled his eyes in disgust.

"No, I did not; she's a decent girl Ritchie. What about you? On second thoughts don't answer that, of course, you did, you dirty bastard."

"I sure did, a bit of a slag that one but I gave her a good fucking seeing too. The dirty bitch was moaning with pleasure but I've spoilt it for anyone else now I suppose."

"What the fuck are you on about Ritch?"

"Well, now she'd had a portion of the old Ritchie pork sausage anything else is gonna come up well short."

Ritchie began to laugh but Michael didn't reply, he was tired and all he wanted to do was sleep but it would turn out to be a struggle as he couldn't get Ellie out of his mind. In Barnet, it was the same for Ellie Evans as she lay in the dark with a broad grin on her face but at Sue's home it was a different matter altogether, she cried herself to sleep.

The following week Sue again dragged Ellie to the Worlds End but walking in they found the place full of the usual bikers and could hear the heavy metal pumping out in the room below.

"No! Oh, Ellie, he's never going to come in here with all of these filthy grebo's."

"You don't know that."

"Excuse me! Did you see how he was dressed? Designer gear from head to toe."

"Oh, I see what you mean but we could stay for a while, you never know we might like it and these guys might be great if you gave them a chance."

"Are you out of your fucking mind Ellie!? I wouldn't breathe the same air as them, they're dirty and don't look as if they've washed in weeks."

"Okay, why don't we walk along to a few of the other pubs? Michael told me they're from around here and you never know we might find him."

"Oh Michael is it now, you just want to see him again."

"No I don't, well maybe just a bit but I'm not infatuated with him, at least not like you are with his brother."

Sue began to laugh and a few seconds later they were heading in the direction of The Elephants Head. Sue had now composed herself and Ellie took a step back and let her friend enter first. Again the place was rammed with drinkers and from a small booth in the corner a DJ was playing 'Everybody's Free' by Baz Luhrmann.

"This is a bit more like it."

The volume was so loud that Sue had to shout at her friend about getting a drink. They pushed through the throng of revellers and after placing her order Sue glanced along the bar. Standing at the end with a pint in his hand and looking as fabulous as ever was the

man of her dreams. Dressed from head to toe in black, he stood out from all the others and she couldn't wait to be with him again. Passing a glass to Ellie she motioned with her head and walked towards him with Ellie following closely behind in the hope that Michael was also there. She wasn't to be disappointed; when he saw her he beamed from ear to ear but Ritchie didn't show the same enthusiasm in fact he wasn't pleased to see Sue in the least. True, he had hoped to get another shag tonight but with a better-looking bird and now he would have to try and get rid of this one which he wasn't relishing as with her doe eyes, she seemed to come across as a bit needy. Being as rude as he could, he didn't even acknowledge her but Sue wouldn't take the hint and placing her hand on his arms she smiled sweetly.
"How have you been Ritchie? Had a good week?"
Now he had to speak to her but it was through gritted teeth.
"Alright, I suppose."
He didn't return the question and turned sideways so he didn't have to face her but the silly slag was staring up at Ritchie as she spoke and she took him off guard with her next sentence.
"You fancy going somewhere quieter?"
Glancing at his brother he saw Michael and Ellie had blocked out any sound and were staring deeply into each other's eyes both aware of how they now felt. Ritchie sighed heavily, well; he supposed fucking this one was better than nothing. Taking her drink he placed it with his own onto the bar and then grabbing her hand led her outside. Unlike the Worlds End, there wasn't a side alley so they had to walk along to

find somewhere but at least the night was dry. Turning down beside the canal, they had only got a few yards before Ritchie pushed her up against the wall. Anyone walking along would be able to see them but he didn't care and Sue didn't complain as she didn't want to upset him. The experience was no different from the last time but as he grunted and thrusted it took a little longer so she at least got some pleasure this time. All she wanted was to bag him and hopefully, it wouldn't take too long if she kept giving herself to him. When it was over he again handed her a fifty for a cab but she didn't go home and instead, much to his annoyance, went back into the pub. When it was finally time to call it a night, Michael was a bit disappointed as he'd hoped to see Ellie home again. So had Ellie but she couldn't let her friend down. Outside the girls hailed a cab and Michael quickly stole a swift kiss before Ellie got inside. On the journey home, Sue couldn't stop talking about Ritchie and Ellie tried to show interest even if deep down all she wanted to do was think about Michael.

"My Ritchie's so good to me, it's the second time he's paid for my cab and it's not cheap."

"Your Ritchie? You've only seen him twice."

The comment riled Sue and just like always her response was spiteful.

"Yes, my Ritchie! And at least he ain't like that wet brother of his. If you wait around for him you won't be any further forward by Christmas."

Sue started to laugh and Ellie just smiled, it was better to let her friend think she'd got one over on Ellie than to have a full-scale row, especially in the back of a cab.

Business at the Spires firm was going from strength to strength. After the incidents with Reg Colby and Carol Humphries, the rest of the debtors paid on time. Michael now only ran operations from the office, he was good at it and besides, he had no stomach for the level of violence his brother had started to dish out. It was agreed that he would let Ritchie know in advance of any likely problems and Ritchie would be the one to deal with things out on the street. Michael was the planner and organised armed robberies, contacted any new businesses who would need the so-called protection rackets that they offered and also worked on the recently added drug trade which was still in its infancy for the firm. Regarding the latter, Michael was aware that they had to tread carefully so as not to step on too many toes. They had built their workforce up to twenty so were not afraid of other firms but it was always best to maintain harmony where possible. There was a big job on the horizon and if they pulled it off, it would put the firm on the map as far as other known villains were concerned. The brothers didn't want it to be common knowledge but all the same there would be whispers and with that would come credibility. Michael had been told that a security vehicle would be coming into the city from the Home Counties. It was all very hush, hush and on the advice of a top brass, the company were planning on using just a plain white van so as not to draw any undue attention. The vehicle contained confiscated drugs from a couple of the larger city police stations and for some insane reason, it was deemed to be a better way than using somewhere local. The cargo was bound for the incinerator at Dagenham but if all went well it would never reach its destination. Michael also had it on good authority that this was a first trial run and if it went smoothly, it would become a monthly occurrence. He decided that they should let this one pass and concentrate on the following months van when the powers that be, would be more at ease and confident of success.

At last, the day of the heist arrived and it turned out to be a Friday much to Ritchie's disgust.
"You lot can get off for a while and remember to keep your phones on and your fucking traps shut. If word of this gets out I will know it's come from within and you'll all fucking pay even if you weren't the one who opened his gob."
In unison, the men all muttered 'Yes, Ritchie'. To be honest, most of them were scared of the older brother and those that weren't were happy that the firm paid a good wage, too good to risk losing by speaking out of turn. To a degree they all liked Michael but they also knew never too bad mouth Ritchie in front of him as the brothers were tight and no one meant more to Michael than Ritchie. All of the men went home for their evening meal and it was agreed they would meet back at the unit at nine. When the boys got to the Lamb, Mavis was in the back kitchen at her usual spot standing in front of the cooker.
"Here are my two favourite boys! Had a hard day? I've got a nice mutton stew for your dinner, that'll line your stomachs for tonight."
They looked at each other and then both kissed her on each cheek. Mavis was wonderful and they loved her dearly but when it came down to business, nothing

was shared with either her or Burt. After finishing their meal and helping Mavis clean away the dishes, the boys went up to their room for a while.

"You think Ellie and Sue will be waiting for us tonight?"

"Who?"

Michael gave his brother a look that said 'Don't be a dick'.

"I don't care if they are, I'm only in it for a shag and I hope you've had your fucking way by now?"

Michael didn't reply, his brother could be a complete pig at times and had no respect for women. At eight-thirty they walked into the bar to say goodnight to Mavis and Burt and by the way they were dressed, Mavis knew that they weren't going for a night out. She didn't ask, her boys were entitled to their privacy but all the same, it didn't stop her from worrying. At the unit, everyone was eagerly awaiting their bosses' arrival and the tension in the air was thick. After a quick run-through of the plan, the men split into three groups plus Michael and they travelled in four vans. The security vehicle would be entering Dagenham via Alfred's Way on the A13 and from someone on the inside; the Firm had been given the make and registration number. Michael had parked up in Sainsbury's and walking to the main road he was to watch for the van. As soon as he saw it he phoned ahead to the next man further along on the road. When Teddy Edwards received the call he dialled Ritchie's phone and the line stayed open. As the van approached he gave the word and the others who were already in position on the side of Greatfields Park threw down a stinger. The van swerved from side to side as the front tyres burst on the metal spikes of the trap. The men, now all wearing full-face balaclavas, ran forward like ants and swarmed on the single occupant. Ritchie held up a handgun and as soon as the driver saw it he immediately released the lock on the rear doors. Teddy Edwards, who had now re-joined the gang, reversed one of the vans up behind and the contents were hand balled from one man to the next. All in all, the entire exercise had taken less than an hour and by just after ten they were back at the unit. Ritchie handed out a couple of cases of bears and the toast went out for what had been the smoothest job in history. Unlike his brother, Michael had gone straight back to the Lamb and as he had a pint at the bar he noticed Mavis watching him with a look of concern on her face. Silently mouthing the word 'what?' he waited for her to walk over.

"Is everything okay son?"

"Sweet as a nut Aunty, sweet as a nut. Why do you ask?"

"Because Ritchie ain't with you."

"Oh he's just tying up a few loose ends, said he wouldn't be long."

He didn't show it but Michael couldn't stop thinking about Ellie and for a moment he contemplated going out to see if she was in Camden but he was stopped when Ritchie walked in wearing the broadest grin on his face.

"A pint of your finest please landlady."

Mavis giggled and when the drink was poured the brothers took a seat at the table in the corner.

"Fuck me Molly, I wish every job could go like that one."

"What did we get?"

"You name it, it was there. Five kilos of coke and bags and bags of crack. There's also at least a year's supply of H for several heavy users and what looks like the entire contents of a very large weed den. I ain't done the calculations yet but I'm guessing it will top a mill. All we have to do now is make sure the men keep their traps shut."

"No worries on that score mate, they all know which side their bread is fucking buttered and besides, if they share info with anyone else they will only be setting themselves up. We have a tight crew Ritchie and they all have above-average intelligence. So what's next?"

"We hit it again next month. Our man on the inside says it's going to be a monthly thing and there's no way they will be expecting to be hit again, well at least not so soon."

"I don't know. It seems a bit fucking risky to me Bro."

"I agree it will take a bit more planning and we need to hit it somewhere different, maybe even before they get into London. If we don't do it next month we can forget it. Our man is a greedy cunt and if we refuse, some other firm is sure to take it on board and after that, they will be armed and ready should another robbery occur."

"Does the bloke know who we are Ritchie?"

"He ain't got a fucking clue! All dealings were carried out on a burner and payment was delivered by a courier. So, what do you think?"

Michael took a few moments to mull it over and Ritchie was on tenterhooks waiting for his answer.

"The man from Delmonte he says yes!"

The rest of the evening was spent at the pub, the brothers were on a high but by the time Burt called the last orders at just before midnight, Ritchie and Michael were already in bed and dreaming of all the money they had and were about to earn.

Three months later and on what was quickly becoming their usual Friday night out, the girls had arrived at the Worlds End but when the boys hadn't shown by ten, they headed to the Elephants Head. Sue was getting more and more agitated and uptight when there was no sign of Ritchie and she snapped at Ellie continually.

"Sue, I don't think they are coming tonight, what say we head home."

"Head fucking home! What if I leave and he comes in, what then? Some slag will be in there like a flash and I could lose him. You have no idea Ellie, no idea at all about how I'm fucking feeling!"

"Okay, okay calm down but sweetheart he ain't coming, well at least not tonight. Now I'm going home as I have work in the morning. It's up to you if you stay in the hope that he might come in or you can join me but if you don't and he's a no-show, it's a fucking expensive taxi ride home."

With tears in her eyes, Sue nodded her head and the girls set off for the station. The whole night had been a washout but they both knew that there was always next week and Sue made up her mind that come next Friday, she was determined to track Ritchie down, even if it took her all night. There was no way some other bitch was getting her claws into Sue's man!

CHAPTER EIGHT

The following week it was the same trek into Camden for the girls but this time it was successful and over the next two months the foursome meeting up would become a regular event. The last Friday night things started as they normally did but after they arrived at the Worlds End and when the boys were still a no-show at eleven o'clock the mood quickly changed, while Ellie was a little disappointed, Sue Nelson was distraught. They headed back to Barnet but with hardly a word passing between them. Turning up outside Madam G's hair salon late the following Wednesday afternoon Ellie saw her friend through the window but Sue didn't come inside and instead waited for Ellie to finish her shift. She must have stood out in the cold for a good half an hour and as Ellie swept up the last of the hair from the floor she couldn't help but worry as it was so unlike her friend. Finally, when Gaynor King the owner, at last, told her she could go Ellie pulled on her coat and was out of the door like a rocket. Dodging the rush hour traffic as Ellie ran across the road her face was full of concern. Reaching her friend she held out her hands but Sue just melted into her arms.

"Hello Babe, sorry I couldn't get out any sooner but what on earth are you doing here?"

Her friend's kind tone seemed to make things worse and Sue immediately broke down into floods of tears."

Ellie pulled away from the embrace and taking Sue's hand, led her back across the road and into

Ravenscroft Park. It was quiet so they wouldn't be disturbed and after the two sat down on one of the many benches Ellie hugged her friend until the crying subsided.

"Now calm down, take your time sweetheart and tell me what on earth has happened."

"I'm pregnant!"

For a few seconds, Ellie didn't speak as she took in the enormity of what she had just been told.

"Wow."

"Fucking Wow? How the fuck, am I going to raise a kid on my own, I don't even want one. That cunt Ritchie has done a disappearing act so he doesn't even know about it."

Ellie took hold of her friend's hands again and gently patted them.

"Then my lovely friend, we have to find him and tell him. This Friday we are going back to Camden and we won't give up until you see him, even if we have to call at that pub he lives in."

Sue smiled weakly; she didn't feel her usual self, the girl with the attitude and mouth to go with it, now felt defeated, lost and scared and right at this moment, she didn't want anyone by her side but her dear sweet Ellie.

"Come on, let's get you home and we'll meet back up at the station on Friday night. Make sure you look your best not that you don't always but you know what I mean. You need to make that bastard want you and the baby you have inside. Have you told your mum and dad?"

"Not yet, the old man will go up the wall so I wanted to wait and see what Ritchie will do."

Ellie nodded her head sagely, that was the best idea and she was glad that for once her friend wasn't jumping in with both feet like she usually did.

The Spires brothers had meticulously planned out the next robbery and the security van would be hit at a place named Lewknor just before it joined the M40. Both the road and the motorway were on Aston Rowant National Nature Reserve and just as before, Michael was ahead, Teddy Edwards was further along and the rest of the crew waited nervously with the stinger. Once again it went smoothly but this time there were two men in the cab and one, a naive bloke named Stuart, was stupidly prepared to risk his life to save the precious cargo inside. Jumping out with a baseball bat in his hand, he ran towards Ritchie but stopped dead in his tracks when a shot rang out and he was hit in the foot. As he screamed in agony, his colleague got out and ran to his side.

"You silly, silly fucker! It ain't worth it pal; you should have just let them have it."

"I couldn't Ralph, why should those scum bags get away with robbery?"

Ritchie heard the remark and stomped over to where Stuart lay on the floor with Ralph kneeling beside him.

"Who you calling a scum bag you cunt!"

"He didn't mean it Mister; it's just the shock talking. Please don't shoot us."

"Just make sure you keep your fucking traps shut!"

The van was unloaded and after Ritchie had smashed the radio and handset inside, the members of the firm all jumped into their vehicles and sped off. A mile or so down the road, the cars came to a stop and large magnetic signs were placed on the sides advertising various businesses. The first van set off and after a five-minute gap, the second and third went on their way. Michael had travelled in a car that had been stolen that afternoon which he abandoned when they neared Northolt. He was picked up in the van driven by Ritchie. On the drive back to the city the noise from inside the other vans was loud as the men all cheered and laughed at the great result they'd just had. Back at base, the beers were again handed out and after unloading and reminding the men to keep shtum, the brothers locked up and then left for home. With the adrenalin running through their veins they travelled at speed and were back at the Lamb just a little later than the previous week.

"You fancy seeing if the girls are in the Worlds End?"

"It's getting a bit late but I suppose I could do with some relief. I need to get changed first Molly, I stink and even though that dizzy bird wouldn't complain, I do have my pride. On second thoughts I think I'll give it a miss. A swift pint is in order and then bed, I'm knackered."

Michael didn't mind too much, he was worn out as well but he would have liked to have seen Ellie but there was always next week he supposed.

Earlier that evening the girls had got ready and Ellie couldn't wait to see Michael. To date, they hadn't done any more than kiss but she liked the fact that he wasn't pushy and that he seemed to respect her. There was just one problem; tonight could turn into World War Three after Sue spilt her guts about the baby and Ellie was worried he wouldn't want to see her anymore but then again, if that turned out to be the case at least it would show her what he was really like. As they travelled on the train Ellie looked at her friend who appeared so forlorn and very quiet which was so unlike her.

"You okay Hun?"

Sue sighed deeply, this had all gone so wrong and not how she had planned, she wanted the fairy tale, the adoring boyfriend and the happy ending and now, well now he could tell her to sling her hook and there was nothing she could do about it.

"Nervous that's all."

"It will be fine sweetheart, one way or another tonight things will get sorted. Best case, he wants to marry you, worst case we bring the baby up together."

Her words didn't have the effect Ellie had hoped for and now the tears started to fall.

"Stop that right now! At the moment you have nothing to cry about and besides, you'll smudge your make-up."

Sue instantly stopped crying and sniffed loudly as she ran her index finger under each eye.

"How's that?"

"Perfect, you look beautiful as always."

The girls started at the World's End and then went backwards to the Faltering Duck. Next, they tried the Elephants head and the Twelve Pins but there was no sign of the Spires brothers. It was a two-mile walk to Holloway Road and on the way they called in at the Black Stock, the Bedford Tavern, the Eaglet, the Enkel Arms and lastly the Big Red but it was still a big fat blank when it came to locating Ritchie Spires. Finally, they reached Holloway Road and as the

Lamb came into sight, Ellie who had been like a woman on a mission, stopped and turned to her friend.

"Now are you sure about this Sue because once we go inside, well there's no going back."

"Am I sure!? Of course, I'm fucking sure!"

"Okay, no need to bite my head off. Come on then, let's do this."

It was now ten forty five and the place was still busy. It was a real drinker's pub, nothing fancy décor wise and, it was also a mostly music-free zone. An upright piano sat on the far wall and Ellie imagined there must be some right old knees up at times. Yet to have a drink they were both thirsty and as they approached the bar Mavis walked over to serve the strangers.

"Hello my little darlings, what can I get you?"

Sue stepped forward and eyed the woman.

"I'll have an orange juice and my friend here will have a coke."

"And?"

"What do you mean and?"

Mavis had now taken an instant dislike to the young woman with no manners.

"A please wouldn't go amiss."

"Please!!!"

Ellie nudged her friend in the side; this wasn't the time for rudeness or sarcasm not if they wanted to find Ritchie. Taking their drinks over to the corner they sat and waited to see if the boys would make an appearance but just like the robbery the previous week, Ritchie and Michael had returned to the pub, had a swift pint and were now upstairs in bed. When the last orders were called Ellie realised this had been a futile search and she could see the pools of tears as they began to form in her friend's eyes.

"I won't be a minute sweetheart, you wait here."

Walking up to the bar she smiled in a friendly way at Mavis and beckoned for her to come over.

"I'm sorry to bother you but we are looking for Ritchie Spires."

Now Mavis was suspicious. She took a step back and just stared at Ellie for a moment.

"You ain't Old Bill are you, only they get younger and younger all the time?"

Ellie wanted to laugh at the absurdity of the question but unlike her friend, she didn't want to come over as rude.

"No I'm not Old Bill, I'm a hairdresser from Barnet and my friend has been seeing Ritchie for a while but now he seems to have disappeared."

"Well, he's not here at the moment but maybe your friend over there should take the hint. Maybe my Ritchie has given her the elbow?"

The coldness and cruelty in the landlady's voice instantly got Ellie's heckles up.

"Your Ritchie as you call him has been banging Sue every week for the last two months and now she's up the duff and he ain't got the first idea about what's going on."

For the first time in an age, Mavis was momentarily speechless.

"Just give me a minute love."

Walking through the door Mavis stopped in the rear hallway that led to the cellar and puffed out her cheeks in shock. Could this really be true, was she about to become a kind of adopted grandmother?

Suddenly she smiled, if it was true she would love a baby in her life to spoil and look after. Smoothing down her dress she patted her hair and then walked back into the bar.

"As I told you, the boys ain't here but I will have a word when they get in. Come back tomorrow night if you can and I will make sure Ritchie is here, let's say about eight?"

Ellie nodded, thanked the woman and then walked over to her friend.

"He ain't here Sue but the landlady said she will have a word with him and if you come back tomorrow night she'll make sure that he's here to see you."

"I suppose it's something. You will come with me won't you?"

Ellie was dreading this, Saturdays were always the busiest in the shop and she didn't finish until six thirty. It wouldn't be worth going all the way home so she would have to take her spare clothes to work and change at the shop.

"Of course I will that's what best friends do for each other. Come on let's get home I'm bleeding knackered."

The next morning and even though for him it wasn't a work day, Ritchie was up first. Walking down the stairs he sniffed loudly but there was no aroma of bacon and when he entered the kitchen Mavis was seated at the table nursing a cup of tea with a face like thunder.

"Everything alright Aunty, Burt pissed you off again?"

"No, he hasn't and no it isn't. Sit down; I need to talk

to you."

"Can I just get a cupper?"

"No! Sit down now!"

In all the years he had lived at the Lamb Mavis hadn't raised her voice to him or Michael not once and to say this was out of the ordinary was an understatement. Doing as he was asked and with a quizzical expression on his face, Ritchie sat down. Mavis now felt guilty and her motherly instinct kicked in so she stood up and fetched the teapot and a mug. He waited until she had poured him a brew but she wasn't forthcoming straight away. Last night as she'd mulled over the news it had begun to bother her. Too many young men were happy to have their way regardless of the consequences, she saw the results every day down the market with young girls pushing prams, young girls who looked down on their luck and who were now tied with no chance of escape.

"I had some visitors last night."

"Not the Old Bill!?"

"No, not the Old Bill but it might have been better if it had been. The visitors were two young women by the name of Sue and Ellie"

"Fuck me, not those two old slappers. I'm sorry about that Mavis they shouldn't…"

Mavis banged the palm of her hand down on the table and her action startled him into silence. She could be fiery; he'd seen that first-hand in the past but never with him or Molly.

"Don't you dare call them that! I understand you've been getting your end away with the one named Sue. I didn't take to her but I suppose she had a right to be unfriendly. The old slag you referred to is now up the duff with your kid!"

"What!?"

"You heard me. I don't suppose you thought of protection, it's always the same old story with blokes, you're all led by your cocks. So?"

"So what?"

Just then Michael entered the room and he was also disappointed that he couldn't smell bacon. About to enquire about his breakfast, he stopped when he saw Mavis and his brother seated at the table.

"What's with the raised voices you two?"

Mavis's sour expression looked set in stone and Michael prayed his brother hadn't upset Aunty to the point where they would be kicked out, this was the only real home he had known and he loved Mavis and Burt as if they were his parents. Turning to face Ritchie, Mavis tapped on the table with her index finger.

"Well, are you going to tell him or should I?"

Pulling out a chair Michael sat down but his gaze never left his brother as he waited for an explanation. When Ritchie began to run the fingers of his right hand through his hair, something he always did when he was pissed off, Michael knew that whatever had happened, it must be bad.

"That fucking Sue has only gone and got herself up the fucking duff!"

Now Mavis was angry, more than angry, she was seething and her voice had gone up a couple of octaves as she spoke.

"Got herself pregnant!? I know your education wasn't up to much boy but I'm sure even you are aware that it takes two to make a baby so why are you putting all

87

the blame on her? I must say, you have disappointed me, Ritchie Spires, really disappointed me!"

Suddenly Michael's face broke into a broad grin and when Ritchie saw it he wasn't happy and kicked his brother under the table.

"What's so funny you soppy twat?"

"Sorry bro but I've always wanted to be an uncle and it ain't so bad, it's not like you've got to walk her down the aisle or anything now is it?"

Mavis couldn't believe what she was hearing and waded in before Ritchie had a chance to reply.

"He most certainly has. Why should the poor little mite spend his or her life with the label of illegitimate, or worse still as a bastard, just because your brother couldn't keep it in his pants? Michael, I expected better from you."

"Well I'm going to ask for one of them tests before I commit to anything, the baby could be any fuckers and I ain't getting saddled with a kid that might not even be mine!"

Mavis slowly shook her head, how times had changed. In her day there would be no questions asked but back then girls tended to keep their legs closed for quite a while before they let their boyfriends have their way. If it did finally result in a pregnancy then without question, they would be hastily married before the birth.

"So you're going to make her wait until it comes into the world!?"

"I didn't say that Mavis. You can have a test done now before it's born."

There was nothing left to be said but the atmosphere at the Lamb remained tense for the rest of the day.

Mavis went shopping and stayed out until just before opening as she couldn't bear to even be in the same room as her boys at the moment. Burt wondered what on earth was going on as she hadn't shared the news with him yet and he was getting fed up with the sullen face of his wife throughout the lunchtime service. The boys spent much of the day up in their room talking and Michael could see that his brother felt frustrated at being trapped but even he knew that Ritchie couldn't just abandon Sue or come to that his own baby.

"Look Ritch, it's happened so you just have to deal with it and you'll love the kid when it gets here, maybe you will even come to love Sue one day."

"I doubt that very much and besides, it ain't just the kid Molly, it's the thought of being tied down to one woman. I can't stand it, I really can't fucking stand the thought of it. You know I never imagined getting married, least of all being forced into it. Spending my entire life with one person has never interested me in the least."

"I didn't know that. I want to get married but I understand what you're saying. There's a big difference between falling in love and wanting to tie the knot to being told it's what you have to do. You could always refuse bro."

"How can I? Mavis would never forgive me and I wouldn't hurt her for the world."

"Well, let's just wait and see what develops tonight. We're all assuming that Sue wants a ring on her finger but maybe she doesn't. Now that really would be a turn-up for the books."

Ritchie smiled at his brother's words but inside he

was willing those words to come true so he'd be off the hook. He wouldn't shirk his responsibilities and the kid would never want for anything he would make sure of that but marriage? Oh please God no.

CHAPTER NINE

That day Sue phoned in sick at Walk Easy, just the thought of all those stinky, sweaty feet made her feel like heaving. There was also Gloria and her incessant questions and happy chatting all day and since Sue had first opened her eyes this morning it was a no-brainer that she wasn't going in to work. The call hadn't gone down well as Gloria would now be left with just the Saturday girl for help and Marlene Collins wasn't the brightest bulb in the box.

"Well, I hope you really are sick Sue and it's not just a hangover from last night. Head office frowns on behaviour like that you know and if they call the branch I'm not lying for you."

"Bloody hell Gloria! I hardly ever take a day off apart from my holiday and yes, I am actually sick."

With that Sue slammed down the phone, she was livid that the old cow had challenged her and it wasn't a complete lie anyway as the last few days had seen the onset of morning sickness. Hearing her daughter retching for two days on the trot, Sue's mum Karen had an inkling of what was going on. Finally emerging from the bathroom Sue flopped down on one of the dining chairs and her complexion was as white as a ghost.

"Cup of tea and a slice of toast darling, it will help settle your stomach."

Sue looked at her mum with daggers, just the mention of breakfast made her feel like heaving again.

"I know what's going on you know?"

"What are you talking about Mum because I ain't in

the mood today?"

"You're pregnant aren't you?"

Sue's mouth hung open, how on earth did she know, did her dad know as well?

"I was the same when I was carrying you, couldn't keep a thing down for the first three or four months and I always found dry toast helped a lot. So, who is the father?"

Sue placed her elbows on the table and held her forehead in her hands, this was all she needed.

"I can't talk about this at the moment Mum; I need to go back to bed."

Standing up she had to steady herself with the back of the chair, if this was what pregnancy was like she was going to make sure it never happened again.

"Will you wake me up about four mum, we can have a chat then if you want?"

When the minute hand hit the hour Karen Nelson had tapped on her daughter's bedroom door and then walked inside. Sue was sound asleep and she hated to wake her but if she didn't do as she'd been asked she would be in the firing line of her daughter's wrath and under normal circumstances it was bad enough but after all of the sickness this morning Sue would be like a bear with a sore head. Taking a seat on the side of the bed she gently stroked Sue's brow until her daughter woke up.

"Hi my darling, you feeling any better?"

"A bit thanks. Sorry about earlier mum but I just didn't have the strength to explain. Does my dad know?"

"Not yet sweetheart, I wanted to find out the facts

before I tell him. You know what he's like and I don't want him going off like a bottle of pop if there ain't any reason to. So, you going to tell me how this mess happened?"

"I met a bloke."

"Well, I gathered that much love."

Sue smiled; at times like these, she really did love her old lady. A lot of girl's mums would have kicked them out as soon as they realised but Sue knew that would never happen to her.

"Oh Mum, he's so handsome and he has his own business."

"That's nice my darling but what's he think about the baby?"

"He doesn't know yet, I'm going to tell him tonight. Ellie's coming with me so you don't need to worry."

"Do you think he will want to do the right thing by you?"

"That's what I'm hoping for. Will you put off telling Dad until we know what's going to happen? I just need some peace and him reading me the riot act won't help matters."

"Of course, I will sweetheart. Now get yourself up and I'll run you a nice bath."

When her mother closed the bedroom door Sue could feel the hot tears stinging as they rolled down her cheeks. She knew after the way she normally treated her mother that she didn't deserve such kindness.

Ellie had worked her socks off and it felt as if the whole of Barnet wanted their hair washed and set today. The Saturday shampoo girl hadn't turned up so Ellie had done all the washes herself and her fingertips now felt like wrinkled prunes. Glancing at the wall clock she was glad to see it was almost five thirty meaning she only had just over an hour left although she wasn't looking forward to tonight and just hoped that her friend was okay.

As Ellie had changed her clothes at work, she was the first one at the station. With only five minutes to go until the train left, she was getting anxious but suddenly she spotted Sue slowly walking along the platform.

"Thank the Lord; I didn't think you were coming."

"Well I ain't got much choice have I?"

Her tone was sharp and Ellie wrinkled her brow.

"I'm sorry Ell, I'm just so uptight and I've been throwing up for most of the day. Gloria at the shop wasn't best pleased when I rang in sick but I just couldn't face it. I never thought being pregnant would make you feel so awful, plus I've been thinking about Ritchie, what if he tells me to fuck off?"

Linking her arm in her friends, the two boarded the train and luckily it wasn't too busy.

"I'm sure he won't but we'll never find out if we don't go and one way or the other you need to know what your future holds, with or without Richie Spires. If he turns out to be a complete cunt and doesn't want to do right by you, then you won't be alone babe, you have your family and you'll always have me I promise."

The words which had meant to sound kind instantly had Sue in floods of tears and she wiped her eyes with the cuff of her jacket before she let out a short giggle. She realised that it must be her hormones as her emotions had been all over the place all day.

"Ellie Evans!"

"What?"

"You used the C word and I know how much you hate it."

"I know but sometimes it's the only way to express myself, he'd just better do right by you Sue or I'll be using that word a lot more."

After changing trains at Finsbury Park, two stops later the girls emerged from the underground. They didn't mess about and headed straight for the Lamb, when they got outside Sue stopped dead in her tracks.

"I can't go in, I can't do this Ellie really I can't!"

"Don't be so silly of course you can, you have to sweetheart. Come on, I'll go in first."

Due to it being a Saturday the pub was full of regular drinkers and there was a lot of shouting and jovial banter going on. Mavis had been continually looking at the door ever since they had opened for the evening, just in case the girls came early and when she spied Ellie she breathed a sigh of relief. Ritchie and Michael were sitting at the table in the corner and when Michael saw Ellie, he nudged his brother in the ribs with his elbow. Ritchie exhaled deeply, he wasn't looking forward to this and it had been playing on his mind all day.

"What should I do Molly, should I invite her over here or take her through to the back?"

"Maybe the back will be best as it's a bit noisy in here and besides, you don't want the world and his wife knowing your business and the fuckers in here are a nosey bunch of cunts at the best of times."

Ritchie stood up and walked over to where the girls now stood at the bar. Sue smiled weakly and Ritchie did something that was really out of character, he bent and kissed her on the cheek before taking her hand and leading her through to the living quarters. Ellie grinned and then made her way over to Michael.

"Alright?"

"I am now that you're here Ellie. This is all a bit of a fucking turn-up for the books ain't it?"

"You can say that again."

"This is all a bit of a fucking turn-up for the books ain't it?"

She mockingly punched him in the shoulder for being stupid but it still made her laugh. In the back kitchen, Sue took a seat at the table and Ritchie grabbed a bottle of scotch and two glasses. Pouring one he handed it to her but she shook her head.

"Sorry sweetheart, of course, you can't have a drink, I wasn't thinking. Well, this is a bit of a mess ain't it?"

"I don't want anything from you Ritchie but I just wanted you to know that's all. Our baby has a right to know who its daddy is and I didn't want her or him just turning up out of the blue on your doorstep in a few years."

Her words took him by surprise; she didn't want a ring on her finger!? Her hands were trembling but she was smart and the reverse psychology had worked as he gently took her hand in his.

"I know this baby wasn't conceived through love or planning but no kid of mine is being born out of wedlock. Now I do want a DNA test done but you can't blame me for wanting that."

Sue sharply pulled her hand away.

"Are you calling me a slag?"

"No, of course not but I'm willing to devote my life to you and the little one so I just want to be sure for my own peace of mind."

"Ritchie Spires, I have only slept with two men in my entire life!"

As the lie fell from her mouth she didn't flinch and continued as if this was all his fault, that she was entirely innocent in the conception.

"The first, took my virginity when I was fourteen, he was wet behind the ears and it was a complete let down. You are the second. It hurts that you've asked but I will take a test as soon as possible. I'm not easy Ritchie, it's just that I fell for you the moment I saw you and having sex was my stupid way of showing it. Ridiculous I know and in hindsight, we wouldn't be in this sorry mess if I hadn't but we can't turn back the clock so we have to make the best of it."

Suddenly Ritchie got down on one knee and Sue couldn't believe what she was seeing.

"Sue….., Oh my God, I've just realised I don't even know your last name?"

"Nelson."

"Well Sue Nelson, will you marry me?"

Laughing and crying at the same time, she stood up and the two embraced. As happy as she was, it wasn't the same for Ritchie Spires, his heart felt heavy as he realised that his days of womanising were over, well at least for the time being.

"We need to go and tell Mavis, she's been like a bear with a sore head all day."

"Who is Mavis?"

"Mavis and Burt own this place and they took me and Michael in years ago when our parents, though I use that term very fucking loosely, well to cut a long story short we couldn't live with them anymore.

Mavis is like a mum to me and my brother and we both adore her. I will warn you though; she ain't no fucking pushover."

In the bar, it was drinks all around, except for Sue of course. Ellie couldn't believe that her oldest friend was getting married and would soon be a mother. All the regulars congratulated the couple and Ritchie had so many drinks bought for him that he soon began to feel the effects. When it was at last time to leave Ritchie paid for a cab to take the girls home and it was agreed that he would go to tea at Sue's the following day, something else he wasn't looking forward to. Karen was still up when Sue walked in the door and when she saw how happy her daughter was and heard the news; she danced around the living room. They still had to tell her father Joe but that could wait until the morning, for now, she didn't want anything spoiling her girl's happiness.

Ritchie had hardly slept and was just lying there staring at the ceiling when Michael woke up the next morning.

"You okay?"

"No not really but there ain't much I can do about it. I've got to meet the future fucking in-law's today! Forty-eight hours ago I was on a high, we'd just pulled off a blinding heist and life was good. Now? Well now I'm tied to a woman I don't love, I'm not sure if I even like her that much and with the added burden of a kid on the way."

Michael hated seeing his brother so down but there wasn't anything he could do about it, though Ritchie's loss of freedom was turning out to be Michael's gain as the impending nuptials meant he would see a lot more of Ellie. Still, he had to try and talk Ritchie into some kind of positivity.

"Life's a bitch at times bro and things happen when we don't want them to but sometimes they turn out to be the best things that could have happened to us. Instead of seeing the negative in everything, just go with the flow and see what occurs. I mean, if it don't work out you can always get a divorce."

Ritchie lay there in the dark and mulled over all that Molly had just said and his brother was right, he wasn't tied down for the rest of his life. He would see how it went and if it did go tits up, he could get rid of her if he wanted.

"Sometimes Molly you are a clever cunt do you know that?"

They both laughed and then Ritchie pulled the duvet up over their heads and at the same time let out a long and very stinky fart. Molly started to cough and wretch and they were soon laughing like schoolboys.

Down in the kitchen, Mavis was singing as she prepared the breakfast. Hearing her boys upstairs laughing made her smile. Suddenly things had taken an upturn, not only did she have a wedding to look forward to but also the arrival of her first, so to speak, grandchild.

In Barnet, it was full steam ahead preparing the afternoon tea. Earlier Karen had taken Joe to one side and shared all that was going on. At first, he wasn't happy about the pregnancy, in all honesty he had hit the roof but once his wife explained that their oldest would be getting married very soon, he came around. Sue could be a right bitch at times and most of the upset in the house was caused by her, now she would be leaving and he was relishing what the peace would be like. The spare chair that was usually stored upstairs was brought down. The boys, Terry and Gary, were bathed and wearing their best clothes and had been sternly warned by their father that they had to behave or suffer the consequences. Karen had prepared an array of sandwiches and there was no cheap ham in sight. At four on the dot, Ritchie rang the doorbell and Sue almost ran along the hallway to let him in. After the initial introductions, the conversation soon became awkward until Ritchie asked Joe if he followed the football. A lifelong Arsenal fan, the two instantly hit it off and while Sue and her mum discussed wedding options, the two men chatted about the up-and-coming season. Sue's brothers were soon excused from the table and were allowed to turn on the television so long as the volume was kept low. A little after six thirty Ritchie decided he'd spent an acceptable amount of time at the house and that it was a good time to be on his way. After arranging for Sue to come over to the pub tomorrow evening, he headed for home but even though the afternoon had been a success, his heart was still heavy.

"So Dad, Mum, what did you think?"

"Well girl, I must admit I was a bit sceptical at first but what a bloody nice fella, you could do a lot worse than him."

"Mum?"

"Oh he's so handsome Sue, I can see why you fell for him and that baby is going to be a real looker. I tell you something, if I was twenty years younger I wouldn't say no if...."

"In your dreams woman, now how about you make your own Richard Gere a cuppa?"

As Joe walked over to his chair and undid his trousers as his ever-expanding waist had taken in far too many sandwiches this afternoon, Karen and Sue burst out laughing.

Ritchie didn't go to the station instead he walked for quite a while. When he'd finally got everything straight in his head he hailed a cab. He would give this relationship his all, at least for now but he was also going to take the Spires firm to the next level. Hopefully, the kid would be a boy so that he could take over one day and if not, well they would just have to have another one, after all, it hadn't taken much to get her up the duff in the first place. Thinking about that, Ritchie realised that once they had tied the knot he would have sex on tap, however, and whenever he wanted it, whether Sue did or not. All in all, he supposed things could have been a lot worse.

CHAPTER TEN

After deciding, much to Gloria's annoyance, to take the whole of the week off sick, the next day Sue walked into the lamb just before afternoon closing and Mavis led her straight through to the kitchen leaving Burt to close up alone.

"Cuppa tea sweetheart?"

"Oh yes please Mrs McAllister and I'm sorry about the first time I came here, you know, coming over as rude as I did. I was so scared about the reception I would receive and how Ritchie was going to take the news, not to mention his family."

"Don't you worry about that my love I completely understand and please call me Mavis, after all, you'll soon be part of the family as well."

When the tea was made and had been poured into Mavis's best china cups it was time to start planning.

"So my darling, when are you hoping to get wed and what sort of thing do you want?"

Sue's politeness and the answer she was about to give had been well rehearsed. Knowing that she had to get the woman on her side and also that she didn't want to come over greedy, she surprised Mavis with her reply.

"Well, as I'll be quite a way on when the test results come through I thought just a quiet ceremony at the registry with close friends and family and if you don't mind, a small reception back here?"

Mavis grabbed the young woman's hand and as tears formed in her eyes, she dabbed at them with the bottom of her apron.

"Oh sweetheart, you've made an old woman very happy and of course you can have it here. It might not be fine dining but I'll put on a bleedin' fine spread and tell your mum and dad that it's on me and Burt."
"Thank you so much Mavis you really are kind and Mum and Dad will be relieved, what with my two brothers there ain't much spare cash to splash around."
"I understand Sue, small mouths are always hungry. Now how about a piece of my fruit cake?"
"Oh thanks but not today, I have to get off and meet my friend, we're going to look at dresses."
Mavis smiled, all brides were the same and wanted to get their dresses before anything else, she supposed it was the fairy tale they were looking for. Walking Sue to the door Mavis kissed her on the cheek and then went back inside. It was mission accomplished and as soon as Sue heard the door close she vigorously rubbed at her cheek. She didn't head straight for home, instead, she went up West to her favourite charity shops and picked out a cream designer gown that she had fallen in love with a couple of weeks earlier but hadn't bought it at the time as it had been a bit too big. With her wedding dress purchased she decided it was now time to go home as her feet were swollen and she felt really tired, this pregnancy game wasn't a lot of fun. Even so, she was deliriously happy and went to catch the train with a spring in her step.

The test results came back three months later and thankfully due to her slim build, Sue wasn't showing too much and could still fit into her dress. When the letter had dropped onto the doormat at the Lamb,

Ritchie's heart had sunk to the bottom of his stomach. Somewhere deep inside he had hoped for a negative result but that wasn't to be. While waiting for the news, the couple had been spending a lot of time together and Ritchie realised that Sue wasn't as bad as he had first thought, they didn't have much in common but the sex had gotten better, she gave an amazing blow job and after they talked a lot about the future he could see that they both had plans and dreams albeit slightly different. They both wanted a beautiful home and for Ritchie to take the firm to the next level which all seemed to be happening but Sue continually referred to the business as his and he had to keep reminding her that it was half Michael's. He couldn't see that even before they were married she was plotting and planning for her husband-to-be to take over and force his brother out. After the pregnancy result the ceremony was hastily arranged for two weeks and when the day finally arrived Sue barked orders at everyone including her bridesmaid and best friend Ellie. Back at the reception Mavis had prepared a traditional spread and Sue grimaced when she saw the bowls full of jellied eels, cockles, sandwiches and sausage rolls. The table groaned with food but it wasn't what she had hoped for, it was tacky and common but she knew better than to say anything this early on. Music played through an old boom box that Burt had bought in the late seventies and was still extremely proud of. He had hit it off with Joe and Karen Nelson from the moment they were introduced and it was something Mavis was happy to see as her husband could be quiet to the point of rudeness at times especially if he didn't know someone. Terry and Gary Nelson were running all over the place causing havoc but for once their parents didn't chastise them. Karen had warned the boys to behave before leaving home but the message seemed to have fallen on deaf ears. Ellie and Michael smooched when the slow songs were played and Sue stared at them with envy. It was obvious they would soon be going strong and she wished her new husband would look at her the same way Michael gazed at her friend. Ritchie spent all afternoon propping up the bar with the rest of the men from the firm and when it was time to cut the cake, a strawberry sponge made by Karen, he almost fell over. Sue grabbed her husband's arm to steady him and the look on her face said it all.

"You could have at least stayed sober today Ritchie."

"Did you hear that lads, fucking nagging me already?"

The room was in uproar with laughter but Sue was devastated. She was beginning to wonder about the saying 'Be careful what you wish for' maybe she had got it all wrong. As a wedding present, Mavis and Burt had paid for a room at the Savoy Hotel but it was ruined by the excessive amount of drink Ritchie had consumed, he was even too drunk to consummate the marriage and Sue lay in the dark crying while her husband snored his head off beside her.

The next morning after breakfast, they moved into their new home. The flat was in a small newly renovated block which had recently gone up for sale at Gilbeys Yard but it wasn't what Sue had dreamed of and after giving in her notice at the shoe shop she

105

spent her days aimlessly strolling around the market and canal. Within a couple of months of getting married, Ritchie hated it, he hated being tied down and questioned about where he was going and when he'd be home. Most days after work he would return to the Lamb and the warmth and laughter that his brother still enjoyed made him long for the days of a few weeks ago. Mavis sensed his unhappiness and after a while, she decided to pull him to one side for a chat.

"What's up, son? You look so down in the dumps lately."

"I don't know how much longer I can take in Aunty."

Mavis sighed heavily, it was always the same with newlyweds and Burt and her had been exactly the same but they had to take time to settle in and really get to know each other.

"Marriage isn't easy for anyone in the beginning love, especially when you've been forced into it. You have to allow a time of adjustment, it must be the same for Sue you know."

"I realise that but she's on my fucking case before I go to work and starts again as soon as I get in. I've been going home later and later but it makes no difference and her cooking is shite and nothing like yours duchess. Look at this."

Ritchie pulled on the waistband of his jeans and she couldn't deny that there did seem to be a bigger-than-normal gap. His words made Mavis laugh but deep down she knew things were coming to a head. She had been right about Sue from the off and whenever they called at the pub it took all of the girl's effort just to say hello. She and Burt were never invited over to the flat, something she would have loved but Mavis didn't have the heart to share her opinion of Ritchie's wife because if she did, she knew it might just be the straw that broke the camel's back and she didn't want to be responsible for the break-up of a marriage. If and when that happened, the decision had to come from Ritchie.

"It will get better I promise you and when that baby comes along Sue will have her hands so full that she won't have time to worry about where you are sunshine."

Mavis was correct and on December the twenty-ninth, baby Daniel Michael Joseph Spires came into the world. Ritchie was elated and after visiting the hospital twice he then went on a two-day party bender, after all, it was the New Year. Since his brother's wedding, Michael and Ellie had become close and were spending every spare minute together. Ellie's mum Eileen, had really taken to her daughter's boyfriend, he spent a lot of time at their home and was always polite and respectful so it was no surprise when at the stroke of midnight on New Year's Eve, he got down on one knee in the small from room at Old Ford View. Eileen jumped to her feet with joy as soon as her shocked daughter said yes. No one at the Lamb was surprised; they all knew that Michael was head over heels in love with the girl, you couldn't be off of seeing it as it was written all over his face. Ritchie wasn't happy and told his brother he was making a big mistake just as he had but Michael wouldn't listen. Even though she congratulated them, Sue was jealous pure and simple, now the limelight would be off of her and little Danny and there was nothing she could do about it.

On January the second, Sue and Ritchie were due at the registrars to legally register the baby's name. Ritchie had agreed to meet Sue outside the offices at five to two and had promised that he wouldn't be late, their appointment was at two and when he still hadn't arrived at five passed Sue was seething. Deciding she would go in alone, she was shocked when the registrar informed her that without a signed declaration, she wouldn't be able to add the father's name. About to reschedule Sue suddenly got so angry that she told the registrar to go ahead and list her son as Daniel Nelson. Ritchie would go mental when he found out but she didn't care it served him right. Sue was also informed that they would be able to add the father to the certificate at a later date. That afternoon at the Lamb Ritchie was full of apologies but he never asked to look at the birth certificate so for the foreseeable future Daniel would remain a Nelson and not a Spires.

It was soon time for Ellie and Michael to tie the knot and Ellie spent the night before her Wedding at the Lamb. Eileen hadn't been able to get out of her shift at work and as she didn't want her girl to be alone so had asked Mavis if Ellie could stay at the pub. Michael had been shipped off to a friend's house as Mavis didn't want him to risk bad luck by seeing his bride before the ceremony. News of the wedding had the locals drinking in earnest and Mavis and Burt were rushed off of their feet so Ellie had spent the evening alone in the back room. By ten Ellie had decided to have an early night and when she was woken by the bedroom door opening at just before eleven, she thought it was Mavis popping in to check on her. Suddenly she could smell stale beer in the air and giggled.

"Michael is that you? You know we can't see each other until tomorrow you naughty boy."

When the bedclothes were roughly pulled back and her nightie was lifted she could feel her body go ridged. A hand was suddenly forced between her legs, it was so rough and she let out a whimper as she realised this wasn't her Michael, he wouldn't treat her like that. Her attacker must have entered through the back door, which was always kept locked but maybe Burt had gone out to the backyard beer store and forgot to lock it when he came back in. Her head whirled; she just couldn't believe this was happening to her. It all seemed to be playing out in slow motion but it was really only seconds and as she tried to scream nothing would come out but suddenly she got her voice.

"Get off! Get off of me!!!!!"

She could feel he was aroused as her attacker hissed in her ear.

"Shut your trap you dirty slag, you know you want it, have done since the night we met."

A hand suddenly clamped down hard over her mouth. With all her might, Ellie, scratching and punching tried to fight him off but she wasn't any match for a man. Her hand clawed at his face but it was futile and seconds later he forced himself inside of her. She was dry and the pain was excruciating but still, the assault continued. As her attacker grunted and thrust until he ejaculated Ellie tightly closed her eyes as she tried desperately to block out what was happening to her. As quickly as it had all begun it was over but in fear, she didn't move an inch until she heard the bedroom door close and the man descend the stairs. Jumping out of bed she ran to the bathroom and locked the door behind her. Ellie could see blood under her fingernails and was desperate to remove it. Running a bath and when it was as hot as she could stand she stepped in and winced in pain when the heat burnt her skin. Ellie scrubbed at her body until it was raw but she just couldn't stop not even when all traces of him were gone. She tried to muffle her sobs but it was difficult, she also knew that she shouldn't be washing and that she should have called the police but she just couldn't. To start her marriage with a rape hanging over her head would be more than she could bear and besides, what would Michael think of her now, would he always look at her as damaged goods?

The next morning at breakfast her eyes were still puffy and she was very subdued but Mavis just took it as pre-wedding nerves. When the full English breakfast was put down in front of her, Ellie thought she was about to be sick. Pushing the plate as far away as she could, she smiled weakly.

"I'm so sorry Mavis you've gone to so much trouble but I just can't eat a thing. My stomach is in knots." Mavis smiled and winked.

"Don't you worry sweetheart, my Burt will polish that little lot off before you know it. Burt!!!! Your breakfast is ready."

The wedding was again held at the Registry Office but this time there were just six people in attendance, the bride and groom, Ritchie, Eileen, Mavis and Burt. Sue had made the excuse that the baby was a little bit under the weather so she wouldn't be able to make the service. Throughout the entire thirty-minute ceremony Ellie couldn't take her eyes off of Ritchie but he wouldn't look in her direction. Down his face were two long scratch marks and as soon as Ellie set eyes on him, she knew who her attacker had been. To the others, he explained the marks on his face had been caused by falling over last night after he'd had a skin full but Ellie knew the truth and struggled to stop the tears from forming. Eileen could see there was something wrong with her daughter and it broke her heart, was Ellie having second thoughts? There was no party afterwards and Ritchie disappeared as soon as the ceremony was over, not even waiting to have his photograph taken with the rest of them. It had hurt Michael immensely but he didn't comment as he didn't want anything to spoil Ellie's day. Later that evening, the newlyweds flew off to Italy for a week-long honeymoon and it turned out to be idyllic. They walked along the beeches, napped in the afternoon and spent leisurely nights eating by candlelight in intimate restaurants. Her husband was so tender with her that the bad memories of her wedding eve started to dim and not seem so bad. When it was time to leave neither of them wanted to go home but to make things a little easier, Michael promised to bring his wife back again on one of their future anniversary's. Back in London as soon as she had returned home from the hospital, Sue began her meddling. She started by making snide comments about Ellie to Ritchie, saying that she had changed and that she was changing Michael. Ritchie hadn't been listening until he heard the mention of his brother's name. He was gutted that while Molly had been away he hadn't called him once but that wasn't true. Sue had answered Ritchie's mobile on Molly's first attempt and informed her brother-in-law that her husband was in a meeting, she then deleted the call. The second time he phoned the flat and again Sue answered and said Ritchie was out for the evening. After that Michael gave up but when he returned he did ask his brother when he sensed that Ritchie was giving him the cold shoulder.

"What's up with you, kid keeping you up all night?"

"Oh fuck off Molly and no he isn't, Danny's a good baby and sleeps through the night. I'm just a bit pissed off that you couldn't even be bothered to give me a call while you were away."

"I did call you, twice in fact. Both times I spoke to Sue and she seemed to be making excuses so I didn't bother again."

Ritchie didn't reply to the statement but when he got home he immediately confronted his wife.

"I don't know what you're on about; I haven't spoken to your bleedin' brother."

"Well, he said he spoke to you, twice!"

"Oh that's right, take his word over mine. There's been no phone calls to the flat, have you checked your mobile?"

Suddenly he felt guilty for accusing her and when he went back over his call log there was nothing recorded, the seed of doubt had been set and Ritchie had to eat humble pie and apologise to her.

The day after they had returned from honeymoon, Ellie had gone round to Sue's flat as she was confident that Ritchie would be at work. The newlyweds had purchased a beautiful lace christening gown in Italy and she couldn't wait to give it to her best friend but she wasn't greeted as warmly as she'd hoped. Excitedly waiting at the door she was dumbstruck for a few seconds when Sue opened up and just stared at her.

"What do you want?"

"Excuse me?"

"Look, I have a lot on and I need to feed Danny."

For a second Ellie wondered if her friend knew what had happened but then she came to her senses, of course she didn't know, how could she?

"Okay, I won't stop long it's just that we bought you something in Italy."

Sue's expression instantly changed and she stood aside so that Ellie could enter. In the smartly furnished front room, Sue almost snatched the parcel from her friend's hands and couldn't wait to see what designer item she had got. Her face dropped as soon as she saw what was inside.

"What the fuck is that?"

"It's a christening gown silly."

"I know what it is but it ain't for me is it?"

Ellie's brow furrowed, she couldn't believe what Sue had just said.

"Well no, it's for your son. Sue, whatever has gotten into you?"

Sue flopped down on the sofa and sighed deeply.

"This marriage and motherhood lark isn't what I thought it would be. I hardly go out, well not at night.

113

His nibs in there, cries constantly unless he's in Ritchie's arms and Molly stirring the shit hasn't helped."

"I'm sorry darling but I ain't got the foggiest what you're on about. How has Michael stirred the shit?"

"He told Ritchie that while you were on honeymoon he tried to call him twice but he fucking didn't."

The sentence was like a red rag to a bull because what Sue wasn't aware of was the fact that on both of those occasions, Ellie had been with her husband.

"Sue that's a bloody lie and you know it."

"No, it's not and I would have thought as my best friend you would have my back instead of siding with that wanker you married."

"I know he phoned because I was there when he tried. I don't know what your game is Sue but you can stop it right now. If you're trying to split them up it's not going to happen, they are brothers for God's sake and have always had each other's back. Nothing will come between them, ever!"

With that Ellie turned on her heels and walked out slamming the door as she went which instantly woke the baby and as she took her first step on the stairs she could hear him screaming his lungs out. She was seething with her friend but couldn't help but allow a thin smile to form on her lips.

CHAPTER ELEVEN

That night when Michael got home Ellie was full of nerves but she still shared all that had happened with Sue. Before the wedding, Mavis had given her a few tips and one of them was to never lie to your husband or keep anything from him as the truth would always come out in the end. Ellie had already broken the latter rule by not telling Michael about the rape so she certainly wasn't going to keep anything else from him. Standing at the stove making sure Mavis's potatoes didn't burn, she had her back to him when he came in.

"Alright babe, had a good day?"

Ellie just shook her head and that was it, usually, she couldn't wait to see him and would hug him as if she hadn't seen him for weeks when in fact it had only been a few hours.

"What's wrong?"

"I went to see Sue and the baby today to take the christening gown which she was bloody rude about but that's another story. She said you were causing trouble and stirring the shit about making out you'd phoned your brother when we were on honeymoon. I called her a liar and said I was there when you tried to call him."

"What did she say to that?"

"She didn't as I left straight after."

"What's she playing at Ell?"

"All I can think of is that she's jealous and is trying to cause a ruck between you and your brother. Sometimes Sue can be a real bitch and for no reason."

"Well, it's never going to happen sweetheart; me and Ritchie have been tight since we were little. Is Mavis in the bar?"

"Yes, why?"

"No reason but don't mention all of this to her babe. She dislikes Sue as it is so no point in pouring fuel on the fire."

Personally, Ellie would rather that she and Michael had no contact with Ritchie but if it did happen it would tear the family apart not to mention break Mavis's heart and she would do anything to stop that. From then on the atmosphere between the brothers wasn't good but they had weathered many storms before and neither would let it come between them. Soon after, Ellie and Michael moved into their first home on Grafton Road in Kentish Town. It wasn't in such an upmarket area as Sue and Ritchie's flat but it was a house, they were buying it and it also had a small back garden. When Sue found out she was livid and as envious as anyone could be, though she didn't let anyone see that. Just before the move Ellie started to be sick and when it progressed to every morning, deep in her gut she knew why. After taking a test and when she worked out the dates, the idea of having a secret abortion momentarily crossed her mind but it was only fleeting, this baby hadn't asked to be conceived and as much as she hated Ritchie and accepting that the baby could be his, it was also half hers. With all of her heart, she willed it to be Michael's and pushing all thoughts of that horrendous night to the back of her mind, she knew she had to tell her husband and the day after they moved in was as good a time as any. A small BBQ had been arranged

116

and Michael had spent most of the day weeding, mowing the tiny lawn and setting up a new table and chairs. When he had finished and stood back to admire his handy work Ellie took a cold can of lager out to him. Standing in the sunshine they both surveyed their little domain.

"Ell, I don't think I could be any happier than I am right now, what about you?"

Ellie gently touched his arm and when he turned to look at her she desperately stared into his beautiful brown eyes.

"Molly, I have something to tell you babe and I hope you're not going to be upset."

Michael placed the can down onto the table and with a serious look on his face waited for his wife to tell him what was on her mind.

"I'm pregnant. Please don't be angry or disappointed with me."

Grinning from ear to ear, Michael scooped her into his arms and kissed her passionately.

"Why on earth would I be disappointed sweetheart? I'm over the fucking moon."

"Well, it wasn't planned now was it?"

"Some of the best things in life aren't. Please, can we tell everyone at the BBQ?"

Ellie had wanted to keep it just between them for the moment but he was so excited and she didn't have the heart to say no. The BBQ was a huge success and when the food had been eaten, Michael emerged carrying a tray of glasses and a bottle of champagne that he'd been out and bought without his wife's knowledge.

"Everyone, we have some news to share. Ellie?"

"Well, it's happened a bit sooner than we thought it would but as the saying goes 'New house, new baby!'" Mavis let out a cheer and Ellie's mum Eileen began to jump up and down with happiness. Ritchie shook his brother's hand but did not attempt to congratulate Ellie, since he'd raped her he had kept well away and only made conversation when it was absolutely necessary. To himself, he had made the excuse that he had been drunk but he hadn't been drunk enough not to know what he was doing or remember it the following day. When Ellie looked in Sue's direction, her friend smiled thinly and Ellie could tell it was false but she wasn't letting her get away with things this time so walked over to where her old friend sat.

"What a turn-up for the books Sue. Fancy both of us having a baby within a year? They will be able to play with each other."

"When your kid gets here my Danny will be almost a year old and as he grows he will need other children of his own age not some whining little cousin following him around."

The words hurt her deeply and she couldn't work out why Sue was being so spiteful instead of being happy for her. Deep down she had a sinking feeling that her former best friend and sister-in-law was about to cause more trouble within the family and whatever it was, it wouldn't be good.

Michael was insistent that Ellie gave up work straight away and she didn't argue with him, recently she had been disheartened with the hairdressers and had been thinking of changing her job anyway. Her dream of owning a salon, had long since disappeared and all she wanted now was to be the perfect wife and

118

mother. Before her stomach grew too big, she decided
to make the most of her time and get out and about
though she didn't see much of Sue and her friend
never called around to the house. In the beginning, it
had bothered her but after a while, Ellie had accepted
it. Instead, she now spent a lot of time at the Lamb
with Mavis and the two had become very close.
Ellie's mum Eileen was pleased that she had someone
else to rely on as she had to work so much that she
couldn't attend any of the antenatal classes with her
daughter and if there was an emergency it could
prove difficult. As her time drew near, Michael was
adamant that she had to stop using the buses or
underground so he began to drop Ellie off at the
Lamb on his way to work and collected her again
each evening, she told him he was being silly and that
she would rather be in her own home but he wouldn't
hear of it. Just before the baby was born, the firm had
a big job to carry out. It was risky if things went
wrong but if they went well, it could turn out to be a
mega payday. One of Michael's informants, he kept
several on a give information, get paid basis, had
called in at the unit a week earlier. Binzie Garner was
a junkie but different from most in the fact that he
didn't steal from people. Of course shops and
businesses didn't come into that equation but on the
whole, Binzie was trustworthy and his info was
always reliable. He told Michael that he'd heard the
Makenzie firm over in South London was expecting a
large shipment of cocaine in the next week. Michael
passed on Binzie's message to Ritchie and they
discussed the do's and don'ts of stealing from another
firm. When it came down to it they didn't care, the

only firm that mattered was the Spires so it was agreed that they should do the job and Michael began to hatch a plan. Binzie was paid to keep his ear to the ground and watch the comings and goings at the old warehouse and to report back as soon as he heard news of any kind. A few days later the call came in and Michael was told that the delivery was happening that night and that they needed to act fast. Ritchie hastily organised the men and gave them instructions, knowing who they were robbing, there was no need to tell them to keep their traps shut. The Makenzie warehouse was situated at the end of a side track just off of Binfield Road and apart from a large depot that was used to store buses by the Abellio Company who serviced the area, nothing much went on in the Lane so it was pretty quiet. The Spires used the same ruse as they had on the other robberies and as soon as a van came into view and indicated that it was turning into the road, a message was sent by mobile and a stinger was laid. Full-face balaclavas' were worn, the transport vans had been stolen and fake plates had been fitted a couple of days earlier in readiness. The men had been ordered not to speak a word to each other during the raid in case the driver or his passenger was able to identify them. With the vehicle now stopped, Richie tapped on the driver's door window with the tip of his handgun and as soon as the driver saw the gun he immediately turned off the engine and got out.

"Please Mister, I don't want no trouble. Do whatever you need to but please don't shoot me."

Ritchie stared at him for a few seconds and then brought the gun down on the side of the man's head and he was instantly out for the count. Feeling in the driver's pockets, Ritchie removed a mobile phone and throwing it down onto the tarmac, stamped on it until several pieces flew off in all directions. The passenger was in a state of shock and walking around the van Ritchie signalled for the terrified man to get out, hand over his phone and take a seat beside his mate on the ground. After that, everything went like clockwork and within twenty minutes the cargo had been taken and the Spires firm were on their way back to base. With the drugs unloaded, the vans were taken off to be dumped and burnt out and the remaining men all made their way home. When the Makenzie's cargo didn't arrive on schedule, the brothers were informed a few minutes later and were at the scene within half an hour. Tommy, the eldest and head of the firm surveyed the van and when the driver came round he began to quiz him. Brian Makenzie just mooched about; he hated the work, hated being in London and only took part in business because of his brothers. Jock was a different kettle of fish altogether, violence ran through his veins and the least little thing could set him off so if you knew what was good for you, a wide birth was always preferable. Walking over to Tommy he waited to see what came out of the driver's mouth. Lou West was sixty-seven years old and looked every year of that. When he'd retired two years earlier he invested in a white van and did runs for anyone willing to pay. He never asked questions about the cargo he carried and in all honesty, there was little point as much of his work consisted of taking things to the local dump for residents unable to do it for themselves. About a year earlier Lou had been anonymously contacted and asked if he would be interested in doing the odd evening job. When the payment amount was mentioned he jumped for joy and accepted on the spot even though he realised that it wouldn't be legal. He was nervous when introduced to Tommy Makenzie and two of his henchmen but after a short conversation and with the reassurance that he would be paid up fully after each job, he was happy enough to continue. Everything had gone fine until tonight and when he'd loaded the van from the collection point, Lou knew it was the largest amount to date. The rear of the Transit was a quarter full of boxes and bags, so much so that the power steering had been pulling a little throughout the journey.

"Honest Mr Makenzie, I ain't got a clue who they were. The first thing I knew was a stinger was thrown onto the road. I had to jam on the brakes to stop the van and then some bloke in a black balaclava showed me a gun, made me get out of the van and the rest is all a blur."

Jock walked over to where Carl Raymond sat on the kerb and roughly hauled the man to his feet. Carl had agreed to accompany his pal on the drive but it was more for company than anything else. He wasn't a violent man and his day job consisted of working as a gas engineer for the borough council. Jock pulled out a large razor-sharp knife from a sheath that hung on his belt and grabbing Carl by the throat, he slowly drew the tip down the man's cheek. Carl screamed out which instantly made Tommy turn on his heels.

"Right, you cunt! Tell me what happened cause I know you didn't get fucking knocked out! You're in on it ain't you?"

"No, no I'm not! I don't know anything, I swear I don't know anythin' guvnor, honest I don't."

Jock was swiftly losing his temper and his brothers could see by the mad look in his eyes that he was about lost the plot and would do the man some serious damage if they didn't intervene and quickly.

"You either tell me what you know you cunt or the next cut will be me severing your bollocks."

"Look, it's just like Lou said. There were six, maybe eight of them in two maybe three vans. They all wore black balaclavas and not one of them spoke a word so we ain't got a clue where they are from. Look guvnor, I was only on board to keep Lou company, I ain't no hard man, and I've got a wife and two kids at home."

"Well if you want to see them again I suggest you spill your fucking guts!"

Jock froze when he felt Tommy's hand on his arm.

"Take it easy brother, no point in killing an innocent man. Let them both calm down then we'll take 'em back to the warehouse and see if they've remembered anything. You get more results with honey than vinegar and you've already frightened the poor bastard half to death."

Back at the warehouse, the two men were seated on hard chairs in front of Tommy's desk.

"Please Mr Makenzie, I've worked for you for a long time and there's never been a problem. I swear on my kids' lives that neither of us knows anything or we would tell you."

Tommy sighed heavily and after mulling things over for a few seconds he nodded in Brian's direction and the middle brother stepped forward and released the cable ties that were securing the men's wrists.

"What the fuck are you doing?"

"It's okay Jock, believe me, they don't know what's going on."

"Well, I think the fuckers were in on it, robbing bastards!"

Tommy slowly shook his head at his brother's statement and then signalled with his eyes for the two men to leave. Lou and Carl didn't need to be told twice and were out of the building as quickly as they could and Lou had already made his mind up that if the firm let him live he would be retiring for good. Jock was about to complain again but was stopped when Tommy place his index finger on his lips. He didn't speak until he heard the front door close and knew there was no one able to eves drop on what he was about to say.

"Put Pauly, Gordon and Jimmy Moorland on it; tell them to watch them both like a fucking hawk for the next few days. I don't think they were involved but I ain't takin' any fucking chances. I'll tell you both one thing, I don't care if it takes me years, I will find out who robbed us. It's not just the loss of the gear and that's bad enough, it's a matter of fucking principle and no one gets away with robbing the Makenzie's without paying for it dearly and believe me, the cunts will pay."

News soon spread far and wide that the Makenzie firm was on the warpath and they threatened violence to anyone who harboured the robbers but also a reward of twenty grand to anyone who could supply information to them. It was a small amount in comparison to the value of the missing cargo but to

124

the local street robbers and drug users it was not to be sniffed at. Word quickly spread around the manor but there was nothing but silence and strangely even the local snouts, who would sell information on to anyone willing to pay, weren't able to offer any news to the Makenzie's. No stone was left unturned but the theft had been carried out with such professionalism that it would take years before they heard anything about who the culprits were.

The next day at the Spires headquarters everything was back to normal and the precious cargo was now stored on the small mezzanine level above the office and accessed only by an internal metal staircase. Ritchie and Michael had decided that it was too hot to handle and that they would wait a good six months and then sell it on in small amounts so that they wouldn't be suspected in any way.

CHAPTER TWELVE

On Friday, two days after the robbery and when the rest of the firm had left for the weekend, the baby decided to make an appearance but she was two weeks early. Luckily Ellie was at the Lamb but Mavis was worried and was panicking when she called Michael.

"Hello, sweetheart."

"It's coming, it's coming!"

"What, what are you talking about Aunty?"

"The baby, it's coming. What should I do, what should I do!"

Michael could hear Ellie screaming out in the background but instead of panicking himself, he remained calm as he gave Mavis instructions.

"Stop and think, have you phoned an ambulance?"

"It's on its way. Oh Michael please hurry, she's in so much pain bless her heart."

"Just try to keep her walking around and tell her to remember her breathing. I'm leaving now and will get there as soon as I can."

"But what if the baby comes Michael?"

"Let's hope it doesn't sweetheart. Tell her I love her and I'm on my way."

With that, he hung up and after being so calm with his instructions, he was suddenly in a blind panic and couldn't think straight. As he rushed out of the warehouse to get home, his mind was on one thing only and he didn't secure the front door lock. After the robbery, Ritchie had given Binzie Garner ten grand and told him to disappear for six months.

Binzie wasn't stupid, he knew all about the Makenzie's and happily did as he'd been asked but not before he made one last visit. With the Spires payoff he had purchased a cheap van and had been watching the unit for any opportunity to increase the money he would be taking with him on his trip. Binzie jumped for joy when he saw Michael rush out blindly and drive off at speed. Making his way inside it didn't take more than a few minutes to locate the stash and thirty minutes later he had filled the back of his van and was at last on his way to a new life. Reaching the Lamb just as the ambulance was pulling away Michael followed on behind to St Pancras Hospital. He was desperate and didn't bother to find a parking space; he just abandoned his car at the entrance. Running into the emergency department, Michael found his wife on a stretcher with a doctor by her side. Ellie was wired up to a monitor and she looked in so much pain that as he ran over to her he pushed a nurse out of the way to get to her side. Grabbing her hand he smothered it in kisses.

"I'm here babe."

With her hair plastered to her face, Ellie tried to smile but it turned into a scowl as a new wave of contractions began and she screamed out in agony. The nurse gently spoke telling her to breathe and pant which had an instant calming effect and when Doctor Travis came over and assured them that two weeks early wasn't much of an issue, they relaxed somewhat but it seemed that as soon as the words had left the doctor's mouth events took a downward turn and went from bad to worse. The supposedly normal delivery quickly turned into a nightmare. The monitor strapped to Ellie's stomach began to flash and bleep loudly and the fear in Ellie's eyes was evident.

"What's happening, oh my God, Molly what's happening?"

Doctor Travis studied the monitor's reading for a few seconds and then turned to face the couple.

"I'm sorry but the baby is in distress and there is no other option but to rush Ellie into the operating theatre for an emergency caesarean. We can carry this out with an epidural so you will be awake for the birth Mrs Spires. I know it isn't ideal but sometimes nature takes control and it's out of our hands. Nurse could you take Ellie and Michael through to the delivery room please."

Ellie was now distraught and began to scream and thrash about. All attempts to calm her, even by Michael, were futile so the team decided it would be in the best interests of mother and baby if Ellie was sedated.

"No, no! I want to see my baby as soon as it's born. Please, Molly, don't let them do this to me, pleeeeeeease!"

Michael kissed her forehead but he couldn't reassure her, there was nothing he could do and the doctors knew what was best for them all. The procedure was swift and Michael saw their daughter even before his wife and he instantly fell in love. He was still holding her when Ellie was brought out of sedation and when the tiny little girl was at last placed in her mother's arms, Ellie just sobbed and sobbed with relief.

"Ain't she just the most beautiful thing you have ever seen Ell?"

"Oh Molly, we did it, we did it!"

When they had first told her about the caesarean, all of the bad memories had surfaced and she'd thought it was the punishment she deserved for letting the rape happen but now, when she looked at her baby, she felt nothing but love.

"So, what do you want to call her sweetheart?"

Ellie thought for a moment and then with doe eyes looked up into her husband's face.

"Can we name her Beth after my nan?"

"Beth? I like that sweetheart. Welcome to the world little Beth."

Ellie was soon moved to a small side room, it was quiet and private and the new family could have some much-needed time alone. They sat in silence for what must have been an hour just staring down at the little miracle they had created, still not quite able to take in that she was finally here. Michael stood up and yawning, stretched out his arms.

"I'm knackered, this giving birth lark really takes it out of you."

Ellie tried not to laugh but it was impossible, he was funny even when he wasn't trying and she couldn't love him any more than she did right now.

"I had better shoot off now darling and let your mum and Mavis know about the baby and tell them they have nothing to worry about. Mavis must be climbing the walls with concern and you know Burt won't be a lot of help to her. I bet they have both been worried out of their minds and I want to tell them about little Beth in person."

"And I bet you tell my mum first and then Mavis and Burt so you can have a few celebratory pints no doubt?"

Michael stared at her with his mouth wide open in shock.

"Have I hit the nail on the head by any chance?"

She was mocking him and he knew it. Laughing, he tenderly placed a kiss on her forehead and then one on the baby's head.

"I don't know what you think of me Mrs Spires but that is not the case, I'm a father now and I have responsibilities. See you both later."

With that, he was gone and Ellie snuggled down in the bed with her baby in her arms, right at this moment she couldn't be any happier, no matter who the father was and at the same time, she was desperately trying to convince herself that it was Michael.

In Barnet, Eileen Evans was just about to put her key in the lock. She'd been buying food down the market after finishing her morning shift at the shop and was looking forward to a cup of tea and putting her feet up before going off to the Mecca. When she spied Michael walking along the landing Eileen froze with fear. He never came around alone, Michael never just called in to see her, it wasn't his way. Had something terrible happened? As she waited for him to give her bad news, it felt as if the world was standing still.

"Hello, Eileen love."

His tone was so relaxed that she knew that whatever it was it couldn't be that bad.

"Hi sweetheart, everything okay?"

"I take it Mavis didn't call you?"

"No love. Why, what's wrong?"

"The baby's here Eileen, Ellie went into premature labour a few hours ago. Luckily she was with Mavis

130

and I'm sorry I didn't call you but it was manic. It's a little girl and she's a right little blinder."

Eileen began to cry and Michael hugged her until the tears subsided.

"I'm a silly old cow I know but I've had a bad feeling ever since Ellie told me she was pregnant. Oh, darling, I'm just so pleased for you both. My life was always shitty and I didn't want that for my girl, I'm so grateful she met you, Michael, really I am. I take it she's in St Pancras?"

"Yes, and I ain't gonna lie, it was a bit touch and go to begin with and Ellie had to have a caesarean but all's good now and mother and baby are resting. She'll be in for several days, just until they are happy that her wound is healing."

"Tell her I'll call in sick at the Mecca and come and see her after tea. I'm a nan, I can't believe it, I'm a nan!"

Michael kissed his mother-in-law on the cheek and then headed off. He was relishing a pint to wet the baby's head but he wouldn't go stupid as he wanted to go back to the hospital later to see his wife and daughter. He smiled at the thought, he was a dad, he had a daughter and it felt good. Entering the Lamb through the back door he popped his head into the bar and smiled. Mavis saw him and she immediately stopped twisting her hands on the hem of her apron, something she'd been doing ever since the ambulance had left.

"It's a little girl, baby Beth is finally here."

A cheer went up and totally out of character, Burt shouted 'Drinks are on the house!' Just as Eileen had done, Mavis was in floods of tears and Michael took her in his arms.

"Why are you crying, grandma?"

Michael's address had Mavis in more tears, he had called her grandma and it sounded wonderful. Instantly her face became serious when she spoke.

"Are you going to let your mum know?"

"Am I fuck, that old cow wasn't a mum to either Ritchie or me so she ain't getting a look in where my kid is concerned. Eileen, you and Burt are the only grandparents Beth will ever have or need. Now dry your eyes Aunty and let's have a drink to celebrate." Many of the regulars had gathered around and all sorts of questions were being asked and answered like how much did she weigh, did she have hair etc.

Halfway through his second pint and when the atmosphere was still a happy one but had at least calmed down a little, the front door flew open and Ritchie stormed in. Michael didn't even get a chance to tell him about the baby before he kicked off.

"You cunt! Get out the back before I lay you out in full fucking view of everyone!"

"What the…"

"I said, get out the fucking back!"

Mavis was about to intervene but Michael held up his hand indicating for her not to get involved. Turning towards the kitchen doorway he slowly shook his head; there was no reasoning with his brother when he was in this mood but only God above knew what had made him kick off. Mavis sighed heavily, something or someone had pushed Ritchie's buttons and when he was like this anything was likely to happen but she knew better than to interfere. Not wanting to cause any more of a scene in the bar,

132

Michael did as he was asked and when they reached
the kitchen he turned and spoke before his brother
had a chance.

"I don't know what the fuck has got into you Ritch but
my baby has just been born and..."

Not letting Michael finish, Ritch launched into a
tirade of abuse, the likes of which he had never used
on his brother.

"I don't give a flying fuck about your kid or anyone
else's! You are one sloppy, useless cunt, Michael. I
popped back to the unit and we've been cleaned out,
the drugs are gone and all because you couldn't even
lock the fucking warehouse up. Sue is right about
you, you're nothing short of a fucking weight around
my neck. We must be down by a couple of mill
because of you and we won't ever get it back. The
boys will all still want paying and it ain't coming out
of my fucking pocket I can tell you."

Michael was momentarily speechless as he tried to
remember his movements before leaving the unit.
True, his mind was otherwise occupied and now
when he recounted his steps he couldn't remember if
he locked the place up or not.

"Look Ritch, if this is down to me then I'm truly sorry
but I had an emergency and things got a bit hairy for a
while down the hospital. No one has been hurt and it
ain't like the gear cost us anything now is it?"

His last sentence shouldn't have been said, it was like
a red rag to a bull and the next thing he knew he was
lying on his back on the floor with Ritchie standing
over him. Rubbing his jaw he was about to speak
again and try and get his brother to see sense but
Ritchie just leaned over him and in a loud voice spoke

133

in a scathing tone.

"We're done, do you hear me, done! Now you can either buy me out or I'll buy you out but from now on there isn't any partnership, do you hear me?"

Ritchie didn't give Michael a chance to reply and walking out, slammed the door without another word. Mavis had been listening from the bar and when she heard Ritchie leave she went into the kitchen.

"Whatever's going on love? I've seen him mad before but never like this, what on earth did you do darling?"

"I forgot to lock the warehouse and we got robbed. I understand that he's angry but fucking hell Mavis he was a bit out of order."

"Give him time to calm down and I'm sure he'll come around, he's your brother, he loves you and blood is thicker than water and more important than whatever it was you had stolen."

"I hope you're right Aunty but to be honest I ain't so sure this time."

When Mavis heard the details of what had actually gone on and why he had been up in arms she telephoned Ritchie and after reassuring him that his brother wouldn't be there, she asked him to call at the pub on Wednesday. Michael was collecting Ellie from the hospital that day and it had been agreed that he would take her straight home so that she could get settled in before visitors began to arrive. Mavis was on tenterhooks all morning and when the front door to the pub opened and Ritchie stepped inside, she could tell by the look on his face that he was spoiling for a fight. Walking through to the kitchen so that her punters wouldn't be privy to the conversation, she waited for him to join her. Mavis stood with her back against the sink, something she always did when she meant business and she started as soon as he entered. "This is all bloody ridiculous Ritchie and you're making a huge mistake. Your brother loves you dearly and yes he fucked up monumentally but we all make mistakes in life and when all is said and done, no one died and it was only money that was lost."

"Only fucking money! It's over two million Aunty, that's a fucking shed load of cash that could have changed all of our lives forever but now thanks to that fucking muppet it's all gone."

"But he's your brother, Ritchie, you can just cut him off!"

"Can't I? You just watch me."

Mavis tried again and again during the conversation but he couldn't or wouldn't see her side. To her family was everything and while she accepted that Michael should have been more careful, nothing should ever be allowed to come between the brothers. What she wasn't aware of was the fact that Sue had been whispering in his ear at every given opportunity and recently Ritchie had started to agree with the things she was saying.

"If you ain't in agreement Aunty and you're gonna take his fucking side then there ain't anything left to say."

With that, Ritchie walked out slamming the back door as he did.

A few days later Michael received a wad of cash via Mavis. Ritchie had called in again for a few minutes one lunchtime and asked her to hand it over to Michael.

"I'll pass it on but I have to say you are a fool Ritchie

Spires, a total bloody fool."

He didn't reply and handing Mavis the envelope full of cash for his brother, Ritchie stormed from the Lamb swearing that it would be a cold day in hell before he ever stepped foot in the pub again and he was true to his word. Michael wouldn't see or hear from his brother again for almost three years. It broke Mavis's heart and all she could do was give all of her love to Michael, Ellie and baby Beth. After a while, the wounds eventually began to heal but she still thought of Ritchie and baby Daniel and all that she had lost due to some silly argument. Sue had been over the moon when her husband shared what had happened, they may have missed out on a large payday due to the loss of the drugs but from now on all the money would be hers and Ritchie's and she planned on spending it as fast as he could earn it.

Three years later Burt suddenly passed away and Mavis was inconsolable. Ritchie and Sue didn't show their faces at the pub to offer words of comfort and it was something that Michael would never forgive them for. They did however attend the church service and as the coffin was led outside and the mourners stood around not knowing what to do next, Ritchie walked over to where Mavis was standing. He didn't acknowledge his brother but taking Mavis's hand in his he looked deep into her eyes.

"I am truly sorry Aunty. Burt was the closest thing I had to a father."

"Shame you ignored him for the last three years then."

"I know and I'm sorry and I will have to live with that

regret for the rest of my life Aunty."

Mavis could only nod her head. As much as she was grieving, she was angry that Ritchie hadn't bothered with Burt since the day he had stormed out of the pub. The poor old sod hadn't done anything to deserve that kind of treatment and even if Ritchie couldn't find it in his heart to visit, now and again he could at least have telephoned Burt. She was also upset that he hadn't spoken to Michael and come to that, Sue, dressed in her designer gear and gold jewellery, so much of it that it was in bad taste, especially at a funeral, had actually looked down her nose at Ellie. The wake was held at the pub and the place was crammed to the rafters with regulars but after not much more than an hour Mavis said she was going for a lie down. Michael and Ellie worked the bar and as sad as the event was, they had fun serving pints and working side by side.

Since the split in the business Michael had been working at the bookies on Holloway Road and to make ends meet, he'd also been doing a few shifts each week at the Lamb. At times he felt as if he was chasing his tail but not once did he complain. Ellie had managed, much to the annoyance of Mavis and Michael, to get Beth in at the local day care centre. It was council-funded so cheap and it allowed her to start hairdressing again. She hadn't gone back into a shop but worked from home and trade was building steadily. Michael couldn't complain because she was bringing in as much as he was each week and they were now able to afford a few of life's little luxuries. The cash Michael had received from Ritchie hadn't been touched and was stashed away for a rainy day. It would have been easy to blow the fifty grand on holidays and fine living but Michael knew they might well need the money in the future and besides, there was nothing flash about the couple. They both enjoyed the simple life and a Chinese takeaway on a Friday night or a Sunday stroll with Beth was the highlight of their week.

A few months into Ellie going back to work, she received a phone call from a woman named Jane who worked one of the food stalls down Camden lock. Jane said she had a regular customer who was looking for a hairdresser and wondered if Ellie would be interested in taking her on. Not wanting to turn away the much-needed income, Ellie agreed and an appointment was made for the following morning at ten. On the dot, the doorbell rang and Ellie walked along the hallway full of smiles until she opened the door, as bold as brass there stood Sue.

"Sorry about the cloak and dagger stuff Ellie but I knew if I asked you would say no."

"No necessarily but if…"

Sue dismissed her friend's unfinished sentence with a wave of her hand and not waiting to be invited inside, she marched through to the kitchen eyeing up the décor and furnishings as she went. Ellie could only sigh at what she knew was to come and she just thanked the Lord that Michael was at the bookies. Ellie was as polite as she could be and after discussing with her sister- in-law what she would like, the scissors came out and Ellie set to work. All the while Sue bragged and boasted about everything she had and that they were planning on putting Danny into private school when the time came but Ellie didn't once take the bait, instead she congratulated the woman who had once been her best friend but someone she now realised she had never really known. Out of the blue, Sue asked about Michael and what he was doing. For a second Ellie contemplated making his job sound much grander than it was but it wasn't her way and even though she knew this would all go back to Ritchie with a lot of extras added on, she told the truth.

"He's doing okay thanks, he does a few shifts down the bookies on Holloway Road and makes up the rest of his hours at the pub helping Mavis out. Bless her heart, I think it's a bit of a struggle running the pub alone but she won't hear of getting rid of it. We ain't rich by any means but we get by and more importantly Sue, we're happy."

With the cut and blow dry complete which to Ellie looked great, Sue paid and also gave a large tip. When they got to the front door she turned to face Ellie.

"It was nice to see you again but I don't think I'll be back. Ricardo at Madam Jones does a better job and I only came to you because he is away on holiday. Bye."

When the front door was closed, Ellie just stood there dumbfounded. What had all that been about, had Sue only called around to gloat? What hurt even more was the fact that not once had she asked after Beth. When Michael got home Ellie didn't mention her client, there had been enough upset in the family without adding more fuel to the flames and there was nothing to be gained from stirring the pot.

As for Sue, she couldn't wait to spill her guts, telling Ritchie how poor his brother was and that he was working in a back street bookie's to make ends meet but she didn't get the response she was hoping for. Ritchie hit the roof! Of all the places his wife could have gone to get her hair done she had chosen to go to Ellie. He wasn't regretting things with Michael, too much water had passed under the bridge for that but all the same he was livid with his wife.

"You just can't stop fucking meddling, can you? All you want to do is cause aggro and tell people how much money you have. Well, remember where that money comes from Sue and as easy as it comes in it can stop!"

Making tears well in her eyes usually worked but not this time, this time Ritchie slowly shook his head in disgust and then slamming the front door he headed off to the pub to calm down.

CHAPTER THIRTEEN

Almost a year to the day that Burt died, Mavis also passed away. She had never gotten over the loss of her husband and a month earlier had taken to her bed, refusing to get up. Being overweight had taken its toll on her heart and one Friday morning when Michael had come to work early to let the draymen in and after accepting the delivery, he took her up a cup of tea. Knocking gently he didn't wait to be invited in but that was normal.

"Morning my little sweetheart, are you decent? I've got a nice cup of rosie for you."

There was no answer and as he opened the curtains to let in the morning light he had a sinking feeling in his stomach.

"I said, morning sweetheart?"

When there was still no reply and after placing the china cup and saucer on to the nightstand Michael took hold of her hand and instantly let it drop back down onto the bedclothes. She was stone cold and he cried out in pain. Taking a seat beside her he once again held Mavis's hand as he spoke to her.

"You rest now my little darling, back with your Burt, just as it should be. You have been like a mother to me and Ritchie and I will never be able to thank you. Sleep well my angel and I shall make sure Beth knows all about her nanny and what a kind and gentle lady she was."

After Michael had called an ambulance he was forced to hang around, it was a sudden death and as such the police had to attend. The pub didn't open that day or the next, he just didn't have the heart and with the funeral still to plan he didn't have the time. Ellie was brilliant and when he tearfully telephoned and told her she offered to go and tell Ritchie and Sue. As much as it stuck in his craw, Michael knew that Ritchie had a right to know but visiting his brother was something he didn't want to do, so when Ellie suggested that she go, he felt more than a little relieved. Deciding to leave it until later in the day in the hope that Ritchie would be at home, she set off at just after four. Knocking on the flat door she waited nervously for it to be answered and hoped that Ritchie would answer so that she wouldn't be forced to go inside. Ellie wasn't in luck and it was Sue who opened up. There were no warm words of greeting and she just stood there staring at her former friend.

"Hello Sue, I'm sorry to bother you but would it be possible to have a word with Ritchie."

"I take it your gutless husband has sent you around to beg my Ritchie for a job?"

"No, he has not! Why are you always so fucking spiteful Sue, on second thoughts don't bother answering. Now if you wouldn't mind getting Ritchie please."

Without another word, Sue stomped off down the hallway and while she waited Ellie could hear little Danny running about inside and then suddenly he appeared at the front door.

"Hello sweetheart, I'm your aunty Ellie."

Danny gave her a big smile and she was about to bend down and give him a kiss when Sue reappeared.

"Don't you dare touch my son! Ritchie, will you get here please."

142

A bleary-eyed Ritchie Spires padded along the hallway and when he saw her he grinned, as he did so all of the horrific memories of that awful night flooded back for Ellie. The way he had pawed her, his stinky alcoholic breath and the physical pain he had caused, not to mention the emotional turmoil that was still going on to this very day.

"Well, well, well, look who we have here. How can I help you, darling? Where are me manners, come on inside."

"No thanks, I've just come to let you know that Mavis passed away this morning. Michael wanted you to know and I will be in touch again as soon as we've made the funeral arrangements."

With that Ellie turned on her heels and walked out. She couldn't get away fast enough and when she reached the corner of the road and was out of sight of the flat she broke down in a flood of tears. It was as if all of the pain of that night had resurfaced and she now felt as violated as if the rape had just happened. Knowing that she couldn't return home with bloodshot eyes she decided to take a stroll down to Camden Lock, it was always bustling with people and whenever she was down the eclectic vibe seemed to lift her spirits.

The funeral was arranged for two weeks with a service at St Mary Magdalene Church followed by a cremation at Islington Crematorium. It was the same service as Burt had been given and Michael would scatter their ashes together somewhere nice in the future. On the day the Church was packed, Mavis didn't have any family apart from the boys but she

143

was loved by all of her regulars and they had turned out in full to support Molly and Ellie. Michael was surprised when they walked in and Ritchie and Sue were already seated in the front pew. Holding his hand she could feel Michael tense up when he saw them. Ellie didn't want him any more upset than he already was so she entered first so that her husband didn't have to stand next to his brother. Neither of the couples acknowledged one another and the atmosphere was uncomfortable and tense for the entire service. It was the same at the crematorium and Ellie was willing things to be better at the wake which was being held at the Lamb but it was no different. It was the first time Ritchie had been back at the pub in a long time and taking Sue's arm he led her to a seat at the far side of the bar. He further added to the tension by not making any effort to mingle with any of the other mourners, many of whom he had served for years when he was barman. Within an hour of getting back to the Lamb, Davis Seeking from Metcalf and Steward, the local solicitors who Mavis and Burt had used for years, arrived and after introducing himself went on to announce that he was here at Mavis's request to read the Will. A couple of the regulars Larry and George were manning the bar and the cleaner, Annie Coombes, had prepared a small buffet that was set up on the corner table, the table that Ritchie and Michael had always sat at and it didn't go unnoticed by either of them. After an acceptable time had passed, Davis Seeking got to his feet.

"Excuse me gentlemen and I don't want to appear rude but I have several more meetings today so would

144

you both mind coming through to the back so that I can read the Will to you."

Sue was hot on Ritchie's tail. Ellie had remained standing at the bar until Michael clasped her hand and indicated with a nod of his head that he wanted her to be a part of this. Taking a seat at the kitchen table and with Davis seeking sitting at the head, he opened his briefcase and removed a manila envelope.

"If you are all ready, then I will begin?"

Michael and Ritchie nodded but neither of them looked at each other or said a word.

"This is my last will which I updated six months after my darling Burt died. Ritchie, you have hardly been to see me or bothered if I needed anything and for that I am heartbroken. Sue, I think I'm being honest when I say that we never liked each other. I got the mark of you the first time you stepped into my pub and you never changed, always out for what you could get and to stir up as much trouble as you could. I leave to my grandson Danny, the sum of thirty thousand pounds which is to be placed in trust until he is eighteen years of age. Ellie, my dear sweet Ellie I leave you all of my jewellery and there is far more of it than you have ever seen. I have……"

"That's not right, why does she get the gold and I get nothing?!"

Ritchie shot his wife a glance that told her to be quiet. His wife never knew when to keep her trap shut and he was sick to the back teeth of her. Davis Seeking was appalled at the outburst and asked, in a somewhat brisk manner, if he could please be allowed to continue without interruption.

"I have always loved you Ellie and I couldn't think of

a sweeter lovelier woman to be married to my Molly. To little Beth, I leave the same amount as I have to Danny and with the same terms imposed. Michael, you have been my rock and I don't know what I would have done without you since I lost Burt. To you, I leave the Lamb in its entirety. Do with it as you wish my love so long as it makes you happy."

"And that ladies and gentlemen concludes the Will." Davis Seeking asked Michael if he would call in at the office in a few days to sign the paperwork and then with a curt goodbye, he left.

Michael was speechless, the pub was freehold and the land alone was worth a fortune. A thin smile crept onto his lips as he looked at Ellie and winked. Sue stood up and slammed away her chair making it fall over backwards. As she stormed out of the backdoor Ritchie gave one last glance to his brother before walking out. The rest of the day passed without event. The wake turned into a jolly affair as they all reminisced about their old landlady and the scrapes she had gotten into over the years. When the place was at last empty and Michael had secured the bolts on the front door he poured them both a brandy and then took a seat.

"So my darling, what do you want to do? Would you like me to sell this place or should we move in and run it?"

Ellie glanced around the bar, the pub had been like a second home to her and she couldn't bear the thought of some developer coming in and ripping out the fittings, the very heart of the place.

"I think we should run it, let's face it, you have been doing it for a long time anyway."

Michael smiled, he was hoping that she would say that and right at this moment he couldn't love her anymore if he tried.

"The house?"

"Well it seems foolish to keep it, we might as well sell it and invest the money somewhere else."

"Or we could rent it out until we retire?"

"Maybe but it's early days yet Molly, let's just take a few weeks to take on board what all of this means."

Back at Ritchie's flat, the pair were going at it hammer and tongs. Sue was shrieking at the top of her voice and Ritchie knew that when she was like this it was best to let her get it out of her system, so long as she didn't go too far.

"Can you believe it! Those two greedy bastards copped for the lot, well I ain't leaving it like this Ritchie. First thing Monday morning I'm down the solicitor's, we're going to fight this. I bet the old cow was losing her marbles and they sat about waiting like a couple of fucking vultures."

"Be careful Sue, Mavis was like my mum."

"Maybe she was but I'm still going to fight this."

"We can't Sue and at least Mavis left Danny set up."

"Set up! That old cow left him thirty measly grand. Do you know how much that grubby little boozer is worth!?"

"You're out of fucking order! Mavis didn't need to leave our son anything, he wasn't a blood relation and thirty grand would get him through his education if that's what he wants to spend it on. You never liked Mavis but she cared for me and my brother and she was right, I didn't return the favour when she needed me and you did fuck all to help out either you lazy

147

bitch! Molly and Ellie deserve all that they have been given. Now I've had a gut full of you today so I'm off out."

"Oh that's right, go off sulking like you normally do you gutless cunt!"

Out of nowhere, she felt his hand grip her clothing and then the hard stinging slap that almost knocked her sideways. This was the first time her had ever laid a hand on her and she was momentarily speechless as she rubbed at her cheek, while he still gripped at the front of her dress, a little Channel number that had set Richie back almost two grand.

"You hit me!"

"I fucking slapped you and you're lucky that's all you got. You know something Sue, I can't fucking stand to be in the same room as you anymore. I only married you because you was up the duff and I think you set me fucking up as far as that was concerned. You're a sneaky, conniving bitch but if you want to keep being my wife you had better get your fucking act together lady and don't even think about getting a divorcee and coming after my money, I'll put you in an early fucking grave before I let that happen!"

With that, Ritchie stormed out of the flat. Sue took a few moments to compose herself and after reapplying her makeup she went out and hailed a cab over to her parents. They had been looking after Danny for the day but that wasn't why she was going, she needed to bend someone's ear and who better than her mum and dad?

As she walked through the front door of the tired-looking little house that she had grown up in, she turned her nose up at the décor. With all the money she had at her disposal, she hadn't once offered to do up this house or get her mum any new furniture. Entering the front room, her dad Joe was asleep in his armchair as usual and Karen was sitting on the floor playing with Danny. When her mother looked at her Sue burst into tears and the noise suddenly woke Joe.

"What's all the bleedin' racket about?"

"Ritchie hit me and that old cow Mavis has left everything, the pub, her jewellery, everything, to that bitch Ellie and Michael and to think I used to call her my friend."

Sue began to cry again and Karen was soon up off of the floor and placing Danny into Joe's lap, she began to console her daughter.

"Oh don't get so upset love, come and sit at the table and your mum will make you a nice cuppa. What an earth got into Ritchie, hitting you like that, do you want to come back home?"

As soon as Joe heard his wife's words he was out of his armchair and after placing Danny in the high chair joined the two women at the table.

"Now don't go rushing into things girl, marriage is a sacred bond and you can't just walk out on it."

"I know what your bloody game is Joe Nelson and you can pack it in this instance. If our girl wants to come home then she can, there will always be a bed here for her and Danny."

Sue glanced around the living room, there was no way she could ever live back here in this hovel. It took another hour of questions but Joe finally got the truth out of Sue regarding what had happened. Karen hung her head and didn't utter a word, she was always the one to champion her girl but even she couldn't deny that this time Sue was in the wrong. Joe tapped his fingers on the table in a drumming motion before he spoke, racking his brains trying to think of a way to put what he was about to say so that it wouldn't cause his daughter to kick off. Finally, he just came out with it.

"I think you got off bleeding lightly if I'm honest. Many blokes would have knocked seven bells out of you for what you said. Mavis McAllister was a good, decent woman and without her, your husband and his brother would have been on the streets not to mention probably banged up for a lot longer than the time Ritchie did serve and don't look at me like that, I've known for years that he did a stint at her majesties. You forget, when you bad-mouthed Mavis it was as if you were slagging off his mum and no man would put up with that. If it was down to me he should have given you more than a bleedin' backhander. I suggest you go home with your tail between your legs and apologise because if you move back in here, your life will be very different and you will be expected to contribute my girl."

"Joe!"

"Don't Joe me, Karen, we ain't got that many years left until the pension and I can't afford to keep her, let alone in the style she's become accustomed to. Then there's Danny and all the things he needs, are you going to stump up for all of that? In my book, Ritchie Spires is a bleedin' saint putting up with her ladyship for as long as he has. He's a good husband and she doesn't want for anything, if she throws it all away because she couldn't keep her trap shut then she's a fucking idiot. All you've ever done Karen was spoil her and it's done no good, I'd go so far as to say you've actually contributed to making her the spoilt little bitch that she's turned out to be."

"Joe! How can you say that about your only daughter?"

"Easily and thank fuck we had boys after her or I'd be in me bleedin' grave by now. Right, I'm off to the Khazi for a turnout and I hope you've heard what I've said and taken it on board."

As soon as he was out of earshot Karen placed her hand on her daughters.

"Take no notice of him my darling, if you want to come home you can."

Once again Sue looked around the room at the old floral wallpaper and outdated furniture and once again her mouth went into action before her brain had engaged.

"I couldn't possibly come back here, I mean look at the place I've seen better squats."

"Sue! This is your home, always was and always will be. I know it ain't posh like you're used to but there's a lot of love here young lady."

"Maybe there is but I'm used to better now, you can't blame me for that."

Getting up from her seat she lifted Danny out of his chair, placed him into the buggy and then headed towards the front door with no regard for the hurt expression on her mother's face. If eating humble pie meant going home then that's what she would do, anything to get her life back and remain being Mrs Ritchie Spires. The thought of living here again made her see sense and she just prayed that Ritchie would forgive her.

CHAPTER FOURTEEN

Sue and Ritchie soon made up but on his part, it had been with reluctance and for several days she tip-toed around him so that she didn't upset him further. After leaving her parents' house she had pushed Danny in his buggy for a while and soon realised that she had laid everything on the line and for what? He might not have been very loving towards her but Ritchie was a fantastic provider, she was insane to risk all of that. Later that night when they were in bed she had put her head under the covers and pleasured him like never before. Ritchie wasn't a fool and knew what she was up to but nor was he going to turn down a blowjob and his wife, for all her faults, did give good head.

After being left out of the Will, Ritchie decided to build the firm up to an even bigger level and set about by hiring more men than ever. By the end of the first month, his manpower totalled over twenty and each man was given a work schedules and encouraged to hire their own workforce, though Ritchie instructed that three men each was the maximum allowed, it made them remain loyal and less likely to attempt a takeover. The loansharking had increased and they were well known throughout the whole of North London. Long firms were set up, their drug supply also increased and money was pouring in left, right and centre. By the end of the year, the cash was rolling in so fast that he hardly ever gave the Lamb a thought. One of the last men to be hired went by the

the name of Blades and it had nothing to do with his surname of Wilkinson but purely down to the fact that he was handy with a cut throat. It was old school but Blades had been taught by his grandfather who had also been a villain and the man, if given the option would take the razor over a gun any day. On this particular day Ritchie, who was normally at the unit before anyone else, was late. The entire crew, no matter what they had planned for that day, would always meet up for a cuppa before they went their separate ways. Blades worked under Barry Connors and his brother Ronnie neither of whom you would want to look at in the wrong way and if truth be told, it was best not to look at them at all. Blades was not yet trusted as he'd only been in Ritchie's employ for a fortnight and he wasn't aware of just who he was pissing off when he spoke out of turn. Blades was a climber and had plans to work his way up so it seemed only right to stop his boss as Ritchie marched across the concrete. No one had bothered to tell him that you didn't speak to the boss unless spoken to and if you had an issue of any kind you went to the man above you.

"Excuse me, Mr Spires, might I have a word?"

Barry Connors eyes narrowed, he was seething and about to step forward but was stopped by Ronnie putting his arm out in front. How did that little cunt dare to go above him?

"Blades! Leave Mr Spires alone."

Ritchie suddenly stopped and looked at the man who was either naive or had a big set of balls. Blades grinned and his cheeky, boyish smile made Ritchie shake his head and laugh.

"It's okay Barry. Follow me, kid."

In the office, Ritchie took off his overcoat before taking his seat in a massive leather swivel chair that seemed to dominate the room. Blades hadn't yet been in the office and he now felt a bit intimidated.

"Sit."

A smaller chair had been strategically placed in front of the desk and taking a seat Blades would swear that the legs had been shortened so it felt as if anyone sitting there was looking up at Ritchie. His boss had some serious issues of grandeur.

"So, what can I do for you?"

"Well, I don't know if you're aware but before I joined your firm I was working for Blacky Holmes over Soho way?"

Ritchie didn't speak but slowly nodded his head.

"Blacky is about to go down for GBH which means his Tom's will be up for grabs. I don't know if you're interested Mr Spires but they bring in a healthy wedge each week. I told Blacky I would have a word with you and he'd rather another face took over than some of the Yardie's, who would be in like fucking Flynn as soon as he gets sent down."

Ritchie was silent for a moment as he eyed the man trying to work out if he was interested.

"Give me a few hours to mull it over and then come back when you've finished whatever it is Barry and Ronnie want you to do today."

With that, Ritchie looked down at the papers on his desk, a silent signal for Blades to get out. Barry Connors wasn't best pleased with his new hire and he let it be known that if the man ever went above his head again, he would be out on his ear. Blades didn't

154

argue he knew that if he pulled off the deal he wouldn't have to worry about what Barry or Ronnie Connor thought any more.

At the end of the day, he returned to the unit and knocking on the office door, waited to be invited inside. Again he took a seat in front of the desk but he didn't speak.

"I've thought about the offer Blades and it's not my usual mode of business, that said, I would still like to meet with Blacky and see the girls first-hand. How much is he asking?"

"I'm not sure and Blacky can be a greedy cunt at times but if he don't get a buyer he's up the creek without a paddle. I would suggest if you don't mind me saying, however much he asks for you should halve."

"Arrange a meet for some time this week. When's he up in court?"

"Friday."

"Then arrange it for Wednesday afternoon, let's say five o'clock. He'll be on edge by then so if I'm interested and I ain't saying I am until I see the Tom's, he'll be more than willing to take whatever I offer due to the time restraints."

Blades smiled and then getting up, left the room to arrange the meeting. Blacky was over the moon to hear from him and swiftly arranged for all of his girls to be at his office on Wednesday afternoon with strict instructions for them all to be clean and well turned out. Anyone on heroin was told to wear long-sleeved tops and on no account were any of them to be high. Around the same time as the Firm's rapid growth spurt, Ritchie fell in love for the first time in his life.

Out for a drink one Friday night he had met the woman whom he would spend almost the next two decades with but only ever as his lover. The relationship moved fast and within a month, in a small flat in Camden, not too far from his first marital home, was where Richie Spires set up his mistress. Hillary Parker or Hills as Ritchie affectionately called her, was the difference between night and day as far as comparing her to Sue was concerned. Hill's just loved life and loved Ritchie Spires even more. She worked on a small bakery stall in the lock and never asked him for a thing, nor did she ever ask him to leave his wife and child, she had no right to do that but whenever he came to their little love nest and he took her in his arms she melted. He had asked her several times if she wanted a more permanent set-up but the answer had always been the same 'We're fine as we are darling'. Hillary loved her own space and seeing her lover two or three times a week always made it feel like it was their first date. The sex was explosive and unlike with his wife, Ritchie always made sure that Hill's was satisfied.

At home that evening, Ritchie had informed Sue that he would be staying in the city on Wednesday night as he had a late business meeting. She didn't know if it was the truth or not and in all honesty, she'd heard the same thing so many times over the years that she didn't care anymore.

On Wednesday Ritchie packed a small overnight bag and then set off for the unit. It was his way of showing his wife that he would be in a hotel and he didn't realise that she knew exactly where he would be staying and that he probably had an entire wardrobe at the sluts flat. The day passed without event and at five on the dot, Blades came to the unit and the two men then left in Ritchie's Aston Martin.

"Nice motor Guvnor."

Ritchie grinned as they turned onto the main road.

"Work hard and you can get yourself one."

"I doubt that, I can't fucking drive."

Turning left onto Caledonian Road the journey to Soho was taken in relative silence. With traffic, it would take just over thirty minutes. The closer they got to their destination the more nervous Blades became. Ritchie had a reputation for turning on people and should the deal turn sour, Blacky was liable to kick off as well.

Blacky Holmes, real name Geoffrey Lancaster, worked out of two rooms above a kebab shop on Lexington Street. Born in Maida Vale, his father was a wealthy doctor and his mother a social worker though he would never admit to that nor his privileged upbringing. He told anyone who asked that he was from Brixton and his voice had a strong Caribbean accent. In reality, his father had kicked him out of the large family home after numerous arguments regarding Blacky's friends and choice of lifestyle. He was a big man and instilled fear on the spot to anyone stupid enough to challenge him but he could also be charming and quickly had a stable of girls working the streets for him. Ritchie parked up the Aston and glanced all around. The kebab shop was busy with all manner of dodgy people coming in and out and Ritchie guessed they were selling a lot more than doner and shish kebabs.

157

"For your sake, my fucking motor had better be safe."
In this area, Blades knew that was highly unlikely.
"Probably for the best if I stay in the car Boss.
Blacky's expecting you so there won't be a problem,
just go on up."

Ritchie gave his employee a look of contempt before
getting out of the car and going into the door beside
the takeaway. The narrow hallway was long overdue
to be decorated and the staircase was bare wood,
though Ritchie deduced that the lack of a floor
covering had more to do with being able to hear
people coming up rather than a lack of care. When he
reached the top he pushed open a bare door and
immediately the aroma of sex invaded his nostrils.
This wasn't a brothel but the seven girls seated on an
old sofa and two chairs looked like they'd been
around the block a few times. A couple of them
weren't too bad looking, well not in a dim light but he
still wouldn't have dipped his wick in any of them.
"Blacky?"

One of the women, who Ritchie would come to know
as Black Grace, motioned with her eyes in the
direction of the only other door in the room. This time
Ritchie knocked but he had no intention of waiting
around and immediately turned the handle. Seated
behind a desk, he came face to face with a giant of a
man and he couldn't be off noticing a woman's head
as it bobbed up and down on Blacky's crotch.
"Enough Sandra, go back ta de udders."

When the door closed the Jamaican accent which
Ritchie had been told to expect didn't materialise and
surprisingly the voice he heard was well-spoken, his
actual command of the English language was far

better than Ritchie's.

"Mr Spires I assume?"

"You assume correctly but you ain't as described Mr Holmes."

"Please no formalities, call me Blacky. I keep the patois for the Toms and punters, keeps them on their toes."

Blacky then let out a deep booming laugh that made Ritchie smile.

"In all honesty Mr Spires I haven't ever been to the Caribbean but it wouldn't do well for my crew or my girls to know that."

"Please call me Ritchie, so, shall we get down to business?"

"Sure. Now I'm looking for forty grand for this office and my girls. They are all good earners and don't bring back any trouble, even if some of them do look a little jaded."

Ritchie laughed out loud, he didn't mean to as he instantly knew he had offended Blacky but at the same time, the amount being asked was ridiculous.

"Let me tell you how it is Blacky. I don't normally deal with Tom's as they're more fucking trouble than they're worth, no matter how much they bring in. Now the munter's out in that room have already seen their best years and I doubt they charge much at all. How I see it is you won't be around much longer and without a buyer there will be a free for all resulting in you getting fuck all. One-time offer, fifteen K with a view to you buying them back for the same amount on your release, more like a loan I suppose and I will make my money while you're inside. Now I'm not going to argue with you as in all honesty I ain't that interested. Think it over and let Blades know your decision."

With that, Ritchie stood up and walked out. As he made his way to the stairs one of the women winked at him and licked her lips in an attempt to be seductive which made his stomach churn, he was already having doubts about the offer he'd just made. Monica who the others referred to as Gorbechevache and the name had nothing to do with Russia, fancied the visitor like crazy. She had gained her nick name because of her enormously hairy eyebrows and not because she'd had a past acquaintance with the old Russian Prime minister known for his own hairy brow. Monica didn't shave and was hairy all over, something which Blacky had planned on telling her to address but it seemed there was a certain clientele that appreciated hairy women and she was able to charge extra for the service.

"In your dreams, Gorbachevache.!"

"Oh fuck off Sandra, some me like to feel a lot of fur on their chin."

The men hadn't even reached Holloway when Blade's phone rang and it was a short call. Blacky had accepted the offer just as Ritchie knew he would.

"Good bit of business Mr Spires."

"Maybe, it remains to be seen. You get in contact with Blacky tomorrow as I want you to take control of the Toms."

"Me!?"

"Am I speaking a fucking foreign language or something?"

"No Mr Spires, sorry Mr Spires."

"As I was saying. You will take charge, get yourself a

couple of bodies and don't let those tarts get away with a thing or they'll run fucking rings around you. I will require weekly reports and payments. If anyone tries to skim off the top, you included, then they will wish they had never been fucking born. Do I make myself clear?"

"Yes, Mr Spire and I promise you will be able to trust me."

"Good to hear but I trust no one Blades. Now work it well and it could be a right good earner but believe me, you will only get one shot at this. When we get back go and see Barry and he'll make arrangements to sort out Blacky's cash and it goes without saying, keep your trap shut even around the other blokes. The less people that know about my business dealings, the better."

Ritchie dropped Blades back at the unit and then sped off, he had a hot date tonight with the woman of his dreams and he didn't want to be late.

By the end of the week, Blacky Holmes was in court and was sentenced to two years. Sent to HMP Wormwood Scrubs, it was his first prison stint and to say it was a shock to his system was an understatement. Blacky wasn't the only one having a baptism of fire as Ritchie never dreamed that running Toms could be so stressful. Blades had initially taken over as agreed and for the first six months things ticked over nicely but a month later he was back at Biddeston Road with his cap in his hand so to speak. Mid-morning and when Barry led Blades through to the office, Ritchie groaned, if he had come all the way over here from Soho it could mean only one thing, there was trouble.

"Thanks for seeing me Boss and I don't like to bother you......"

"I can sense a but coming, what's up Blades?"

"Well for the last few of days some of the girls have been calling in sick, not all the time but you know a Toms, they don't like losing money. Anyway, I sent Georgie Lake, that's one of my boys, out to have a nose and see what he could find out. Seems, they've been moonlighting for Glenmore Henry, a Yardie who's a real nasty bastard by all accounts."

"A real Yardie this time?"

"Boss?"

"Never mind. Does this Glenmore know they're my girls?"

"Not sure but I don't think he cares boss, he ain't scared of anyone."

"Get the girls who have been moonlighting and take them to the office, don't let them out of your sight until I get there."

Just over an hour later Ritchie got the call from Blades. With Ronnie and Barry Connors, who both had years of violet experience, the men made their way over to Soho in Ronnie's Jag. Climbing the stairs Ritchie made the door fly open and as he stormed in Fifi Long and Sandra Raymond cowered on the old sofa.

"You know why I'm here girls, better still you know why you're here?"

Suddenly Ritchie lunged forward and viciously grabbing Fifi by the throat lifted her from the sofa as he did so.

"Who's the cunt you've been working for?"

The man's eyes were wild and Fifi Long was suddenly frightened, more frightened than she was of Glenmore Henry, more frightened than she had ever been in her life. As quickly as he'd grabbed her, Ritchie allowed the woman to drop back down again. "He threatened to kill us Mr Spires if we didn't work for him."

"Blades, keep them here until tonight and no one comes in or out until I get back. Understood?" Wide-eyed, Blades vigorously nodded his head in fear. He had never been witness to his boss kicking off but he'd been warned and after this little show of violence, he didn't want to be on the receiving end. Not a coward by any means, in fact on occasion he could be downright vicious but even Blades knew to court aggravation would be a stupid act.

CHAPTER FIFTEEN

Back on the street, Ronnie Connors turned to his boss.

"Where to next Mr Spires?"

"Take me to the office, I have some real business to attend to."

The journey was taken in silence, Ronnie and Barry knew when their boss was in a bad mood and this was one of those times. When he was seated behind his desk Ritchie gave instructions that he wasn't to be disturbed. Sighing heavily he thought back to when it had been him and Michael taking on the world and he wished his brother was here now but it was a wish he would never share with another living soul. Ritchie knew that Michael would have been against getting involved with Blacky Holmes in the first place and now with this recent trouble, he was wondering what the fuck had possessed him. Telephoning Sue and telling her he had business so he wouldn't be home that night he then called Hill's and told her he was staying over. Just the thought of seeing her suddenly made everything feel better and by seven that night when he returned to Soho he was a man on a mission. Ronnie and Barry had driven to Soho in a transit van. Ritchie already had a plan in mind and he couldn't bear the thought of being in the same vehicle as a couple of Toms so had driven himself in his Aston. The area looked far seedier at night and he grimaced as he stepped from the car and made his way up the stairs. Fifi Long and Sandra Raymond were still seated on the old sofa when he walked in and the look

of relief on Blade's face made Ritchie inwardly smile.
"Tarts been giving you a hard time, have they?"
"No Mr Spires but they don't half fucking whinge a
lot."
Ritchie walked over and Fifi flinched as she pushed
he body as far back into the lumpy old couch as she
could. He didn't bother with her this time and instead
spoke to Sandra Long, a woman in her forties who
had more miles on her than a clapped-out old banger
and knew the score, knew she should never have
bitten the hand that fed her but she was scared and
Ritchie Spires should have made sure that this kind of
situation had never arisen in the first place. They had
worked hard for Blacky and had always felt safe but
they never saw Ritchie and to the Toms, Blades was a
bit of a wet weekend and someone was liable to take
over any day, putting their livelihood in jeopardy.
"So, how does it work? How do you pay that cunt!?"
"He phones us up when he wants us to work and
honest Mr Spires we ain't got no choice, not if we
want to keep working. The bastard threatened to cut
us if we refused didn't he Fifi?"
"That's right Mr Spire, threatened to slice both of our
faces. I know we ain't much to look at but punters
won't touch someone who's scared, it's like
Brenda…."
"That's enough."
Turning back to Sandra Ritchie motioned for her to
continue.
"He sits in the window of the chip shop at the bottom
of Old Compton Street and watches us. When a
punter comes along and business is agreed we take
them down the back of Tibury Court unless they're

staying at the Premier and then if we're lucky we get to use a bed. When it's done we take the cash back to Glenmore. He takes the fucking lot Mr Spire that's why we can only do a couple of nights a week or we wouldn't be able to live."

"When are you next working for him?"

"Tonight."

"Ronnie, bring the van around."

Barry and Blades escorted the girls outside and when they were all in the van they headed towards Old Compton Street with Ritchie following behind. Parking up down Tilbury Court, Fifi and Sandra were instructed to walk to Old Compton and when Ronnie came along and they were sure Glenmore Henry was watching them, they agreed to a threesome and then with arms linked they headed back. Ten minutes later Fifi was instructed to call Glenmore and tell him that the punter wasn't playing ball and wouldn't pay them. She also told him that they was in the back of a parked van down Tilbury Court and needed his help. The women were then told to go home via Rupert Street so that Glenmore wouldn't see them and wait to be called. Ritchie got into the back of the van while Ronnie, Barry and Blades hid out of sight. Ritchie watched Glenmore through the black-tinted windows as he swaggered down the Court. Stopping at the van he slowly circled the outside but when he couldn't see anyone in the front seats he walked to the backdoors and hammered hard with his fist.

"Open up mon and let me girls out."

Suddenly the back door flew open and Glenmore came face to face with Ritchie.

"Who the fuck are you mon?"

Ritchie didn't reply and as quick as a flash Ronnie pulled a canvas bag over the Jamaican's head while Barry pushed him forward so that he was half in and half out of the van. Glenmore fought and kicked but he was overpowered as Barry cable tied his hands behind his back. Ritchie jumped out, smoothed down his jacket and then turned to Blades.

"Tell the girls to get back out to work. Ronnie, take this piece of shit to the unit."

With that, Ritchie got into the Aston and drove off. He had thought this sort of business had ended long ago but now here he was back in the thick of it and it pissed him off. Ritchie sighed heavily; Hill's was waiting for him back at the flat so he wanted this over with as soon as possible.

Blades sorted the girls out and then made his way back and he planned on taking his time as he didn't want to witness what was about to happen to Glenmore. By the time Ritchie arrived, Ronnie and Barry had unloaded the cargo and their prisoner was now seated in the middle of the unit, tied to a chair which sat on a large plastic sheet. Walking over Ritchie roughly pulled the bag off of Glenmore and a large mound of dreadlocks tumbled out as he shook his head. Ritchie had already decided that his victim wouldn't be leaving the unit alive, the Jamaicans were hard bastards and this Glenmore Henry would never let the matter drop and when healed would seek out revenge. Ritchie had instructed Blades to instil to the girls, with violence if necessary, that they were never to mention what had gone on to another living soul.

"So Mr Henry, thought you could take over my girls did you? Thought you could just fucking rob me and

I'd take it?"

"Fuck you mon!"

From his top pocket, Ritchie pulled out a cutthroat razor and flipped it open to reveal the highly polished blade.

"You do know you're not getting out of here alive don't you?"

Glenmore couldn't take his eyes from the razor and they were now bulging with fear.

"Look mon, I just tried me luck. A brudder needs to make a dollar, you know what a mean?"

"Not with my fucking girls, you cunt!"

"Come on mon, we can sort dis out can't we?"

"Not a fucking hope you piece of shit!"

"Please I'm sorry mon, let's say no more."

So as not to get splashed, Ritchie stepped to one side and with one swift movement drew the razor over Glenmore's throat and a whoosh could be heard as blood hit the plastic on the floor. Ritchie looked at his men but there was no change of expression from Ronnie, Barry or even Blades, who had arrived a few seconds too soon.

"Get this cleaned up and I want no trace or we'll have all the fucking Yardie's in London coming back at us."

Ronnie stepped forward.

"A few years back when I worked for Mickey Colletta he had a man. Old Harry Cunningham a pig farmer from somewhere in Norfolk. It costs but no questions asked."

"You got his number?"

"Sure have Boss, I always hold on to a good contact."

"Give him a call and take the money out of my desk,

there's fifteen grand in there, will it be enough?"
Ronnie nodded his head and with that, Ritchie walked
from the building and made his way over to Hillary's
and some much-needed peace. Ronnie made the call
and then told Blades and Barry to disappear as Harry
didn't like too many people being around. By eight
that night and after Ronnie had wrapped and tapped
Glenmore's remains, there was a short sharp rap on
the front roller door. Opening up, Ronnie stepped to
one side as Harry and his son Henry stepped into the
unit. Usually, they had a woman with them but not
this time.
"Long time no see Harry, how have you been
keeping?"
"Bootiful me old darling thank ya, now where's me
pigs dinner?"
"No Martha today?"
"She's on hog duty, got a pregnant sow due any time."
Ronnie led the two men through to the scene of the
murder and Harry nodded his head.
"Bit a the ol black, hay? No worries, me boars ain't
fussy. You got me cash?"
"I have Harry but I'm not sure what you charge these
days?"
Harry Cunningham eyed the man suspiciously. He
hadn't seen Ronnie Connors for a long time, not since
the Colletta days and he was on his guard.
"Five."
Ronnie disappeared into the office and opening
Ritchie's desk removed five thousand pounds. When
he returned to where Harry and his son were standing
Harry already had his palm open. Ronnie handed over
the money and Harry nodded for Henry to remove the

cargo. Within ten minutes the two countrymen were on their way home and Ronnie had locked up the unit. It had been a tiring but interesting day though he wasn't upset that it was over. In Camden, Ritchie had enjoyed a fabulous home-cooked meal and was now lying on the sofa with his head resting in Hillary's lap.

"You okay Ritchie, only you don't seem yourself?"

"Yeah I'm fine babe; I just had to carry out a bit of unpleasant business today. It was something I would never have got involved in when Michael was around and it's bothered me."

"Why don't you phone him sweetheart and put things right?"

"Sadly it's too late for that but it don't stop me thinking about him, especially when times are tough. You know we were always there for each other no matter what, that's until my bitch of a wife came on the scene and started stirring the shit!"

Hillary didn't reply, Ritchie's family was his business and she would never interfere. Stroking his head she bent over and kissed him.

"I think I know what will make you feel better."

Ritchie Spires grinned from ear to ear, what a woman!

CHAPTER SIXTEEN

South Lambeth, in an area nicknamed Little Portugal, due to its large Portuguese population, reigned a relatively new firm if you can call two decades new. The Makenzie brothers dealt in anything, no matter how horrendous and violent, not to mention illegal. They had quickly earned a reputation for the punishment that they and the rest of their firm administered, which was notorious for its level of viciousness, not to mention the fact that it was often very unnecessary violence. In total, there were three brothers, Tommy, Jock and Brian, all of whom had migrated down from Glasgow some twenty years earlier after their mother had passed away. Old Maggie Makenzie had raised her boys single-handed and had taught them all to fight, to the death if it was called for. Their father was a drunk and had disappeared from the scene as soon as the youngest, Brian, had been born. Maggie worked two jobs to support her little clan and all three brothers loved her more than anything else in the world. As the boys grew she discouraged them from having girlfriends, telling her sons they would only get in the way but in truth, she was jealous of anyone coming between her and her boys. Tommy Makenzie was the oldest with his brother jock following on two years later and a year after that, Brian had come into the world. Business had started when the boys were still in school and by the time they were all in secondary they already had a reputation as bullies who you didn't cross on any account and who without question, you handed over your lunch money to when asked.

By the time Tommy left school he already had a lengthy police record and at the age of seventeen would begin his first prison sentence. It was only a two-year stretch but was swiftly followed by a five and then an eight-year incarceration. Finally after being released at the age of twenty-five, Tommy knew it was time to start his own crew and hadn't intended to include his brothers but when Jock, the fieriest of the brothers, had insisted, Tommy had relented with Brian reluctantly following suit. With a band of five additional men, the small firm terrorised the local area of Possilpark by way of loan sharking and robberies. Tommy had learned so much on the inside and now planned everything so meticulously that they didn't even get their collars felt much less get arrested for anything. Maggie couldn't have been prouder, but when she suddenly passed away from a brain haemorrhage at just forty-eight years of age, Tommy decided it was time for them to relocate. His choice had been London where within the first few months of the move they would swiftly earn the reputation of being real hard bastards and men you didn't cross. Tommy was tall, dark and handsome with a good physic but the same couldn't be said for Jock. The stereotypical description of a Scot couldn't have been more fitting. He was of average height with a mop of unruly, curly, ginger hair and a freckled face. Brian was just Brian, plain in looks and somewhat gentle in his demeanour which at times riled his brothers. Where Tommy was a thinker and a planner, Jock would wade straight in and what he lacked in stature he more than made up for in his ability to fight. At times Tommy felt it was like having a wild animal at his side, handy when called for but a nuisance to keep under control. Settling in Brixton for no other reason than it was the first place on the map that Tommy's pin had gone into, the brothers shared a flat on Ferndale Road. The building was a converted Victorian terrace and the boys had the ground floor unit. They had only been in residence for a few days when late one night reggae music began to blare out from the flat above. Jock was out of bed in seconds and running up the stairs began to pound on the door. When a six-foot Jamaican answered it didn't deter Jock and barging in he ripped the power supply from the wall. Baron Grant was the local ganja dealer and rather than take on the little scot, he admired the man's attitude and fearlessness. Within a few days, the Makenzie's and Baron were in business together and Tommy was soon introduced to all of the local villains. The Scots, as they came to be known by other firms, were accepted without question and business moved swiftly along.

A small unit on Binfield Road in Little Portugal was acquired and within two years the Makenzie's were firmly on the map and now ruled the area with an iron fist. Sometime later Baron Grant mysteriously disappeared but no one ever questioned where he had gone and many accepted that his body was probably propping up one of the many new builds that had begun to spring up in the area. The boys were now dealing in cocaine and heroin although they were still the go-to firm for cannabis and any other recreational drug but only on a wholesale basis. Tommy was greedy, greedy to the point that apart from his brothers he wouldn't share anything with anyone else and was always in fear of being ripped off. Business was good and they soon began to import, it was risky but the rewards were far greater than buying from other suppliers. By the time their fifth anniversary came around, Tommy had his own flat and so did Brian. Jock had remained at Ferndale Road as he liked the area but he had no friends and women shied away from him when he tried to chat them up. Seeking out the company of prostitutes was his only way of getting any sexual relief but even then the girls would only visit once. Jock had sick sexual desires and no amount of money could buy what he wanted the women to do, when they refused he would get violent and often the girls would leave the flat bruised and battered but their pimps knew better than to complain. Brian, unbeknown to his brothers was gay and he sought out comfort in London's West End, namely Soho. He was discreet and respectful and shied away from rent boys preferring to cop off via chatting up men in bars and he usually honed in on the married ones, they were easy to spot and would always keep their mouths shut. Getting seen was Brian's biggest fear as he didn't know how his brothers would react and he wasn't about to take the chance of finding out. Tommy was different to Jock and Brian in so many ways and when he had a night off would venture across the water and drink in any local pubs he came across. The Camden area was his favourite, his face wasn't recognised and he could be just a regular bloke but he didn't chat with anyone and looked like a lost soul as he stood alone at the bar nursing his pint. Women didn't interest Tommy and he was far too money-orientated to share his life with anyone but he was content in his own way.

Five years after the robbery which still played heavily on his mind, Tommy ventured into Holloway and by chance came across the Lamb. It was instantly a place he liked and soon, whenever he was able to get a night off, it became his regular. The landlord Michael kept a good pint and the landlady was friendly and would often prepare the regulars a sandwich if they were hungry. Michael would chat with the Scotsman but the themes of conversation were kept light with football being the main topic. Mavis had taught him early on that you never spoke of politics or religion as it was a sure way to start an argument and Michael followed that rule to the letter. It must have been around a year after Tommy's first visit that Michael found out who the man was. Freddy Walton who had moved to Holloway three years earlier from Lambeth, happened to be in the bar one night when Tommy walked in. As soon as he saw the man Freddy downed his pint in one and then much to Michael's amazement, walked straight out. Now Freddy was a heavy drinker and most nights had to be shown out of the door well past closing time so for him to leave so abruptly was totally out of character. The following day, Freddy was one of the first in at lunchtime and made a beeline for Michael. Ellie was serving so she didn't take much notice when her husband went to the side of the bar and was in deep conversation with Freddy.

"Alright, Fred?"

"I am now thanks."

"What on earth happened to you last night?"

"When I saw that cunt at the bar, I knew it was time to be on me way. You do know who that Scottish bastard is Molly?"

Michael pursed his lips and slowly shook his head.

"No idea. He drinks in here from time to time, I think his name's Tommy but that's about it, why?"

"He's only fucking Tommy Makenzie, you must have heard of the Makenzie firm from over in Lambeth?"

"Of course I have but why would Tommy Makenzie be drinking in here? Pint?"

Freddy nodded his head and then took a seat on one of the bar stools.

"Back when I lived over Lambeth way I had a few friends who had dealings with the firm and they are one bunch of fucking nasty bastards. Seems the oldest, that's Tommy by the way, well he likes to drink where he isn't well known, safer for him I suppose but I swear on my life that's him, Molly."

"Well thanks for the heads up pal, that one is on the house by the way."

Fred nodded his head as Michael moved away to start helping Ellie serve but all the while his thoughts went back to that robbery several years earlier.

The years swiftly rolled by, Beth grew up and Tommy Makenzie continued to use the Lamb to drink about three or four times a month. The subject of his business was not raised and for that Tommy was grateful, this was his special place, the only place where he wasn't judged or challenged and God help

176

anyone who tried to spoil that for him. By now he knew Michael must have been aware of who he was but the landlord showed no fear and always treated him as just another punter. The topic of work finally came about one Thursday night. It was unusually quiet and Michael was sitting at the end of the bar reading a magazine when the door opened and in walked Tommy Makenzie. Looking up Michael smiled.

"Evening Tom looks like you're stuck with me for conversation tonight."

"I can think of worse Michael."

Molly poured Tommy's usual drink of a draught Guinness and walking back to his seat he passed the pint to his customer.

"Busy day?"

"It's always a busy day in my line of work. You do know what I do work-wise?"

"I've heard the whispers Tommy but in the pub trade it doesn't do to take any notice of gossip and in here you are a friend like all of my other regulars."

Tommy Makenzie took a sip of his drink and then smiled in Michael's direction.

"Well thank you. By the way, you can take all of those silly little whispers and fucking double them. Maybe then you just might be close to what I do."

The expression on Michael's face changed, he now felt fearful and for a second he thought back to the night of the robbery when his life as he knew it had fallen apart. Tommy recognised the signs and laughed.

"No need to worry pal, that part of my life is separate and this part is my private time. I never do or talk

177

about business in my private time. "

"Glad to hear it. Can I ask you just one question though, Tom?"

"Fire away my old son but whether I answer honestly is another matter."

"Do you like what you do?"

Tommy took a moment to mull over the question. He'd never given much thought about whether he liked what he did but he did like the money that the lifestyle gave him.

"It's okay I suppose, with hindsight it wouldn't be my chosen career but the pay is good. I know people think we dish out too much violence but in this game Michael, if you don't then the local little gob shite's would be on you in seconds and before long you would have nothing left."

Michael nodded his head sagely as he took a sip of his drink.

"So you don't get any problems then?"

"You get aggro in all jobs but on the whole, it's pretty good. Only once did some cunt take me for a mug and ripped me off."

"And what happened to him, if you don't mind me asking that is?"

Tommy placed his drink onto the bar a little too heavily and Michael could see the fire and anger in his customer's eyes, so much so that he wished he hadn't asked."

"Never found out who it was but if I ever do, the cunt won't know what's hit him. It's played on my mind for years and I'd give anything to find out who it was."

Michael then changed the subject and was relieved that he and Ritchie's secret was still just that. With the

remote from the bar, he switched on the television.
"Sky's showing Arsenal tonight, fancy a look?"
"Don't mind but they ain't no Rangers, now there's a real man's club."
Michael laughed but he was glad that there would now be silence while the match played, hopefully by full-time Tommy Makenzie would have called it a night. Over the ensuing years, the two men would become friends. They never socialised away from the pub and they weren't what you would call bosom buddies but it was an easy, mutually respectful friendship that Michael liked.

CHAPTER SEVENTEEN

Michael and Ellie had run the Lamb continually since Mavis's death and apart from annually decorating, the place hadn't changed a bit. It was now fashionable for youngsters to frequent traditional pubs and the bar was packed out every weekend much to the pleasure of Beth who was now of drinking age but not to the ageing locals who continually moaned to Michael and Ellie that they couldn't get a seat and it wasn't like that in the old days when Mavis and Burt had been in charge. Beth had so many friends that her parents had lost count and on many an occasion Michael had tried to warn his daughter that they were probably using her just to get the odd free drink but she wouldn't hear a bad word said about any of them. A quiet girl, Beth Spires was not only beautiful she was loyal and clever and kind, if a little too trusting. In a month she was due to go off to university, something her parents were dreading. It wasn't that they didn't trust her but for so long it had just been the three of them and they had already accepted that empty nest syndrome was going to hit them both hard. Beth's place at the University of Leicester had been secured by her fantastic grades and she planned on studying computer science for the next three years. She hadn't decided yet if she would remain after that time to gain her Masters, life was short and she wanted to see as much of the world as she could. She was free for the first time in her life and was now excited to experience all that life had to offer. When Ellie had tried to give her 'The Talk' a few days before she left,

180

Beth had started to laugh which instantly stopped the conversation.

"Please Mum, I'm not stupid and besides, I have no intention of getting saddled with some spotty boy, I'm keeping my hand on my snatch and no man is going anywhere near it."

"Beth Spires! What a terrible expression."

They both laughed and after a loving embrace, Ellie let the subject drop as she was happy with what her daughter had said. Beth was motivated, had planned everything down to the last little detail and couldn't wait to get started, she loved her parents dearly but they were overprotective and at times she felt like she was being smothered. Gaining her freedom was scary and she knew they wouldn't be around to sort out her problems but maybe that was a good thing, maybe it was time to be an adult and figure life out for herself. She hadn't yet shared with them her decision to find work and support herself through Uni. Beth knew about the money Mavis had left to her but she wanted to do this by herself and in any case, she would have far more fun spending it if she decided to take a gap year.

Finally, the day arrived and with the car packed to the roof and Beth crammed in the back like a sardine, the three of them set off on the two-hour drive. Much to her mother's delight, Beth was to spend her first year in halls so she would be protected to some extent but when they arrived and looked at the buildings it was nothing like Ellie and Michael had been expecting, nor was it in the grounds of the university. There was lush greenery surrounding the purpose-built blocks but it was still a ten-minute walk to campus. Beth could see that her parents weren't happy so she decided to tackle the issue head on.

"What's wrong? I can see by your faces that it isn't what you were expecting."

"Well I imagined you'd be safer sweetheart, you know if you were right next to the university as I assume they have security patrols."

"God Dad! For someone coming from one of the roughest areas of London, you can come across as a bit naive at times. This place is as safe as anywhere, students have been using this kind of accommodation for decades and as yet I haven't heard of anyone being murdered."

"Beth!"

"What? Please don't keep on or you'll spoil it for me and I've been so looking forward to this day. Let's all just have a nice time shall we?"

Ellie gave her husband a roll of her eyes and they both let the matter drop, at least for the time being. It took several trips up and down the stairs and by the time they had unpacked the car, the small room was full to bursting with all the stuff her parents had insisted she bring with her. Standing in the doorway with her hands on her hips, Beth knew it couldn't stay like this.

"Oh, Mum! I can't have all of this in here. Let me go through it all and you and Dad will have to take some of it back. Why don't you both go and have a coffee while I get stuck in without either of you interfering?"

"Well say what you feel Beth, don't mind our feelings will you?"

"It's not that Mum but you'll insist I keep everything.

182

I mean for God's sake, who needs five sets of winter pyjamas and why have you packed a chiller box and icepacks? Give me strength!"

Michael looked at his wife; he could really do with a drink. When she smiled at him he winked and as they set off for a café or better still a pub Beth started on the task at hand. The stuff she came across was ridiculous and within half an hour she had reduced her chattels to more than half. Opening the door to start stacking the boxes in the corridor she stopped when her eyes met those of the most handsome boy she had ever seen. He was tall, muscular and dark and when he offered his hand she stood up and stared into his eyes.

"Daniel Nelson, I'm up the hall in room nine pleased to meet you?"

"I'm Beth, Beth Spires and it's nice to meet you too."

"That's strange, some of my family have the surname Spires, where are you from?"

"London, can't you tell by my accent? It's actually a well-used surname in Scotland and Ireland not to mention Germany and France, so I very much doubt were related."

Daniel laughed and no more was mentioned on the subject of names.

"A few of us are going out for a drink later, a bit of a get-to-know-each-other thing. You up for it?"

"Oh yes, that sounds wonderful. I can't wait to meet new people and thank you by the way."

Beth realised that she was coming over too wordy and too strong so she immediately changed tactics.

"Well, I will if I get my room straight, my parents have brought everything but the kitchen sink."

Daniel laughed, it wasn't the first time he had received this kind of response and in the past, he had made full use of it and had charmed the girl into his bed but this girl, this Beth, well, he knew instantly that she was somehow different.

Okay, if you can make it we are meeting up in the common room at seven."

By the time her parents returned, there was no sign of Daniel and Beth intentionally didn't mention him. To do so would result in the Spanish inquisition from her father and she was too tired to get into a heated argument about taking her time and not rushing into a relationship. The farewell was awful and when the tears had subsided and after Ellie had hugged her daughter for the tenth time and made her promise to phone every day, Beth watched as the car pulled away. Alone for the first time in her life, she stretched up her arms and grinned from ear to ear. The boxes still hadn't been unpacked but she was exhausted so lying on the bed she decided to take a nap. When she eventually woke and looked at her phone she saw it was nine-thirty, she had missed out on the opportunity to get to know the handsome stranger and she wanted to kick herself. Deciding that she should at least tidy her room, her mind continually filled with thoughts of those beautiful brown eyes that may well have captured her heart.

On her first morning as a resident, it was the induction and she wasn't due in the common room until ten. Fixing herself tea and toast in the communal kitchen, Beth mulled over what to wear. She didn't want to look too stuffy but at the same time, she

184

wanted to be smart. Opting for a pair of navy trousers and a crisp white t-shirt, she grabbed her bag and headed off out. As she made her way over to the campus she studied the other girls she passed. Some were newbies like her and others were in their second and final years. You could easily tell the newbies who looked as uptight as she felt, whereas the seasoned students didn't have a care in the world. Her dress wasn't out of place but jeans were the main attire which she was glad of and tomorrow she would fit right in. Suddenly she heard someone call out her name and as she spun around she came face to face with Daniel. When Beth saw him she could feel her heart skip a beat.

"Shame you couldn't make it last night we had a great time."

"Oh sorry about that but to be honest I fell asleep. I only meant it to be forty winks but then I woke up and it was getting towards ten."

Not wanting to stop talking for fear this Adonis would walk off; she continued the conversation as they walked and at the same time she couldn't be off noticing how many of the other girls were eyeing him up.

"Did you go anywhere nice?"

"Only the student bar but I met some cracking people. We're meeting up again tonight, fancy it?"

Beth felt all warm inside as she smiled, it was an emotion she had never experienced before and she liked it.

"Would love to thanks."

"Great, I'll call for you at seven then?"

With that, he was gone and Beth had to breathe in

deeply to compose herself, it felt like he had taken every ounce of oxygen she had.

Dressed to impress in a sexy little black number, Beth was sitting waiting on the bed and he was bang on time. They started in the student bar and Beth inquired if any jobs were going. Sadly they had already been taken but she didn't let it bother her.

"Are you self-funding?"

"Trying to and I'm sure something will come up."

"Well I've heard the library is hiring, it's a bit nerdy but it's better than nothing."

She thanked him but it was getting so noisy that they were having trouble hearing each other speak. When he'd finally had enough Daniel pointed towards the door and ten minutes later saw them walking around the grounds of the university.

"So Daniels Nelson, where do you hail from?"

"Originally, London. At least that's what I've been told but my parents moved out to Hertfordshire before I started school. My dad works in the city so he stays there a lot in the week and tries to only come home at weekends but I think that's more to do with my mum than work though."

Beth looked shocked which made him laugh.

"Not the happiest of marriages in the world I'm sad to say. As far as I know, my grandparents still live in London but I've never met them or at least not that I know of."

"Oh, that's hard. I couldn't imagine not having both of my parents around all the time. That said they can be a bit overpowering when it comes to me but I know they are only trying to protect me. I suppose being an only child made them more protective. It's sad about

your grandparents as well, family feud or something?"
"Not sure they don't speak about it but what a coincidence; I'm an only child too."
By midnight and when they were getting tired and with the added fact that it was an early start tomorrow for both of them, Daniel suggested they call it a night. A true gentleman, he walked Beth to her door and as much as she longed for him to kiss her he didn't. Taking her hand he stared into her beautiful big blue eyes.
"I'm so happy that I've met you, Beth Spires."
"Likewise Daniel Nelson, likewise."
Inside Beth leaned back against the rear of the door. Grinning from ear to ear she wouldn't have been able to explain how she was feeling if she tried but she hoped it was the same for him.

Over the next few weeks, the young lovers spent almost every evening and weekend together but on the last Thursday night Beth told Daniel that she had to go home for her grandmother's sixty-fifth birthday celebration. Daniel was a little disappointed that she hadn't invited him but he didn't say anything.
"I would rather stay here with you but it's her retirement and she would be so disappointed if I didn't go home. I'm so sorry babe."
"It's fine sweetheart and who am I to spoil your Nan's big day, after all, we have the rest of our lives to be together."
When her last class of the week finished at eleven Beth caught the train. It was much quicker than driving and it meant that her dad didn't have to leave

the pub as Friday lunchtime was always busy. When she walked into the back kitchen Ellie was standing stirring something on the stove just as Mavis always had or that's what she'd been told. Turning and seeing her daughter it was as if Beth had been away for months as she ran over and wrapped her girl in her arms.

"Alright mum, I've only been gone for a few weeks."

"And those weeks have felt like a lifetime Sweetheart. Just wait until you have your own child and you'll know exactly what I'm talking about."

"Nan here yet?"

"No, she had to do the lunch shift at the Mecca but she's coming straight here afterwards. I asked her where she wanted to go tonight but she said she'd rather stay over and have a few drinks so I'm doing a nice roast chicken. So, tell me all about it, you made many new friends?"

Beth's cheeks immediately flushed and Ellie started to laugh.

"I know that look; you've met a bloke haven't you?"

"Leave it out mum; I've met lots of people. Where's dad?"

"In the bar but you've changed the subject bleedin' quickly ain't you? It doesn't matter; you're here until Sunday so I'll get it out of you one way or another."

Beth waved her hand in dismissal as she walked through to the bar. It was heaving with all manner of people, office workers who were already well-oiled and looking forward to their weekend, builders who had been in London working for the week and who should have been on their way home to their families but after swearing they would only have a couple of

188

pints were now plastered and wouldn't make it home until Saturday to face the wrath of their wives. At the far end and almost huddled together were five or six of the old timers, all eyeing up the newcomers and muttering under their breath but which no one took any notice of.

"Hi, dad!"

Michael stopped what he was doing, grabbed his daughter by the hands and stared lovingly into her eyes.

"Ain't you a sight for sore eyes, your mother has been doing my head in since you left darling', she's missed you rotten."

"It'll get better dad, she will get used to it sooner or later. It's not that I don't miss you two but I'm a big girl now and it's nice to have a bit of freedom and make my own decisions. You do understand don't you?"

"Of course I do love but I will never admit that in front of your mother, it would be more than my life is worth."

Just then the door opened and Eileen Evens walked in carrying an arm full of flowers she'd received from her workmates. The regulars burst into a round of 'Happy Birthday to you' which made her smile from ear to ear but the only person she wanted to see was her granddaughter.

"Bethie!!!!!"

"Hi Nan, here let me give you a hand with those. Mums in the kitchen, come on through. So, how's it feel being a pensioner?"

"Cheeky little cow, I can still give you a run for your money not to mention a backhander if you get too

189

lippy young lady."

The weekend was a huge success but it was over all too soon. Beth had fallen back into her old routine so easily that for a second it had crossed her mind whether to go back or not. Her bed was so comfortable and her mother's cooking was good old-school tasty fare but when she thought of Daniel, her heart melted so there was no choice to make.

Late on Sunday afternoon Michael and Ellie dropped Beth off at Kings Cross station and when she stepped from the train in Leicester, Daniel was there waiting for her and she fell into his arms.

"How did you know what train I'd be on?"

"I didn't, I've met every train since noon."

There and then Beth knew she had fallen in love, it felt so good to be with him again and as much as she loved her family, she couldn't, even after such a short time, imagine life without him. That night they sealed their relationship and when he realised that she was a virgin, Daniel felt honoured that she had chosen him to lose her virginity too. It had been awkward and it was painful for Beth but from then on they couldn't get enough of each other and Daniel spent more time in Beth's room than he did in his own.

By the end of their first year and when it was time to pack up and go home for the summer, neither of them couldn't hide their heartbreak. Even though they had secured a house share together for the following year, something Beth was yet to tell her parents about, the idea of being apart for the holidays for even a second was something they hated. It would also now feel lonely in bed and they had both been dreading the thought of sleeping alone.

"Come back to Hertfordshire with me, I can't bear to be without you for six weeks."

"Oh Daniel, it's the same for me but if I don't go home it will break my mum and dad's heart."

His face fell and she couldn't stand to see him so crestfallen.

"What about if you come and stay at mine for a weekend, say in two weeks and then I can return the visit a couple of weeks later? That way we'll keep everyone happy and we won't go too long without seeing each other."

Daniel scooped her up in his arms and twirled her around until they both fell over onto the bed.

"I take it that's a yes then?"

Daniel saw her off on her train and the journey for both of them was spent deep in thought. Back in London Beth gave it a few days before she broke the news to her parents but it still went down like a lead balloon. Michael looked suspicious and Ellie was hurt that their girl didn't want to spend all of the holidays with them.

"Who is he? What's his name? Darling, we don't know anything about him?"

The question instantly got Beth's heckles up and she didn't hold back.

"For God's sake will you listen to the pair of you? Stop treating me like a child, I'm almost twenty and you act like I'm still in nursery school. His name is Daniel Nelson and he's from a wealthy family in Hertfordshire. His dad works in the city and mostly commutes home at weekends. That's about all I can tell you at the moment but I will add that he's the

kindest, most lovely man I've ever met, well, all except for you Dad. We've been together for almost a year so it's not like he's a bloke I've only just met."
"Almost a year!"
"Yes, mum and I didn't tell you about him for precisely this reason."
"So you're keeping secrets now, are you? You never did that when you were living here."
"It's not a secret Dad but I just wanted to take the time to get to know him. It might not have come to anything and I would have still had you two on my back. Thankfully it has and you can both meet him soon enough okay?"
"Well, I still ain't at ease with things but like you rightly said, you're an adult now and we just have to learn to let you live your life. Do you fancy helping me behind the bar tonight?"
"You mean you trust me to pull a pint after last time?"
They all laughed but Beth knew that underneath they were hiding their feelings; she just hoped when they met him they would love him as much as she did.

CHAPTER EIGHTEEN

The taxi pulled up at the entrance to the drive of a large detached property named Spires House, on Whitehall Road in Hitchin. Daniel paid the driver and signed heavily as he walked the gravel length of half a football pitch to reach home. Finally, he stepped up to the open Roman-style porch and placed his key into the door lock. Calling out as he always did even though he knew there would be no reply, he dropped his bags in the large hallway and made his way through to the impressive kitchen that was always so pristine it could have been a show house. No one dared to use it in case they messed anything up, even a spot on the work surfaces and his mum would do her nut. Opening the fridge Daniel removed a carton of milk and drank directly from it. A thought crossed his mind and he grinned for a second, if his mother had been here she would have given him a right mouthful. Walking up the grand staircase he entered his room and flopped down on the bed, he was missing her already and he didn't know how he would cope. Placing his Beat headphones on, one of the many gifts from his mother last Christmas, Daniel didn't hear her call out or come into his room. Tapping him on the foot she stood at the end of the bed with her hands on her hips and a frown on her face.

"I wish you wouldn't just leave your bags in the hall, this isn't a doss house you know."

"Nice to see you too mum, been out shopping have you?"

The sarcasm didn't go unnoticed and she quickly shook her head. Her son was as stubborn as his father and God help the woman who got saddled with him. Still, he was her son and she loved him dearly even if he did do anything he could to wind her up.

"You hooking up with Arthur during the holidays."

"Why on earth would you ask that?"

"Because he will be coming over."

"Oh fuck off mum, he's a complete wanker."

"Daniel! Please don't speak like that, you're at University now but you sound just like an East End barrow boy. I've invited Arthur, his sister Lavinia and his parents George and Tamsin over to dinner tomorrow night so I hope you will keep a civil tongue in your head and not embarrass me. Your dad wants to butter him up, George Farringdon is the captain at the new golf club and your father wants a membership. You never know, you might like the sister. She's a year younger than you and very pretty."

"Yeah, like anyone in that family is good looking, not."

"Daniel!"

Danny ignored his mother and placing the headphones back on his head he closed his eyes which she knew was the sign to get out of his room. He spent the rest of the day there and dinner was some microwave crap that his mum brought up on a tray. She wasn't much of a cook and would do anything not to have her kitchen used for anything. At least there would be good grub tomorrow as he was certain that caterers would be coming to the house. It must have been well after midnight when he heard the front door close and his father throwing his keys into the silver dish on the hallway table. He didn't even bother to pop his head in to say high which was fine by Daniel. He didn't like his dad, never had and it hadn't taken much working out that his parents were forced to marry as he was on the way, still, he wondered why there had never been any other kids it would have been good to have a brother or sister to share things with as he was growing up.

It wasn't until breakfast the following morning that Daniel got to see his parents together but it was nothing to write home about. The breakfast table in the kitchen was immaculately set and was adorned with all manner of fresh fruit and warm muffins. He knew his mother would be watching like a hawk for any crumbs to be dropped, so she could be there in seconds with her trusty brush and dustpan. He smiled for a second when he imagined it tied to her waistband. Taking a seat Daniel stared in his father's direction but the man was so engrossed in his newspaper, that he didn't put it down until Daniel's mum placed a plate of eggs and bacon in front of him. He didn't welcome his son and only managed to mumble a few words at the same time as reaching for the salt.

"Got any plans for the summer then?"

"No not really but I have asked a friend to come over in a few weeks, just for the weekend."

"Male or female?"

"Richard! Don't speak to him like that. You haven't laid eyes on our boy for almost a year and the first thing you say to him is filled with suspicious undertones."

"For fucks sake Sue! I didn't mean anything by it and

besides, he ain't exactly been interested in the fairer sex now has he?"

"What, you mean like you were Richard? And please don't call me Sue, you know I hate it. When the Farringdon's arrive tonight please call me Susan, you owe me that at least Ritchie, after all, I'm only hosting this dinner for you."

Daniel let out a loud sigh and it was a little too noisy for his father's liking.

"Don't fucking sigh at me you little cunt. You should be grateful for all that you have, when I was your age I was out ducking and diving, not living the life of fucking luxury in some University room all paid for by me I might add."

Daniel could feel his blood begin to boil; he had never wanted to go to university in the first place and had only agreed after a lot of pressure from his mother and the realisation that he could at least get away from this hellhole for a while.

"While we're on the subject Dad, why have you never told me about your parents or mums come to that?"

Ritchie threw his knife and fork down onto the china plate making Sue's face contort at the thought of her best breakfast china getting chipped, not to mention and unbeknown to her son, the idea of her family history coming out.

"And nor will I, mine were a couple of complete cunts and I wouldn't have wished them on my worst fucking enemy. Now, I'm off out for a game of golf with Sid so you two can chew over the fat regarding what I've just said but believe me, you won't get much out of your mother, she's only ever been ashamed of her lot."

196

"Richard!"

Danny looked from his mother to his father and then back again. Sue dabbed at her eyes with her napkin but he didn't know if they were genuine tears as she had a habit of turning on the waterworks whenever it suited her.

That night and after both Danny and Ritchie had promised to be on their best behaviour, the evening finally got underway. The Farringdon's arrived and the party all went outside for Canapes on the terrace. Sue grinned, it had taken a long time but she was finally where she wanted to be and all thoughts of London, her family and the shitty life she had led back then were pushed to the back of her mind. Looking out over the lawn, Danny stood awkwardly with Arthur on one side and Lavinia on the other. He hated every minute of this charade and when Arthur tried to make conversation his questions were met with single-word replies. Lavinia slowly linked her arm through Danny's and when he looked at her she stared back with doe eyes. She wasn't a bad-looking girl but there seemed to be an empty void where her brain should have been, all she did was continually giggle which quickly got on Danny's nerves and he longed for Beth to be here.

"Dinner is served, Madam."

The rent a butler was so professional and when he looked across the table Ritchie thought he could see the idea forming in his wife's mind, well she could think again, there was no way they were getting a butler. Ritchie gave in to most of his wife's demands to keep the peace but that was a step too far. As much as Danny was missing and wanting to be with the woman he loved, yes, it had hit him like a bolt of lightning last night, he was most definitely in love, Ritchie was dreaming of the same thing as his son. He'd been with Hilary Parker for years now and he loved her more than ever. When her husband had begun to stay away from the house for nights on end, Sue Spires had turned detective. It had now been five years since she'd found out about the mistress but it had taken a lot longer for her to gather the courage to confront the competition but it hadn't fazed Hilary in the least. Unaware of how long the affair had been going on for, Sue had travelled to London and the two women had met without Ritchie's knowledge. After a slap and a few choice words had been exchanged, the women had settled on Hilary remaining a mistress. As long as she was content with that then Sue was prepared to turn a blind eye, it wasn't as if she had to bear her husband's advances after he was fresh from being with another woman, that part of their marriage had ended years ago and was one of the reasons Sue had turned detective and found out about Hilary in the first place. No man, especially one as handsome as her husband, was happy to go without sex so if he wasn't getting it from her then he was getting it from somewhere else. To begin with, she had panicked that he would leave and her life of luxury would come tumbling down but that hadn't been the case and Hilary did her best to reassure Sue that she had nothing to worry about. The set-up suited her and she had no desire to steal Ritchie away. Sue didn't know if the woman had ever told Ritchie about their ~ ʾut she guessed not as it had never been mentioned and all in all, from then on life seemed to move along without any issues.

Taking their seats at the elaborately dressed table, the meal began and the food was everything Sue had hoped for. Foie gras and mini Melba toasts were followed by Seabass En Papillote with seasonal vegetables and the crowning glory was a chocolate soufflé. After coffee had been served, Ritchie and George, on Sue's suggestion, went to his study for a cigar. Unable to contain herself any longer, Sue turned to Tamsin, knowing that it was the woman in the marriage who always got things done and more often than not, made the decisions.

"So Tamsin, how does it feel to be the wife of the Captain of the new golf club?"

"Fabulous darling, we get invited out to so many parties, you would adore it."

"How lovely, now, about Richard joining the club?"

Tamsin Farringdon stared open-mouthed at her host and to Sue it felt like she had suddenly grown two heads or something. Tamsin placed her cup onto the marble table and slowly shook her head.

"Oh I'm dreadfully sorry Susan but I have already discussed it with George and he doesn't think Richard would be a good fit."

"A good fit! Why on earth not?"

"It seems your husband had a shady background and it just wouldn't do for any of his past to catch up with him. I mean, you never know if some gangsters were to turn up one day, what on earth would the members think? I hope you aren't terribly offended but George does take his role very seriously."

Inside Sue was fuming but she only nodded her head

and smiled sweetly as she excused herself. From the kitchen, she phoned her husband and after she explained that he didn't have a cat in hell's chance, she slammed the phone down. Walking onto the back patio she called Danny over and ordered him to do something horrible to Lavinia which would force the Farringdon's to leave. It wasn't in his nature but Danny wanted out of the situation as much as his mother so a few moments later he suddenly put his hand up the young girl's skirt and pulled at her knickers. Lavinia shrieked and jumped back a few steps.

"What on earth do you think you are doing!?"

"Just having a little feel, you know you like it."

"I most certainly do not, you pig!"

Lavinia ran into the front room and seconds later Arthur was called inside and the family marched out vowing never to set foot in the house again. When Danny went back into the kitchen, Ritchie was standing there with his tie lying on the breakfast bar and his shirt undone to the waist. Seeing his son he began to laugh out loud.

"What did you do boy?"

"I just shoved my hand up her skirt, that's all. Frigid little cow screamed blue murder."

"I tried that with your mother but it didn't work, pity she wasn't frigid then I wouldn't have got stuck with the pair of you."

"Richard!"

Danny couldn't help but laugh at his father's words and it was only heightened when he saw how sour his mother's expression was. While in his study Ritchie had downed several glasses of scotch and was now a little the worse for wear and when he began to laugh at his own words, Sue stomped off upstairs. Danny had seen the hurt look on his mother's face and he couldn't work out why they stayed together, after all, it wasn't as if they loved each other or come to that, even liked each other.

"Why are you always so cruel to mum? If you're both so unhappy I don't know why you don't just call it a day and get a divorce?"

"Money son, pure and simple, money. Your cow of a mother would try and take me to the fucking cleaners but if it wasn't for that fact, I'd have been gone a long, long time ago."

"What, even when I was little?"

"I never wanted you boy, she trapped me and I've hated the sight of her ever since. It's because of that bitch that I have no contact with my family."

Danny was confused, this was the first time his father had opened up to him and he wasn't about to let the conversation end even though the words were like a knife in his heart.

"What family dad, I don't know anything about them and I've always wondered."

Ritchie took a seat at the breakfast bar and poured himself a glass of wine from a half-opened bottle that the hired butler had left out. Pointing to the stool beside him, Ritchie motioned for his son to join him.

"Rita and Albie were our parents if you can even call them that. By our, I mean me and my younger brother. Things got really bad so after I gave the old man a pasting, me and Michael moved in with a lovely couple who became our kind of surrogate parents. To cut a long story short, I got in with your

201

mum and got her up the duff and to be honest, I think she let that happen on purpose. Then I had a big fall out with my brother, instigated by your mother I might add and I haven't spoken to him since."

"Doesn't it hurt you, Dad?"

"Of course it fucking hurts but it's been too many years and too much water has passed under the bridge to put things right now."

"What about Mum's family?"

"Joe and Karen? They lived on Moxon Street over in Barnet and were alright as it goes but sadly not good enough for your mum, Sue thought they were common and shut them out of her life without blinking a fucking eye, hard-faced bitch! She's got two brothers somewhere, your uncles but I wouldn't know them if they came up and slapped me, they were just little kids and I can't even remember their names."

Ritchie poured another drink and it was the first time Danny had seen his father drunk. There had always been an invisible barrier between them which had been put up by his father and Danny knew there was no better time to find out why.

"So, why have you always been so distant with me Dad? I know you said earlier that you never wanted me but I didn't ask to be born."

Ritchie was now holding his head in his hands, the alcohol had made him maudlin and full of self-pity and Danny was sure he saw a tear drop onto the granite work surface. He didn't feel guilty about asking, being pushed away for so long had made him numb to any feeling towards his father.

"I know you didn't and I was wrong, I think back then

202

a part of me resented you so much for tying me down that I punished you. I'm sorry son."

Ritchie sniffed hard and with one hand wiped his eyes and with the other, he nipped snot from his nose and wiped it on his trousers.

"You got a girl?"

"Yeah, and she's the most beautiful person I have ever met both inside and out. I'm going to stay with her and meet her family the weekend after next and then she's coming here a fortnight later. The summer break is a long time to go without seeing each other, I never thought I would feel this way Dad but she's just fantastic."

"I'm happy for you but I hope you wear a rubber son, they all come over as sweetness and fucking light until they trap you. I know I shouldn't have said a lot of what I have about your mum but you don't know her, not really, not like I do."

"If you're so unhappy Dad why don't you just leave and fuck the money."

For a second Ritchie didn't reply as he thought about Hilary and all that he could have with her but then it crossed his mind that maybe she wouldn't want him if his funds dried up and he was too old to start again. The firm still carried out the odd robbery but business was now mostly legit and he couldn't do another stint at Her Majesties, not at his age. Ritchie had an office in the city and traded foreign currency and he'd turned out to be good at it, it was what had paid for all of this, the house, the cars and Sue's never-ending visits to boutiques and high-end shops where she would regularly drop two or three grand.

"I'm too old son, maybe it's a case of better the devil

you know and anyway, your mother knows when she's gone too far and I can soon get her back in line. She keeps a nice house so things could always be worse."

"So you've never met anyone else?"

Danny was fishing as he'd had an idea about Hilary for a long time.

"Yes, and I still see her. Never loved a woman like I do her."

"Does mum know?"

"Not sure but if she does she has never mentioned it, probably suits her."

"What's her name?"

Ritchie stayed quiet. Hilary was his and he wanted to keep it that way, sharing her could end up backfiring for him and he didn't want that to happen for all the money in the world.

"Sorry kid but I don't want to talk about her."

Daniel shrugged his shoulders and then saying goodnight left his father in the kitchen. He would never understand some people and his parents were at the top of that list, he just hoped and prayed that Beth's family were better than his own.

CHAPTER NINETEEN
Two Weeks later

Since the only heart-to-heart he'd ever had with his dad happened, Daniel couldn't get out of his mind all that Ritchie had told him. He was struggling to even be in the same room as his mother and he now saw her in a completely different light. In the past, he had always felt sorry for Sue regarding the way his father treated her but now the tables had turned and it was Ritchie he felt sorry for. He didn't say anything to his mother but she could tell something was bothering him but she didn't ask for fear of hearing anything that would upset the apple cart of her almost perfect life. He couldn't wait to get away and if there was time this weekend Danny had decided that he wanted to try and find some of his long-lost family but only if Beth was okay with it. They had missed each other terribly and this weekend, fingers crossed, would probably be spent entirely in the bedroom, well that's if her parents allowed them to sleep in the same room. Beth had been on tenterhooks since she's woke and now his train was due in at any moment and she was as nervous as she'd ever been. The two weeks they had been apart had felt like a lifetime and she was worried that either he wouldn't come or that he wouldn't feel the same about her. They hadn't been together that long and young men could soon lose interest if another pretty face was on the scene but Beth needn't have worried, as soon as he stepped onto the platform and saw her in the distance he dropped his bag and began to run. Daniel didn't give her the chance to speak as he swept her up into his arms and covered her face in kisses.

"I take it you've missed me then?"

They both started to laugh but Beth quickly brought the emotional reunion to a halt.

"Danny you need to go and get your bag. I've been watching it out of the corner of my eye but this is London babe and anything left unattended doesn't stay around for long. I tell you, they'd have your bleedin' eyeballs and come back for the lashes if you gave 'em half a chance."

He noticed that her accent had changed, it was stronger and the only description he could muster was that she sounded like a cockney; his girlfriend was home and had easily fallen back into what her life must have been like before they met.

"You do make me laugh Beth. I couldn't wait to get here and I've got so much to tell you but it can wait until later. Do you think we'll get any free time while I'm here?"

"Not if my parents have anything to do with it, why do you ask?"

"I've just found out about some family that I didn't know existed and I would have liked to have looked them up. I didn't mention you as I didn't want to be questioned but my father told me that we have family not too far from where you live and also in Barnet. By the way, what's the sleeping arrangements?"

"Horny are you? Well, I'm afraid you're on the sofa, my parents are very old fashion but I don't know why as I bet they were shagging well before they got married, not that I'm suggesting anything but, oh I feel stupid now."

206

"Don't be so silly, I didn't think anything of it." Daniel meant what he'd just said but marriage to Beth was definitely on his to-do list, just not yet. After he collected his bag, Beth introduced him to the underground which fascinated him. It wasn't that Danny was naive but he had led a somewhat sheltered life, his mother had made sure of that and on the odd occasions that they had come to London to see a show or to go shopping, Sue had insisted on getting taxis everywhere. He had attended St Georges School in Harpenden and then on to St Margaret's for his senior years so roaming the streets of London had never been available to him. Both schools were private and even though they were not that far from home Sue had insisted on Daniel being a weekday boarder. It went down well with her snobby friends and Ritchie didn't mind as it was one less thing to worry about, though he often complained when the fees were due to be paid. Danny had spent his youth either at the schools or at home in Hitchin for the holidays and now for the first time he felt alive and being with Beth was the icing on the cake.

Walking in through the back door of the Lamb, they found the kitchen empty, it was opening time and both of her parents were behind the bar. The kitchen was small in comparison to the Hitchin house, not to mention very dated but Daniel loved its cosiness. Pots and pans hung over the top of an ancient-looking range cooker and two armchairs sat on either side. On cold winter days, it must have been so warm and comforting and for a fleeting moment, Danny envied his girlfriend.

"Come on and I'll introduce you."

As she took him by the hand Beth could feel his hand shaking with nerves.

"You okay? They don't bite you know."

Danny didn't reply and slowly followed her through to the front bar and was instantly put at ease when Michael walked over and smiling, offered his hand.

"Dad, this is Daniel. Daniel, this is my dad but everyone calls him Molly."

"Pleased to meet you, Daniel, Beth has talked about you nonstop."

"Dad! I have not! Why is it that parents always try and embarrass us, it's a wonder you haven't got the old photo album out to show him my naked baby pictures?"

"I'm saving those for later."

Beth jokingly punched her father in the shoulder as she led Danny over to where Ellie stood. It was unlike her mother but Ellie didn't speak and her face was as white as a sheet. She looked as if she had seen a ghost and was rooted to the spot. His cheekbones and colouring and those eyes, she remembered eyes just like them from so many years ago and the name Daniel and the Surname Nelson, it couldn't be but suddenly she had a bad feeling and she couldn't shake it off.

"Mum? Mum, are you okay?"

There were suddenly a million questions running through her head and she was desperate to sit down with this young boy and quiz him until she was satisfied that it was only her own stupidity that was making her feel this way. Gathering every piece of inner strength she could muster Ellie smiled at the visitor.

"I'm so sorry, please forgive me. I just had a bit of brain fog, probably because I've just started the menopause or at least that's my excuse."

"Mum!"

They had been back a little over ten minutes and in that time both of her parents had managed to embarrass Beth so God only knew what they would come out with over the next two days, especially when her nan arrived.

"We're going through to the back for a cuppa, want one?"

"No thanks love I'm fine. Dads left forty quid on the table for you to get a takeaway, I wanted to cook but you know how busy Friday nights can be. Your nans not coming over until tomorrow night so at least Daniel's will be spared for a while longer."

Ellie leaned in and after kissing her daughter on the cheek, offered her hand to Danny.

"Nice to meet you sweetheart and I hope we get the chance to sit and talk properly while you're here."

"Likewise Mrs Spires."

When the couple had settled in the kitchen and were seated at the table with their tea, Beth broached the subject of earlier.

"So, tell me all about this long-lost family."

Danny started at the beginning and told her about the dinner party and the Farringdon's. When he got to the part about Lavinia Beth could feel the jealousy start to invade her mind but she didn't get the chance to question him about it as Danny continued to talk almost nonstop. Beth just sat and listened as her boyfriend revealed all about his small but very dysfunctional family. When he at last finished she

just stared at him wide-eyed for a few seconds.
"Wow! You certainly are a strange lot; I couldn't
imagine my parents being like that. Oh I'm sorry, that
sounded rude and I "
"Don't be silly, it's made me realise that we know so
little about each other. So, what other family do you
have?"
"There's only mum and dad and me Nan, if there is
anyone else then they've never mentioned it. I know
there was a woman called Mavis once who brought
my dad up, this was her pub actually but she died
when I was very young so I can't remember her."
"Haven't you asked your dad about his real parents?"
"No, I figured if he wanted me to know he would
have told me and anyway, if I had questioned him and
he'd got upset that would have broken my heart. It's
strange but the three of us have always been so close,
not forgetting me Nan of course, well I didn't ever
feel like I needed anyone else. Does that make sense
Danny?"
"Completely! Now come and sit on my lap and let's
discuss what we've got coming up this weekend."
Beth giggled, she knew it was a double entendre and
he most definitely wasn't talking about their daily
schedule. Tiptoeing up the stairs they managed a
quickie in the bathroom; Beth hadn't dared to use her
room as it was directly above the bar and the
floorboards creaked badly. That evening they shared
an Indian takeaway from Bengal Spice which was
situated on Holloway Road. They decided to walk
and collect the food rather than opt for a delivery as it
allowed them more time to talk away from the noisy
pub.

210

Saturday morning was spent with Ritchie and Ellie but after a full cooked breakfast, it was time to start getting ready for opening. Ellie still wasn't happy, she hadn't managed to get any time alone with the visitor and her thoughts were weighing heavily. The young couple were now free until this evening so Ellie suggested they go out for a few hours.

"Mum and Dad will be busy as the pub stays open all day on Fridays. They usually take a nap before reopening but not on Fridays as it's so manic. So, shall we start to look for your family? It's the only chance we'll get as they will want to show you off to the regulars tonight and tomorrow they've arranged for Old Lenny Rayner to look after the pub so they can take us out to Sunday lunch and then you've got a train to catch. Did your dad give you an idea where to start?"

"No, and he'd go mad if he found out. The only reference he gave was that Mum's parents lived on Moxon Street in Barnet. I don't know what number though, as for my uncles, I haven't even got their names."

"No matter babe, we'll start with the local, everyone knows everyone in a local boozer or at least they do in this neck of the woods."

Getting the train to Barnet, they were both oblivious to the fact that it was the same route Sue and Ellie had used all those years ago. It wasn't an area Beth was familiar with so when they walked from High Barnet station she stopped to ask Mike Fallen one of the men at the ticket desk where was a good local pu' ˙ʰ ˙ˠ could go to.

"Well, the Barrington is nice, a bit upmark(

that's what you're after?"

"No not really, I'm looking more for a good old fashioned local."

"Then it's got to be the Olde Mitre, the place had been open since Adam was a boy. Full of locals but it can get a bit leery at times sweetheart."

"Oh that doesn't worry me, I'm used to it."

Beth took directions and after thanking the man the pair made their way along the High Street. It didn't take more than a five-minute journey and they were soon standing outside the pub. The inside was nice and the host was warm and friendly, to Beth, it was a good sign. After getting their drinks and ordering a bowl of chips to share Beth led the way outside into a surprisingly pretty beer garden. A few minutes later the landlord came over to the table with their food. Placing the bowl down he was just about to walk away when Beth stopped him.

"Excuse me but we're trying to find a local family and wondered if you might be able to help?"

The landlord eyed them with suspicion, a trait almost bread into any Londoner and Beth knew the expression instantly.

"It's okay, were not the Old Bill or anything. My parents own a pub in Holloway, the Lamb, maybe you've heard of it?"

"Not Molly?"

"Yes that's right, he's my dad."

"Well blow me down; it ain't half a small world. I'm Harry, Harry Fenn, so who are you looking for sweetheart?"

Harry now had both palms flat on the wooden table and was leaning over slightly.

"It's my friend's grandparents, he hasn't ever met them but we have it on good authority that they live or lived on Moxon Street, Mr & Mrs Nelson?"

The landlord scratched his chin for a few seconds and then smiled.

"You mean Joe and Karen?"

Daniel was getting excited and couldn't stop from adding to the conversation.

"That's right, my nan and grandad. I think I also have two uncles but I don't know their names."

Sighing heavily, the landlord took a seat on the bench next to Beth.

"I'm sorry to say that Karen passed away several years ago and Joe had a massive stroke and went into a care home a couple of years ago now. By all accounts, he can't speak or recognise anyone."

"And my Uncles?"

"Look, you seem like nice people so I'll tell you what I know but it ain't much thank the Lord. There was your Uncle Gary, a nice bloke as it goes, well he joined the army and never came back to the area again so I ain't got any idea where he is or even if he's still alive."

"And the other brother?"

Daniel was fast losing hope that there was no family left to find. He wasn't upset more like disappointed and his face spoke volumes. The Landlord was hesitant for a few seconds but when he saw Danny's sad expression he decided it wouldn't do any harm to continue.

"Terry, that's who you mean and regarding him, I would walk away now sunshine and pretty fucking quickly if you want my advice. All I know is that he

ain't the kind of geezer you want to get mixed up
with."
"Well I do, my relatives have all gone except for him
so please tell me what you know."
"I can't swear to it as I only know what I was told by
other regulars but it appears your uncle Terry was a
right nasty bastard, a fucking bully in my eyes.
Anyway, he went to work for a firm over in Lambeth
named the Makenzie's and by all accounts they are
vicious bastards as well. There's the oldest Tommy,
who runs the firm and then there is Jock who's a
complete psycho. There was another brother Brian
but I never heard too much about him. Listen to me,
sound like a right old woman, now where was I? Oh
yeah, I haven't heard anything about your uncle Terry
for the last couple of years so whether or not he's still
involved I'm not sure. I don't want my name
mentioned if you happen to find him but do
yourselves a favour and walk away. From what I
remember, your old man is a good geezer and he don't
need the likes of the Makenzie's in his life, in his pub
or you getting mixed up with them."
Beth smiled and thanked the Landlord for his
honesty. She wasn't sure what Daniel would want to
do but she hoped with all her heart that he had taken
on board all that they had been told. She'd heard the
stories and knew what the type of men described
could be like. Sadly Daniel didn't and he was even
more determined to find his one living relative.

The rest of the weekend passed without event. They
spent time with Beth's Nan Eileen who instantly fell
in love with Daniel. They also enjoyed a roast with

Beth's parents at the Audley in Mayfair after Molly had read rave reviews about it in the Standard. It was good but as Michael proudly stated and not quietly either, it still didn't match one of his wife's Sunday dinners. Ellie nudged him hard in the ribs with her elbow and Daniel couldn't help but laugh. He liked this family and would love to be a part of it one day. Just before they were set to leave and head to the station for Daniel's return home, Beth and Michael went to the toilet and Ellie gently pulled Danny to one side.

"I hope you've had a good time Danny and it's been really lovely to meet you but I don't even know your parents' names, I think we'll be seeing a lot more of each other and it would be nice to be on first name terms in case they ever telephone for Ellie."

Danny grinned; he must have scored some points if she wanted to know about his parents.

"My mum is called Susan and my dad is Richard and to begin with I thought it was strange as you all have the same surname but Beth told me Spires is quite common, especially in Scotland."

"But, but I thought your last name was Nelson?"

"Oh, mum just put that on my Uni application, I think there was some kind of mix-up when she did my registration of birth and she never got around to changing it but I am a Spires really. My dad was a bit naughty back in his youth and mum didn't want anything coming out and scuppering my chances so it worked out for the best I suppose."

Ellie could physically feel the blood drain from her face and she momentarily turned away so that he didn't see. Thankfully Beth then returned to the table and a few minutes later they were all in the car and heading for Kings Cross. Michael and Beth got out to say goodbye to Danny but Ellie remained seated in the car and as Beth waved him off she couldn't get out of her mind how rude her mum had been and as soon as she got into the car she angrily turned on Ellie.

"What the fuck was that about?"

"Ellie don't talk to your mum like that, though in her defence and to be fair I did think you were acting a bit strange Ell."

Ellie knew they wouldn't let the matter drop so until she could try and sort this mess out without hurting her daughter too much, she had to lie.

"If you want the truth then I'm sorry but I don't like him, Beth."

"Mum!"

"Well you wanted to know and now you have it. Now if you don't mind I would rather not talk about it as I have a raging headache."

The drive back to the Lamb was taken in silence and you could cut the atmosphere with a knife, something that rarely occurred between the threesome. Michael decided to let things cool down a bit and then he would have a word with his wife. She had no reason to dislike the boy, he was polite and friendly and it was obvious he adored their daughter. Whatever the problem was it bothered Michael; this was so unlike his Ellie.

CHAPTER TWENTY

Back at the pub, Ellie went straight upstairs and wouldn't show her face again until the following morning. Poor old Michael was forced to run the bar alone because Beth was also sulking and had refused to help him when he asked. Whatever was going on it needed sorting, why were the women in his life always the ones to get into a strop? He would never understand the female species but it could never stop him from loving them.

After having a restless night's sleep, Beth was the first down in the morning and not wanting to be around her mother she quickly downed some cereal, washed and dressed and was out of the pub before her parents got up. When Ellie heard the back door close she knew it was her daughter and she was out of bed like a shot but had to be as quiet as she could so as not to wake Michael. If he caught her there would be hell to pay and she would have no way to explain why she was snooping about in their daughter's room. Carefully turning the knob on Beth's bedroom door she slipped inside and closed it behind her. Taking her time Ellie went through each drawer desperately looking for something that would tell her where Daniel lived but there was nothing. Suddenly she spied Beth's backpack in the corner of the room and when she opened it and found her daughter's address book she prayed it would hold the answer. Luck was on her side and Ellie soon found the Hitchin address. Quickly getting dressed, she was just finishing off

217

checking her handbag when Michael appeared in the kitchen.

"Morning sweetheart, you feeling a bit better today?" When she didn't reply, Michael pulled Ellie around to face him and his look was one of concern. She was desperate to share what was going on but couldn't, the past rape would break his heart, not to mention that their daughter, her daughter, was possibly having sex with her own brother.

"A little I suppose. I was thinking of taking a few hours off today, I need a break, Molly?"

"Sure babe whatever you want, where is it you're off to, anywhere nice?"

Ellie quickly racked her brains trying to come up with a plausible tale that he would accept without question. "Well, I didn't tell you as it didn't seem worth talking about but when I was down the cash and carry the other day I bumped into Lorraine Brackham. You don't know her; we were at school together, longer ago than I care to think about. Anyway, I hadn't seen her for years, she moved out to Welwyn Garden City after she got married. It was nice to see each other again and she said she was having a bit of a school reunion today at her house and invited me. I didn't say I could definitely make it but well, with all the upset from yesterday, I think I would like to go Michael." Ellie had at least thought to use a different location just in case Michael mentioned in passing to Beth where she was going. That girl was as sharp as a pin and had he have said Hitchin, she would have put two and two together in an instant.

"Okay, love, whatever you want. You seen Beth this morning?"

"No, but I heard her go out earlier, she's probably catching up with friends as well."

Ellie felt awful about lying, it was something they had sworn never to do but she couldn't think of any alternative. Hopefully, when she spoke to Sue they would be able to stop this relationship in its tracks but if not, well she didn't even want to dwell on that scenario.

"Want me to drop you at Kings Cross?"

"Thanks, darling but you'll have your hands full so I'll get the tube. I haven't done that in a long time either so it will be nice. I'm not sure what time I will be back but it could be late."

"No worries just let me know when your train is in and I'll get old Stan to come and fetch you."

"No, don't bother him love, I'll get a cab."

Kissing Michael for a second longer than she normally did, Ellie grabbed her bag and headed out of the door. For a Monday it was unusually quiet, the commuters had already made their way into work and the tourists seemed to be thin on the ground. Now seated on the train Ellie could feel the knots in the pit of her stomach and throughout the thirty-minute journey they didn't relent. Exiting the station Ellie hailed a cab and asked the driver to take her to Whitehall Road. It was a five-mile drive and would take nearly a quarter of an hour but Ellie was so wrapped up in her thoughts that she didn't attempt to make conversation. After asking the cabbie to drop her at the top of the road, she slowly walked along until she found a sign saying 'Spires House'. The road was in a nice suburban area with a mixture of the usual detached and semi-dwellings, all except this

219

one. You couldn't see the house from the road but Ellie knew it was going to be impressive. She hadn't considered what she would do if Daniel was at home but this had to be sorted out and the sooner the better. Gripping her handbag strap tightly to her shoulder and with her head down, Ellie began the walk down and only God knew what would greet her at the other end.

Sue had just finished getting ready as it was her weekly 'ladies that lunched' meeting and she was trying to think of something new she could brag about. There were eight of them in total; all married to wealthy businessmen and who all had a fantastic lifestyle. Maybe she would talk about her up-and-coming holiday to Necker Island, a holiday that hadn't even been booked yet. Sue knew Ritchie would go mad at the five grand a night price tag but it was a private island and after all, you couldn't really top that in bragging rights. Somehow she would get him on her side, after all these years she had turned her conniving ways into an art form. Smiling, she took one last look in the mirror and happy with what she saw, was about to open the front door when the bell rang. Sue's brow furrowed, if that was Angie the cleaner she was in for a right mouthful, Sue didn't like any of the tradespeople coming to the front door. When she opened up and was ready to let rip, all she could do was stand there dumbstruck with her mouth wide open.
"I bet you didn't expect me to ever darken your doorstep, Sue."
Still, Sue didn't respond and Ellie just walked inside

without an invite leaving the door wide open.

"You might as well close that bloody door because I'll be here for a while. We need to talk Sue and you ain't going to like what I have to say."

For the first time Ellie had taken charge and as she marched into the kitchen, Sue, doing as she'd been told, closed the door and then quickly ran after her former friend.

"So, what's all this about?"

"Is Daniel here?"

"No, not that it's any of your business and what's he got to do with any of this, whatever this is?"

"He's been seeing my Beth for quite a while now and spent this weekend with us."

The look on Sue's face was one of horror, after all the money they had spent on his education, how and why on earth would he choose to see a girl from a shabby back street London pub?

"Well Ellie, as much as I'm not happy with that snippet of information, there isn't much you or I can do about it. Now if you don't mind I have an appointment that I don't want to miss."

Ellie and again without invitation, took a seat at the breakfast bar and plonked her handbag down onto the highly polished granite work surface much to Sue's annoyance. Picking up the bag and placing it onto the floor Sue reached for a wet wipe to clean the surface.

"Why don't we do a bit of reminiscing? You remember back to the day me and Michael got married? I know you didn't attend because you'd just had the baby but can you remember Ritchie having a long scratch down the side of his face?"

"I don't recall, look what's all this about only I'm due

to meet friends."

"Well, I can certainly recall and it was nasty, ran all the way down his cheek. That scratch dear Sue, was made by my fingernails. That bastard came to the pub and raped me on the eve of my wedding."

"I don't believe a word of this, my Ritchie would never do anything of the sort. Now like I said...."

Ellie didn't let Sue continue, the situation was far too important to allow her sister-in-law to push the problem away.

"You can believe what you want but it's the truth and you know very well that unlike you, I don't tell lies, Sue. That's not the end of it either. It has always played on my mind but over the years I've tried to convince myself that Beth was Michaels."

"So why are you trying to stir the shit now!"

"Because, when Beth applied for Uni and I helped her complete the forms, there was a question regarding next of kin. It just raked everything up again; I couldn't rest so I applied for a DNA test kit."

"But they're brothers, it would be the same."

"You're wrong Sue, I asked a doctor and the DNA of two brothers is only about fifty per cent the same. I sent off a sample of Michael, mine and Beth's hair which I took from our hair brushes. When the result came back it stated 'no match' and my nightmare had come true. Now you and I both know that I never slept around and apart from Michael there was only the rape so it's not rocket science to work out who Beth's father is."

Sue's complexion was now as white as a sheet. Taking a seat next to her old friend she could only look at Ellie with tears in her eyes.

"So, so what do we do now?"

"Well, this could tear both of our families apart if we ain't careful. Who am I kidding; it will definitely tear us all apart no matter how we handle things. As much as it fucking pains me, Sue, we have to work together on this. I will keep chipping away at Beth, tell her that Daniel isn't right for her and you do the same at this end. Hopefully by the time they meet again, which if you didn't know is the weekend after next right here in this house when my girl comes to visit for a couple of days, their interest in each other may have cooled. If it does, then Michael and Ritchie might never find out because if that happens only God knows what Molly would do."

Sue didn't need to think long about what had been said. Firstly she didn't want Ritchie to get into a fight with his brother, or for it to be the final nail in the coffin of her sham marriage. Lastly, there was Daniel to consider, strangely he was last on the list of why this relationship was so wrong and even though Ellie hadn't heard her friend's thoughts, she knew exactly what order they came in; Sue only ever put herself first. For now, they had to work on their kids and just wait so the two women swapped mobile numbers and agreed to keep in contact until this was all sorted out. With that Ellie walked from the house and headed for the station, it would be a long walk but she needed to clear her head. A few minutes later Sue's car came roaring passed but she didn't stop to give her sister-in-law a lift, she was late and her friends were waiting. She still planned on sharing the news about her holiday, after what she'd just heard it was the least she deserved.

Back at the Lamb, trade was quiet and Beth now sat at the corner of the bar reading the paper while Molly washed and polished glasses. Things were still tense and Michael knew that he had to try and sort it out before Elli came home.

"So, you in a better mood today sweetheart?"

"Me! It was Mum who was being a total bitch!"

"Watch it! Have a bit of respect, your mum loves you dearly and if she behaved strangely then she had her reasons. Think about it Beth, when have you ever known Mum to be rude or offhand with anyone?"

Beth chewed on the tip of her index finger as she mulled over what her dad had just said and he was right, her mum was the salt of the earth, everyone loved Ellie Spires and Beth had never heard a bad word said against her mum.

"I think you need to sit down with her and instead of shouting, calmly ask her why she didn't take to Daniel. You get more results with honey than vinegar you know."

"Mum always says that."

"I know she does but it's true love."

Just then the backdoor opened and Ellie came in and made her way to the bar.

"That was quick babe, reunion not up to much?"

Ellie gave a weak smile and slowly shook her head, all the while her eyes never left those of her daughter.

"No, just a load of old women bragging and boasting about what they've got. Not my scene at all."

Motioning with a nod of her head, Ellie walked into the kitchen and Beth stood up and followed. Michael had plenty of experience when it came to girl talk and this was one of those situations. Even though there

224

were no customers, he decided it was best if he stayed in the bar. Hopefully, by the time he had read the newspaper, they would have sorted things out. In the kitchen, after Ellie had made tea, mother and daughter took a seat at the table.

"So, what was all that about yesterday Mum and why don't you like Danny?"

Ellie took hold of her daughter's hand and stared deeply into the most beautiful hazel eyes.

"Sweetheart, you know sometimes when you're in someone's company and you might have only just met but you take an instant dislike to them and before you start, it's got nothing to do with him taking you away from us. Of course, I want you to eventually meet someone but you still have a lot of studying to get through. It's nothing personal but I just couldn't take to the boy, I'm sorry that you don't like hearing this but we can't all like the same things. There's just something about him sweetheart."

Beth instantly pulled her hand away from her mothers, so much for talking calmly.

"You are making no sense mum, no sense at all. You can't just say you don't like someone without a reason and my Danny gave you no reason whatsoever. I love him Mum and I mean really love him. I don't want this to come between us but if you keep pushing that's exactly what will happen so please don't make me choose because you won't be the winner!"

Beth got up from the table having hardly touched her tea but at least this time she didn't angrily stomp off. Making her way up to her room she lay on the bed and ran over all that had been said but it was ridiculous and she couldn't for the life of her work out

225

why her mum was being so nasty. Well, she just had to get through the next two weeks and then she would be with him, if his parents liked her then nothing could come between them. If Ellie continued on this path, then Beth would leave, it wasn't long until Uni resumed and until then maybe she could stay at Danny's house.

CHAPTER TWENTY-ONE

Over the next two weeks, Ellie continually tried to talk to Beth about Daniel but all she ever got was Beth holding her palm up, she flat-out refused to discuss anything about him with her mother.

In Hitchin it was even worse as until Sue had met the girl there wasn't anything bad she could say about her or if she did, Daniel would become suspicious. On the day Beth was due to visit, Sue was on tenterhooks. As for Daniel, he was like a dog with two cocks and couldn't wait for Beth to arrive as this time they wouldn't be sleeping apart. Just before he left to collect her at the station, Sue called him into the kitchen.

"What's up?"

"About this weekend, I have put your friend in the bedroom next to mine."

"What? Why?"

"Because this is my house and while you sleep under its roof you will obey my rules. I can't stop whatever you get up to at Uni but here there will be no bloody bed hoping, do I make myself understood?"

Without a reply, Daniel turned on his heels and stormed out. He would try and talk to his dad about it later but if he still didn't get any joy then he would just sneak Beth into his room when his parents were asleep. Since Ritchie had opened up to him Daniel felt they were on a lot better terms, he was a man of the world and would understand and if anyone could change his mother's mind it was his father. As soon as she'd heard the door slam, Sue got on the phone to

Ellie. Beth was already on her way so the two women were free to talk without the fear of being overheard. The conversation was strained as they had no interest in each other except for the current mess that was threatening to shatter both of their lives.

"Hi Elli, it's Sue. I've just spoken to Daniel and told him there would be no sleeping together this weekend and boy he wasn't happy."

"Thanks for that Sue, it's disgusting just thinking about it. So when do you hope to start putting my girl down."

"As soon as I can but I couldn't do it before I have even met her. I'll keep you posted over the next two days but hopefully, your girl will be on her way back before the weekend even gets started."

With that, the call ended and Ellie joined her husband in the bar. She was more upbeat than she'd been in the last two weeks and Michael breathed a sigh of relief.

On Friday afternoon as Beth stepped onto the platform she looked all around but she couldn't see him and panic began to set in. It was a relatively small station compared to Kings Cross so there weren't too many places to hide; suddenly she heard her name being called and then spied him standing behind a barrier. There hadn't been an inspector on board and now she had to show her ticket but as soon as the barrier opened she ran into his arms.

"I've missed you so much, Danny."

"I've missed you too babe, come on let's get out of here."

"Can we go somewhere quiet; I need to talk to you?"

Danny's smile momentarily disappeared but

reappeared when she kissed him again on the lips only this time with so much passion.

"Can it wait until later sweetheart, only mum is waiting to meet you and if we're late it will piss her off? We have two whole days to talk and…….."

He didn't finish his sentence as they both knew what he was referring to. Ritchie had taken the train into the city so Danny had used his dad's Aston Martin to collect her and the drive was over in a matter of minutes. Beth was in awe of the car but when they entered the drive up to the house her mouth hung open in shock.

"Oh my God! Is this where you live?"

Danny laughed and shook his head; his girl could be so funny at times. When the car stopped he quickly got out and running around to the passenger side, opened the door and took out her bag. Hidden from sight in the upstairs bedroom, Sue was watching, normally she loved aggravation but this time it was different, this time she knew her son was about to get his heart broken. By the time Danny and Beth walked into the hallway, Sue was halfway down the stairs. Grinning like a Cheshire cat, no one would have known in a million years what she was up to.

"Mum, this is Beth. Beth, my mum Sue."

"Pleased to meet you, Mrs Nelson.

Sue laughed and took Beth's hand.

"Nice to meet you too Beth but it's Mrs Spires, not Nelson."

Beth was a bit taken aback as to why the woman didn't want Beth calling her by her first name, it seemed a bit unfriendly but she didn't ask questions, there would be plenty of time for that later. Ritchie,

229

for a change, arrived home early from work as Sue had insisted that they show a good front for Daniel's girlfriend. The four enjoyed a pleasant dinner and then Ritchie retired to his study and Daniel and Beth went up to his bedroom to listen to music or at least that's what he told his mother. Unlike Elli, Sue, much to Beth's happiness, seemed far more relaxed about them spending time alone in a room together. Daniel put on some music and then lay beside Beth and it wasn't long before he began to get amorous. Beth placed her hand on his arm and shook her head before propping her back up against the headboard.

"It's probably the wrong time but then I don't think there will ever be a right one. Danny, we need to have a serious talk."

Inwardly he began to panic, did she want to end things, had she met someone else?

"What's wrong babe?"

"There's no easy way to say this so I'm just going to blurt it out. I'm pregnant!"

For a second he didn't reply as he desperately tried to process the news. Sitting beside her he ran his hand through his hair just as his father did whenever he had a problem.

"You sure?"

His question rattled her and Beth's reply was harsh.

"Of course, I'm fucking sure; I did another test before I left just to be certain."

"Okay, calm down sweetheart there's no need to bite my head off."

Leaning over the bed, Beth reached into her backpack pulled out a pregnancy wand and handed it to him. Sure enough, there was a red cross showing a positive test.

"So, do you want me to get rid of it?"

"Beth! Of course I don't, it's our baby and he or she might have come along at a bad time but we'll manage somehow and we will both love it with all of our hearts when it gets here. How did it happen, putting the obvious aside of course?"

"Remember when I had a chest infection about three months ago and the doctor gave me amoxicillin tablets? He forgot to tell me that they can interfere with the birth pill and even stop it from working. No one is to blame; this was just an unlucky accident."

"Have you told your parents yet?"

"You're joking aren't you, my mum will go ape shit and my dad will probably want to knock seven bells of shit out of you, at least until he calms down that is. I'll tell them when I get back, which by the way will now be tomorrow. Sunday afternoon is usually quiet after the lunchtime trade."

Holding her close he gently stroked her back trying to comfort her. Danny knew he would have to leave Uni and get a job to support her and the baby but it didn't bother him that much, he had never wanted to go there in the first place and it was only down to pressure from his mother that he had enrolled.

"What about your studies?"

"I can take a year off and then complete the final year and you?"

"I'm leaving and don't try to talk me out of it Beth. If I'm being honest I hate the fucking place and only stayed because I met you. Are you sure about telling your parents this early on?"

"What in case I lose it or something?"

"No of course not, it's just. Oh, I don't know, don't you think we should leave it a while at least until it's sunk in, with us I mean."

"No, I don't, I would rather face the music now before I'm as big as a house and can't walk away from my mother's rantings. Maybe we should tell your parents first?"

Danny didn't know how his mum would react but his dad wouldn't be happy, not after what he had recently shared regarding getting tied down but Danny didn't feel like that, he loved Beth with all his heart and he would love the baby they had made together.

"Okay. My dad goes to golf on a Saturday morning but when he gets back we will break the news and please don't worry darling, everything will be fine we just have to wait for them to calm down and realise how happy we are and then I'm sure they will be glad for us. You don't think your mum will be pissed off that you told my family before her?"

"It's not up to her so she'll have to lump it. You do still want me Danny don't you?"

"Of course I do and I want this baby too."

Beth smiled but it was weak and inwardly Danny was trying to convince himself that what he had just said was true. He wanted Beth that went without question but a baby; he wasn't sure at least not yet.

The next day they both stayed in Danny's room until they heard Ritchie's car drive away. Ten minutes later Sue also left the house to do the weekly shop at Waitrose on Bedford Road. It was a ten-minute drive and Danny knew how picky his mum was with the food, even Waitrose didn't go unscathed when it came down to fresh produce so they had at least an hour and a half before she came back. About to wake Beth and ask if she'd like some breakfast he was stopped when the bedclothes flew open and she rushed into the en suite bathroom. He could hear her throwing up and then retching for what felt like an age. Smiling to himself he knew not to ask if she fancied playing around as the answer would be a firm 'No' with a few expletives added. Ten minutes later she emerged looking as white as a sheet.

"You okay?"

"Yeah, but it takes its toll out of you. It's been like this for a couple of weeks now and it's been hard throwing up and keeping it quiet so my mum didn't hear me. To begin with I thought it was a stomach bug but when it didn't stop, I think deep down I knew and that's when I took a test, five to be honest. It took that many for it to sink in and for me to accept it wasn't a faulty test kit."

A short while later they heard Sue return but remained in Danny's bedroom unto he saw his dad's Aston Martin pull up in the drive.

"I suppose we'd better get it over with now they're both home?"

Beth sheepishly raised her eyebrows and got off the bed. Still in their nightwear, she gripped his hand for support as they made their way downstairs to the kitchen. Ritchie was in the middle of making a bacon sandwich and Sue was just about to read him the riot act for getting oil on the splashback but stopped when her son and his girlfriend walked in.

"And good morning to you two, that's if you can still call it morning as it's almost lunchtime. What would you both like to eat? Beth?"

"Thanks, Mrs Spires but I'm good."

"Daniel, what about you, love?"

"No thanks, mum. Can you just sit down for a minute; we have something to tell you both."

"But I was just about to…."

Danny was losing patience, he was nervous and just wanted to get the news out, at least then they could start making plans and there was still Beth's parents to tell and he wasn't looking forward to that. Sue took a seat at the breakfast bar next to Ritchie waiting to hear what this important news was but Danny had stalled much to his father's annoyance.

"Well, come on then spit it out, my bleeding sandwich is getting cold."

With a gentle nudge from Beth Daniel finally let the cat out of the bag.

"Well, it's happened a lot sooner than we would have liked but it seems we are pregnant."

"We are pregnant? You soppy sod, you mean you've got her up the fucking duff! I told you about…"

Ritchie's sentence was cut short when suddenly they all turned to look at Sue as she screamed out 'NO!!!!' and then ran from the room. The three of them could only stare until Ritchie broke the silence.

"What the fuck was all that about?"

"Danny, go and see if your mum is okay, this has all come as a shock. I just hope my mum reacts a bit better."

Sighing heavily Danny kissed Beth on the cheek and gave his dad a warning glare to not upset his girlfriend before walking into the hall and going upstairs.

"Take a seat sweetheart and rest your legs. So, you're up the duff then?"

Beth could only nod her head; there was something about Ritchie that made her feel on edge. He hadn't been that friendly since she'd arrived and she'd begun to think that he didn't like her, that she wasn't welcome.

"You reckon your mum and dad will be okay with this?"

"No actually I don't but there isn't a lot I can do about that. We're going to London tomorrow to tell them after the lunchtime rush is over."

Ritchie looked confused which made Beth smile.

"They run a pub Mr Spires and Sunday lunch times are always busy."

"A pub hey. Whereabouts?"

"I doubt you would have heard of it but it's in Holloway."

The words had seemed to take forever to get out of her mouth and the moment he heard the first two letters, it felt like the air had been taken from his lungs and for a second he thought his sandwich was about to reappear.

"Danny says you work in London, maybe you know it but then again maybe not as it's a bit of a spit and sawdust kind of place. The locals all love it; my parents have been there for years and…"

"What's it called sweetheart?"

"The Lamb, why?"

Ritchie had just been about to place another mouthful of sandwich into his mouth but it dropped from his hands and as he stared at the young woman, who until yesterday had been a complete stranger, all colour drained from his face.

"Are you alright Mr Spires?"

"Your dad, what's his name?"

"Michael but mum and his friends call him Molly. I'm sure when we all get together you're going to get on well, there's nothing bad to say about either of my parents."

Ritchie pushed his right hand through his hair and with the other he bit down on the nail of his left index finger. This was a nightmare, he had never been certain but now looking into her eyes, Ritchie knew it was his daughter steering back at him. Suddenly the front door slammed and then Danny appeared.

"What's going on boy?"

"I honestly don't know dad. I realise that neither of you would be happy with the news but Mum's gone off her nut. I tried to get some sense out of her but she wouldn't talk to me and she's just grabbed her bag and car keys and left. Didn't say where she was going either, what a fucking mess!"

Beth was shocked to hear him swear, she was always dropping the odd fuck but Danny? never, at least not in front of her. All sorts of scenarios were spinning around in Ritchie's head and for a second he wondered if his wife was on her way to London but she didn't even know about the past, how could she?

"Let's just all calm down shall we? Give your mum a bit of time to digest things and let this bombshell sink in and then I'm sure she'll be back and taking over with plans about baby gifts and stuff. You know how she is Danny, has to be in control all the time and the rug has been well and truly pulled from under her."

Danny smiled but deep down her wasn't sure, he had

never seen Sue react like this about anything before.

CHAPTER TWENTY-TWO

At the end of the lunchtime service, Ellie was about to call last orders when her mobile began to ring but with old George Chase belting out a bad rendition of 'Underneath the Arches' on the piano she couldn't hear a word of what was being said to her. Showing Michael her phone she pointed to the door indicating that she needed to go out to the kitchen to take the call.

"Hello?"

"Ellie, it's me, Sue. I need to see you now!"

"Don't be daft, you're in Hitchin and I'm trying to empty the bar if I'm ever to get me feet up for a few hours."

"I'm out in your backyard."

Ellie didn't say another word as she quickly opened the door and slipped outside. Sue was trying to hide the best she could but it was near on impossible as the small yard was barren with just a fence surrounding it.

"What the fuck is going on?"

"She's pregnant."

For a brief moment, Ellie's world stood still as she desperately tried to take in what had just been said to her.

"Ritchie knows as well, I just ran out and drove over here I didn't know what else to do. Oh, Ellie what a fucking mess!"

Ellie was pacing up and down as she tried to work out how to handle things.

"Right, there's nothing for it. After Beth has left to

come home, you have to tell Danny. It's up to you if you miss out telling him about the rape but he has to know about how this will affect the Baby Sue. Tell him he has to end things and then I will work on Beth and try to get her to have an abortion."

"An abortion!?"

"Sue, we're talking about incest here. That innocent baby could be born with all sorts of disabilities, are you prepared for that because I certainly ain't. On top of that, there is the legality of it all; if anyone was ever to find out they could both end up in prison"

"Okay, okay I get it. I'll drive them to the station in the morning and then talk to Danny on the way home. Wait to hear from me before you say anything to your girl. What a way to reconnect hey?"

It was rhetorical and Sue was out of the gate and on her way back to the car before Ellie could comment. When the pub closed for the afternoon Ellie made the excuse that she was tired and needed to lay down, anything rather than have to be in Michael's company and not tell him. This was all going to come out sooner or later she just knew it and she didn't know what he would do. Her husband was a kind, gentle man except if anyone hurt or threatened his family, then he could be the most evil bastard on the planet and she didn't hold out much hope for Ritchie if he ever found out about the rape. In Hitchin, Sue did the same as her sister-in-law and avoided her family as much as possible. Unlike his brother, Ritchie didn't question his wife about her behaviour as he really didn't care if she was upset or not or even where she had run off to. Both women were up pacing the floor for most of the night and for once Sue wasn't just

239

thinking about herself, well maybe just a bit she supposed.

With very little sleep Sue was up and dressed early the next morning and had prepared a light breakfast for her son and Beth. Her eyelids were heavy and there were dark circles around her eyes and for the first time, her son would see her without make-up. Ritchie had already left for another game of golf so it was up to her to make things comfortable at least until after Beth had gone home. When she heard them enter the kitchen Sue swallowed hard and turned to greet them with a smile on her face.

"Morning. Now I've just prepared a light breakfast, cereal and fruit. I hope that's alright Beth?"

"That's great and thank you, Mrs Spires."

"You're very welcome and feel free to call me Susan. Now, what time were you planning on leaving for the station, I take it you are going back a day early after revealing your news?"

"As soon as we've had breakfast mum. Why?"

"I just thought I'd give Beth a lift, obviously you'll be coming along for the ride as well. I've got a few jobs to do upstairs so just give me a shout when you're ready to leave."

"Well, I was planning to go with her, Mum."

"Far be it for me to interfere but emotions will be running high so maybe it's for the best if Beth is alone, at least for the time being?"

Danny and Beth looked deeply at each other for a few seconds, almost as if they could read each other's thoughts.

"Danny, I think maybe your mum is right."

With that Sue was out of the kitchen as fast as her legs would carry her. Sitting on the bed waiting for the call she hoped they wouldn't be too long; she was beginning to feel sick and just wanted this all over with as quickly as possible. Twenty minutes later Danny came into the bedroom.

"We're ready now. Mum, are you alright only you don't half look pale."

"Just a bit under the weather son but I'll be okay. Right then, let's get the little lady to the train station shall we."

The drive was taken in almost silence, the lovebirds sat in the back and were too engrossed in each other to talk to Sue and for the entire journey, she was running over in her mind what to say to her boy. When Beth had boarded the carriage and when Danny had watched the train pull out, he got back in the car where his mother was waiting.

"You did like her mum didn't you; only after the way you reacted to the news I had my doubts."

"Of course I did but I do need to have a chat with you Daniel."

As she pulled off of the main road he didn't question where they were going and just stared straight ahead worrying about what it was his mother was going to say. Turning onto Fishponds Road, Sue then turned right into the car park of Hitchin Town Football Club. Switching off the engine she unclipped her seatbelt and turned to face her son.

"What I'm about to tell you will sound ludicrous and to begin with you won't believe it but I swear on my life that it's the truth, Daniel."

Danny just stared into his mother's eyes and was now

241

feeling very scared regarding what she was about to reveal though thankfully for Sue, he was yet to question her.

"I want you to listen until I've finished before you say anything. You have to end things with Beth and I mean like now and the two of you must never see each other again."

He couldn't, wouldn't accept what she was saying, had she lost her mind?

"No way, why would you ask such a thing mum, what's Beth ever done to you?"

"Sweetheart she hasn't done anything. I had a visit a few days ago from Beth's mum, she's my sister-in-law Ellie."

Danny pulled a weird face as he suddenly pushed himself back into the seat.

"What the fuck are you on about Mum, I think you've lost the bloody plot this time."

"It's a small world darling but Beth's dad is your father's brother. We haven't seen or spoken to each other in years, well not until Ellie came to the house the other day. It gets worse babe so prepare yourself."

Now he knew she was over-dramatizing the situation, how on earth could it get any worse?

"Years ago and believe me I knew nothing about it until the other day but well, your dad had sex with Beth's mum and Beth is the result. This has all knocked me for six and I haven't spoken to your dad yet, at the moment I can't even look at him. Michael, Beth's dad, well he's not her real dad but you know what I mean, he hasn't got a clue about any of this and nor has Beth come to that, well at least not yet she hasn't. If it was just the fact that the relationship has

242

to end but it's not, the baby is on its way and only God knows how all of this will have affected him or her, there's a good chance that it will be severely disabled either mentally or physically, not to mention that all of this is against the law. Daniel, you're brother and sister for God's sake."

Sue expected a barrage of questions, anger and rage but there was nothing. Daniel just sat there steering ahead with tears streaming down his cheeks. She gave it a while but when he still didn't say anything she started the engine and drove them home. Danny went straight up to his room and closing the door he spent the rest of the day in bed.

When Beth arrived back at the Lamb there was an hour to the opening and knowing they would soon be busy, Ellie took her daughter upstairs where they both took a seat on the side of the bed.

"What's all this about Mum? Why did you want us to come up here?"

Ellie took her daughter's hand in her own, this was going to be the hardest thing she had ever done.

"Darling I know you're still angry with me and I don't blame you but I need to speak to you and I think after I explain a few things you will understand the reaction I had to Danny."

Beth roughly shrugged her mother's hand away and was about to get up to leave when Ellie grabbed her daughter's arm and stopped her.

"You will hear me out young lady, you have to."

Her tone was sharp and so unusual that Beth's brow furrowed as she sat back down.

"Please bear with me as this is an awful story, one I

hoped to never have to share with you but that's no longer possible. When me and your dad got married we swore to never keep secrets but this one I couldn't share with anyone, well at least not without wrecking my marriage, my whole life come to that. You know we have never shared much about the past or anything to do with family? Well, there was a reason for that but not the reason your dad God love him, used. He had a falling out with his brother over business and they never spoke again. For me, it was a completely different reason. Your dad's brother was the total opposite of Michael, a bully, loud and brash and the woman he married, who used to be my best friend well, she wasn't much different. Anyway, on the eve of my wedding I was staying here with Mavis and Burt, Michael had been shipped off to stay with a friend as Mavis said it was bad luck to see the bride before the service."

Beth sighed and Ellie knew she was being long-winded about sharing her secret and guessed she was just trying to put off the inevitable for as long as possible.

"Sorry, I was regressing a bit. Well, that night I was uptight, coiled like a spring about the wedding I suppose so I decided to have an early night. I hadn't been in bed long when I heard someone come into the bedroom. At first, I thought it was your dad who had sneaked back in but, oh my God I was so wrong. Either Burt or Mavis hadn't locked the back door and, well it was your dad's brother. He raped me, Beth, raped me on the eve of what should have been the happiest day of my life."

"Oh, mum! Why didn't you ever tell me?"

"Because no one else knew and I wanted to forget about it, forget about the whole horrendous thing that had happened to me. I was so happy with your dad that I kind of managed it somehow. Then I found out I was pregnant. I wanted to believe the baby was Michaels, convinced myself of it actually. Then just after you were born Michael and his brother fell out and never spoke again so it seemed like it could all be hidden away."

"So, is Dad my dad then?"

The look of fear and despair in her daughter's eyes broke Ellie's heart but she had to continue if this was ever to be stopped. Slowly, while never taking her eyes off of her daughter, Ellie shook her head.

"I'm so sorry sweetheart, truly I am but Michael may not be your dad, at least not biologically but he is in every other sense of the word. He adores you and if this ever comes out it will break him."

"There's something you should know mum, I'm pregnant."

"I already know sweetheart Sue came and told me yesterday."

Beth looked at her mother wide-eyed; she just couldn't believe this was happening.

"Sue? What's Sue got to do with any of this?"

"Darling, Sue is my sister-in-law and Danny's dad Ritchie is the one who raped me. He's your uncle but also your father."

No, no, nooooo!"

Ellie was panicking and her tone rose as she spoke.

"Calm down sweetheart, please. I'm so sorry."

"I need to speak to Danny."

"I don't think that's a good idea darling, now about the

245

baby?"

"What about it? I'm not having an abortion Mum if that's what you're on about."

Ellie's eyes were full of tears and for a moment Beth felt guilty about her sharp tone.

"Darling you have to understand that it could be deformed or mentally retarded. Your genes are too close together sweetheart; don't you understand that, you're brother and sister?"

Suddenly Beth sharply pulled her hand away and her reply was filled with anger.

"Of course, I fucking understand but there's no way I am getting rid of my baby. You can do all you like Mum but you can't make me. Now I'm going to my bedroom and please don't come after me."

Alone in her room Beth opened up her laptop and began to research incest. Just the thought of it made her feel sick to her stomach but at the same time, she couldn't stop her love for Danny. It was wrong but did they just expect her to turn her feelings off like a tap?

First, she googled what birth defects her baby might have and was surprised by what she read. 'The risk for passing down a genetic disease is much higher for siblings than for first cousins. To be more specific, two siblings who have a child together have a higher chance of passing on a recessive disease to their child so the inbred child has a fifty to one hundred per cent chance of having a rare genetic disorder showing full symptoms if both parents are carriers. Such conditions include metabolic diseases, skin and blood diseases, along with physical and mental development problems, not to mention problems with hearing and vision. To be more specific, two siblings who have a child together have a higher chance of passing on a recessive disease to their child, as they are far more closely related and are much more likely to be carriers of the same diseases. Their child is more likely to get two broken copies of those genes and end up with the disease, but how much more likely? It continued that for two siblings who are fifty percent related such as Beth and Danny, it could mean for any given gene there is a 1 in 4 chance that they have the same copy as each other. Overall, the child of these siblings has a twenty-five per cent higher chance of being born with birth defects. Beth read and reread, that was an average chance and in no way high enough to terminate her baby. If Danny was willing to take the chance then so was she. Next, she read about the legality of an incestuous relationship, even typing the word incest made her grimace but when the answer appeared on the screen she smiled. 'In France, there is no law in particular against two adults (those aged 18 and over) engaging in a consensual incestuous relationship or having children but they are not permitted to marry'. Reading on Beth found that half-siblings were allowed to marry in Sweden and Brazil and for a few moments her heart skipped a beat. Was she getting too carried away? Danny might not want anything to do with her now, she hadn't heard from him and the fact that he hadn't called her started alarm bells to ring. There was only one thing left to do, she would have to bite the bullet and call him. If he dumped her then at least she would know but one way or another she was having this baby with or without him! Deciding that a text would be best Beth nervously tapped in her message.

"We need to talk. Do you want to do it on the phone or in person?"

Seconds later there was a reply.

"Where and when? xxx"

Beth could feel the tears as they flowed freely, he wanted to see her so there was at least some hope and he put three kisses at the end, he wouldn't do that if he was about to break up with her, would he? The couple arranged to meet the next day in Camden Lock at noon, the Lamb would be busy so she would be able to slip out without her parents noticing.

CHAPTER TWENTY-THREE

For the rest of the day, Beth stayed in her room and only ventured downstairs twice to make a drink and get a sandwich. Michael assumed his wife and daughter had been arguing again so didn't bother too much about Beth's absence. Ellie had spent her time behind the bar serving and chatting with customers in an attempt to take her mind off of what was happening within her family but it wasn't successful. After they closed up for the night Michael popped his head into Beth's room but seeing the light was off he quietly closed the door in an attempt not to wake her but Beth wasn't asleep and would end up spending most of the night just staring up at the ceiling crying. At breakfast the following morning, Michael asked Ellie what was going on but the only reply was.
"You know what she can be like'. Leave her alone and she'll soon come around."
It was true, their girl could be a sulker, they had spoilt her and when she didn't get her own way would go into a right strop but to Michael this time it felt different.

The next lunchtime and at twelve on the dot, Michael slid the bolts on the door and opened up. As usual, there were five or six of the old timers waiting outside so it was a busy first few minutes, busy enough for them not to notice or hear when their daughter slipped out of the back door. Beth and Danny had agreed to meet at the entrance to the food market in Camden and as Beth approached she was more nervous than she had ever been. When she spied him sitting on a bench opposite one of the Chinese food stalls her heart began to race. Danny was as nervous as Beth and as soon as he saw her approach he was out of his seat and running towards her. Scooping Beth into his arms he held on as if he was never going to let go.

"Fuck I've been so worried."

"Likewise Danny but we need to talk and here is not suitable. Let's walk down the side of the Loch where it's quieter."

Holding hands they descended the steps that led down to the towpath. There was no seating so they sat on the floor and leaned up against the metal railings. Beth waited for him to begin but when after a few seconds he still hadn't uttered a single word, she took the lead and started to talk.

"So, what do you think of this shit shower we have been dealt?"

"I don't know I've been trying to get my head around it but I can't. The one thing I do know is that I'm not giving you up Beth no matter how wrong it is or what anyone says."

His words were like music to her ears and she was now comfortable in sharing all she had learned on the internet. Slowly so he could take in every word, she repeated what she'd read.

"So our baby might be fine?"

"Yes and if we go to France then our relationship won't be illegal and we can live as a family. In Sweden and Brazil, we can even get married but in all honesty, I'm not bothered about that, as long as we are together then that's all that matters."

Danny placed his arm around her shoulder and

hugged her.

"So what do we do now?"

"We need to leave as soon as possible because if I have the baby here, I'm sure my mum would tell the authorities. I don't know if they would allow us to keep it but I'm not prepared to take that chance. I have forty thousand in my bank account, the inheritance from Mavis who I told you about and there is also twenty of my student loan left. What about you?"

Although this was no laughing matter, Danny couldn't help but smile.

"The same give or take a few hundred and I would imagine my inheritance came from the same source as yours. Good old Mavis God rest her soul. That's roughly one-twenty, enough to keep us going until I find some work. So, when do we leave?"

"I've looked at the timetables and we could get the Eurostar tomorrow night if we buy the tickets today?"

"Then let's go and get them."

With the tickets purchased, they then both visited their banks to withdraw the maximum and also to enquire about transferring the remainder to France, which turned out not to be an issue once they had opened up a foreign bank account. Now it was again time to part ways with the couple agreeing to meet tomorrow night at St Pancras station. The timing couldn't have been better, on Thursday nights the darts team took over the pub and this week it was the playoffs so it would be extra busy and with both her parents rushed off their feet, they wouldn't have time to miss her. When Beth got home she was in a better frame of mind and was even civil to her mother when Ellie asked if she would like a cuppa. Ellie had decided not to question her daughter anymore and instead let Beth decide on her own what she wanted to do. If her daughter hadn't come to her by the weekend then she would have to raise the topic again but for now, she would let the matter lie. That night Beth went through all of her clothing and packed two large holdalls. A lot of her old clothes would be left behind because it wouldn't be long before she would need maternity wear. It was strange but as awful as this situation was, deep down she was excited for the future.

Thursday seemed to drag by but at six, when the darts team slowly began to filter into the bar Beth started to get nervous. There was loud laughter coming from the bar and as she picked up her two bags she glanced around the kitchen for what she knew would be the last time. It was strange as she'd never given the small snug room much thought in the past but now as she did, images of her childhood flashed through her mind. She could remember her first day at school and coming home so full of enthusiasm to a celebratory dinner. Then there were all the silly tears that had been shed over arguments with friends and how her mum had always been there to soothe away her tears. She smiled when she thought of Gary Hopkins her first love at the age of seven and the heartbreak she'd felt when he dumped her for Naomi Parsons. As always Ellie had been there telling her 'The stupid boy was an idiot and there were plenty more fish in the sea' and Beth not understanding what her mother was saying. She smiled when she thought of Andrew Graham and the day he had broken up with her just after her fifteenth birthday. At that age, it had felt like the end of the world but as always, Elli was there to wipe the tears away. Now she was about to go it alone, have a baby without her mum by her side to make sure she was okay and for a moment Beth contemplated staying. Deep down she knew that wasn't an option and when she at last slipped out into the cold night air she sighed heavily.

Reaching St Pancras he was once again waiting for her but unlike Beth, Danny was all smiles.

"You okay babe?"

"I will be when we're on our way, I keep thinking my mum has followed me and any minute she will come running and screaming along the platform."

"You got away alright though?"

"Yeah fine, you?"

"They wouldn't miss me if I was gone for a week let alone a few hours so the answer to your question is yes. I have left nothing behind sweetheart, a person's family has to love and want them and mine don't so I have no regrets."

After showing their tickets and passports they finally boarded the train and could relax. Sitting opposite her Danny took hold of Beth's hand.

"Well, this is it, babe, we're about to start the rest of our lives and we'll soon be three."

Beth smiled until he asked his next question.

"Have you thought what you'll do if, well if the baby has something wrong with it?"

She couldn't believe what she was hearing but it was an honest enough question and she supposed, one that needed to be asked. What angered her was the fact that he had asked what she would do, there was no mention of 'them or we' and it bothered her.

"No, I haven't, I want to have good thoughts while this baby is growing inside me but I know if something is wrong I will still love him or her. I noticed you referred to me in the singular and not us but I won't hold you to anything Danny, anytime you've had enough you're free to go. All I ask is that you tell me first."

She could feel his grip on her hand tighten as he stared into her eyes.

"Sorry, but I ain't going anywhere. I'm in this for the long haul whatever that might bring, so please don't ever doubt me."

At the Lamb, Beth had left the lamp on in her bedroom and propped up underneath was a note. By the time the pub closed at just after midnight, it was the first chance Ellie had to check in on her daughter. Too late was an understatement, the couple had already arrived in Paris and were tucked up in bed at the hotel Beth had booked before leaving London. Ellie's hands began to tremble as she opened the letter and tears streamed down her face as she slowly began to read.

Dear Mum and Dad. We have gone away and you won't find us. I did a lot of research and yes Mum, there is a chance that the baby could be born with problems but there's also a strong chance that it won't. There is nothing on this earth that would make me terminate my child and Danny feels the same. Don't worry, I will let you know when our baby is born but after that, we won't be in contact again. I'm sorry it came to this mum but you putting pressure on me to get a termination made our minds up. I love you and Dad dearly but now my own child has to come first. All my love Beth xx

Ellie was in turmoil, now she would have to tell Michael the whole sordid story. If she didn't then he would search for his daughter for the rest of his life not to mention he would call the Old Bill and report Beth as missing. Well she wouldn't tell him tonight, it was too late and she was tired, too tired to have the past raked up all over again. Tomorrow would be soon enough and in any case, she needed to speak to Sue first, maybe and it was only a maybe, her old friend might know where her daughter and Danny had gone. Michael had been working hard as there had been a delivery that day and moving barrels and crates into the cellar always tired him out, for once she was grateful for the draymen and as she went into the bedroom he was snoring softly.

Using the excuse of needing stuff from the cash and carry, Ellie was out early the following morning. Sue was still in bed when her mobile burst into life and she groggily felt on the bedside table for it.

"Hello?"

"Sue, it's Ellie, have you seen Danny?"

"Not since yesterday why?"

"They've gone; Ellie left me a note which I found last night."

Sue was now sitting up in bed and as she rubbed her eyes her make-up smudged making her resemble a panda but she didn't bother as there was no one there to see. For years now Ritchie had slept in another room, they didn't even have sex any more let alone spend much time together and she knew he would

255

always prefer to be with his mistress.

"Let me go and see if he's left anything, I'll ring you back in a minute."

Getting out of bed Sue stretched and yawned, unlike her friend, there was no urgency as she slowly padded along the hallway to Danny's room. The bed was still made but the wardrobe doors were open and when she peered inside the rails were empty. Knowing she would now have to call her friend back she decided it could wait until she'd had a coffee. The door to Ritchie's room was open so she knew he'd already left for the day so at least that was one less thing to worry about. Ten minutes later and just as she was about to take a seat at the breakfast bar to have her coffee her mobile rang again. Ellie was desperate and felt like tearing her hair out, what was taking Sue so long to get back to her, maybe Danny was still there. With that thought she again began to panic, if that was the case it would mean that her girl, her beautiful daughter, wherever she was, was alone.

"Well?"

"Bloody hell Ellie, I haven't even had my coffee yet."

"Your coffee! Fuck me Sue, do you realise how important this is? If they've run away then there's no way I can't tell Michael all that has happened."

"Now just you hold on a minute Ellie. If you open up that can of worms all hell will break loose and my life will be in ruins. Ritchie would probably leave me and there's no way I could ever show my face at the Golf Club again."

"Your life! What about the lives of our kids and come to that the life of our grandchild? The poor little mite didn't ask to come into this world and now when he or she does, they could have all manner of things wrong with them. So, did you look in Danny's room?"

"Yes I did and it's Daniel, not Danny. He wasn't there and neither were his clothes so they've obviously gone away together but we'll find them, Ellie. For now please don't say anything to Michael, at least give it a few days in case they get in touch."

Ellie took a moment to think over what Sue had just said and maybe she was right, maybe she was jumping the gun a bit.

"Okay, I'll give it until Sunday but if my girl ain't been in contact by then, well I'll have no choice but to tell Molly and just so you know Sue, it will probably end my marriage as well but I'm prepared for that. My child comes first and it's a damn shame you don't put your boy above your snobby friends at the Golf Club."

Ellie then abruptly ended the call, oh how she missed the old days before mobiles when you could slam the receiver down on someone.

Returning to the pub empty-handed, Ellie made some lame excuse about the cash and carry being out of stock. It was five to twelve and the punters were already queued up outside so there was no time for chatting. Luckily she had gotten out of the situation without any questions. On Fridays, the Lamb always stayed open all day and the stream of customers was relentless but for once Ellie didn't mind, today she was grateful that they were so busy that hardly a word was passed between her and her husband. Before she knew it the front door had been bolted and they both flopped into bed exhausted. At least she had gained some time and deep down she was praying that Beth would call tomorrow so that she didn't have to relive her past nightmare. What would be would be and as she stared at the illuminated clock face on the bedside table she felt as if her time bomb of a life was rapidly ticking away and there was absolutely nothing she could do but wait for the explosion to blast her world apart.

CHAPTER TWENTY-FOUR

On Saturday morning Ellie was up early and when Michael came downstairs he found his wife in the kitchen cooking breakfast.

"Morning sweetheart, Beth not up yet?"

Ellie froze, she hadn't thought about this and was now wracking her brains quickly trying to think of something to say that was believable.

"Oh, she set off early; she decided to spend the day with one of her girlfriends from Uni who lives in Brighton. She said if she was having a good time then she might stay over but would ring one of us to let us know."

"Bless her heart, that girl of ours is living life to the full."

Ellie hated lying to him and had to force the tears that were fighting to escape. Sniffing loudly and making the excuse that she must be coming down with a cold, she placed Michael's breakfast on the table.

"You not having any babe?"

"I haven't really got an appetite love. I'm just going to finish getting ready as I think it will be another busy one today and the shelves were well depleted last night so I need to refill them."

Michael only nodded his head as he shovelled the food into his mouth. He loved a full English any day of the week but on a weekend it always seemed a bit more special. Upstairs in the safety of the bathroom, Ellie finally let her emotions take over and the tears fell thick and fast. This was all so insane and she willed Beth to call her so that they could sort this

259

mess out.

At just before noon Ellie's mobile rang and snatching it from the bar top she walked into the kitchen.

"Hello?"

"It's Sue, you heard anything yet?"

"No, but I meant what I said if they haven't called by closing tomorrow afternoon then I have to tell Michael."

"Oh please Ellie I'm begging you, please don't…."

Ellie ended the call; she was fed up to the back teeth with everything always being about Sue. For the rest of the day she continually watched the clock, it was ridiculous and she knew that but she couldn't stop. It felt like she was on a countdown, like a bomb had been set and there was no way to defuse it.

Sunday morning, D-Day.

Unbeknownst to Michael, Ellie had arranged for Stan to come in and do the lunchtime service. She also asked if he was happy to return that evening if he was needed as she didn't know how Michael would be when she dropped her bombshell. Stan was more than willing so she at least had a backup plan in place. Ellie was standing at the stove when he came downstairs and placing a kiss on her cheek he took a seat at the table.

"Smells good babe, you really have been spoiling me this weekend, done something wrong have you or have I?"

She knew he was joking but as her old mum always said 'Many a true word was spoken in jest'. Placing his breakfast onto the table Ellie left him alone to eat and making her excuses, went upstairs to wash and dress. She was as fast as she could be and when she re-entered the kitchen he had only just finished. Ellie sat down opposite him and her eyes, to Michael at least, looked in so much pain.

"You okay babe?"

"We need to talk and I mean like right now. I've already made arrangements and Stan is coming in to tend the bar so there's nothing to distract us."

"You're leaving me."

"Don't be daft you soppy soft of course I'm not, you're the love of my life and you know that."

"Well, what is it then, you're not sick are you? Oh God no, please tell me you haven't got some incurable illness."

She could see he was beginning to panic which was so unlike Michael. Gently she took his hand and lifting it to her mouth, tenderly kissed it.

"I have a lot to tell you darling and it's going to take every ounce I have to do that but please believe me, I am not sick. Now, you will want to interrupt me and you will get angry, probably angrier than you've ever been but I need you to promise me that you will let me finish what I have to say because if I have to stop I don't know if I'll never be able to continue?"

He already had tears in his eyes and she hadn't revealed anything yet but Michael was a bright man and he knew that whatever was coming would be horrendous and probably break his heart. Slowly he nodded his head and then signalled for Ellie to begin.

"Can you remember on the day of our wedding, the awful scratches Ritchie had on his cheek?"

Ellie didn't allow him to reply, the question was

rhetorical and she needed to finish.

"The night before when I turned in early and Mavis and Burt were working the bar….."

Ellie stopped for a moment when she saw him close his eyes. He thought he knew what was coming and he wished that no matter how awful it was, it was the only thing she would reveal but that was far from the case.

"Oh no, please don't tell me what I think you're going to tell me. That cunt!"

"Ritchie let himself in and he raped me, Michael. I tried to fight him off that's how he got the scratches but he was too strong."

"But why didn't you tell me, how have you kept that to yourself for all of these years?"

"I thought that if I told you, you wouldn't want to marry me."

Now it was Michael's turn to hold his wife's hand as the tears fell freely down his cheeks.

"You silly woman, of course I would. I love you, always have and always will."

"There's more, I wish there wasn't but there is and I have to tell you Michael because it involves our girl."

Michael instantly dropped her hand, sat back in his chair and slowly began to shake his head from side to side.

"Don't tell me, Ellie, don't you dare."

"I didn't know, well not for sure and I suppose over the years I convinced myself but when the University wanted next of kin in case of a medical emergency I had to find out. I sent a sample of mine, yours and Beth's hair away for a DNA test and the result came back negative but Michael you are her father, you're the one who raised her, sat up with her when she was sick or scared of the thunder. That's what being a dad is about, not just being a sperm donor."

"Does she know?"

"I had to tell her sweetheart."

"Why, why did you have to? After all these years you could have left us both in the dark and we would never have been any the wiser."

"Because my darling, there is more. It was a million to one chance but Daniel is Sue and Ritchie's son, that's why I said I didn't like the boy, I was trying to split them up but I wasn't successful."

"Does Beth know about that too?"

"Yes, again I had to tell her but it's made no difference and now they have run away together. Her passport's gone so they could be anywhere."

"Poor little cow she must be going out of her mind!"

Ellie stood up and began to pace up and down, she was wringing her hands and her steps were becoming faster and faster.

"She'll come home when she calms down; you know what she's like and let's be fair, that's a fucking big thing to have to take on board."

"She won't come back Michael because she's pregnant. I tried to talk her into having an abortion but she wouldn't hear of it. She told me she'd done some research and there's a twenty-five per cent chance that the baby will be abnormal, to her it means that they have a seventy-five per cent chance of having a healthy baby and to Beth, it's worth the risk. I don't know if she's being rational or if it's her hormones taking over but she wouldn't budge on her decision Molly."

When Michael spoke his voice was raised, something he rarely did, especially where she was concerned. "For Christ's sake Ell, it couldn't get any fucking worse if you tried."

Storming out he left the backdoor wide open. The heavens had opened and he had no coat but at least his tears were washed away by the rain. He seemed to walk for hours not knowing where to go or what to do about the nightmare he was now living. From somewhere he heard a clock strike five and his thoughts went to the Lamb and the regulars he knew would be waiting to be served. When he walked in Ellie was sitting at the table but as he went to dry off and change his clothes he ignored her, at least for the moment. It was soon time to open up the bar and after Michael had sorted out Stan and made sure his helper could manage alone, he was back in the kitchen to continue talking with his wife. Ellie was still seated at the table and when he walked in he seemed to have aged in just a few hours. Wrinkles and dark circles were under his eyes and she would swear they weren't there first thing this morning.

"How are you feeling sweetheart?"

"As if my heart has been fucking ripped out."

"Michael, can you ever forgive me or is our marriage over?"

"What on earth are you talking about; none of this was your fault, I'm angry at the situation and the fact that you kept it from me for all of these years. The only one to blame in all of this is that cunt, Richard!"

"I know you're angry but you still seem to be taking all of this far better than I thought you would sweetheart."

264

"Well, I ain't got much fucking choice in the matter, have I? That cunt might have tried and failed to wreck my life twenty years ago and there's no way I'm going to let him fucking succeed this time. He will suffer Ellie but I just ain't worked out how yet."

"Please don't do anything stupid honey; I couldn't bear to lose you as well."

Michael tenderly kissed her forehead as he spoke.

"You know me Ell; I'm a planner, not a fighter and I need to take a while to think this through. It's stopped raining so I'm going for another walk to clear my head and work out what I want to do about this."

"Do? What can you do?"

"There's always a solution to a problem love, I just have to find it."

"Want me to come with you?"

"I'd rather go on my own if you don't mind."

Michael then walked out of the back door but he hadn't kissed her like he usually did and that set the seed in her mind that maybe he was done with her. Sitting alone and thinking too much was suddenly stopped when her mobile rang. Glancing at the screen and when she saw who the caller was, Ellie didn't feel like answering but she knew her old friend, knew that Sue wouldn't give up until Ellie spoke to her.

"Hi Ellie, any news yet?"

"No and before you ask, Michael knows. I told him everything, Sue."

"No! What did he say, what's he going to do?"

"In all honesty, I don't know, he's gone for a walk to think things through and thankfully he didn't blow his top or he hasn't yet anyway."

"You don't think he will come here do you, I can't

possibly have any trouble. The circles I mix in, well my friends are, I hate to sound nasty but to be honest they're all snobs and they don't like fighting and bad language."

Ellie couldn't believe what she was hearing but on second thoughts she could. Sue had always been the same so why on earth Ellie thought she might have changed was a stupid idea.

"You obviously fit in well then. In answer to your question, I don't know where Michael has gone so I suggest you speak to that bastard of a husband and warn him just in case. From now on Sue, unless you have any news regarding my daughter I would prefer you not to call me again."

With that Ellie ended the call and switched off her phone. If Beth wanted to get in touch then she could always call them on the pubs landline. Right at this moment Ellie couldn't handle any more upset so climbing the stairs she went and lay down on the bed.

In Hitchin Sue tried to phone Ellie back but when there was no reply she began to pace up and down. How dare she call her a snob? Momentarily she bit down on her index nail and then remembering the newly painted French manicure she inspected her finger for any damage. Thankfully there wasn't any, it wouldn't do to turn up to lunch at the Golf Club tomorrow with bad nails. Ritchie had been in his study all afternoon catching up with paperwork or at least that was what he'd told Sue but he'd really been on the phone several times to Hillary. Today was her birthday and he longed to be with her but a deal was a deal and years earlier, when Danny was small, it had been agreed that weekends were for family. That brought a thin smile to his lips, what family, a son he hardly knew and a wife he couldn't stand. After ending the last call he sighed heavily and then made his way to the kitchen where Sue was still pacing up and down.

"Who's shit in your path?"

"Ritchie I think you should sit down, we need to talk."

"Don't be so fucking dramatic Sue it pisses me off."

"Michael knows you raped his wife."

For several seconds no more was said and the look of shock and guilt was evident on Ritchie's face but the emotion was only fleeting.

"That was bleeding years ago and technically they weren't married."

"So it is true, you are a complete and utter bastard Richard Spires."

"Tell me something I don't know."

Sue walked over to the cabinet and poured herself a large neat vodka. His tone sounded almost smug and she felt like throwing the bottle at his head, she probably would have done but for the fact that it might have damaged her beautiful kitchen.

"Do you know that Beth is your daughter?"

"I had an inkling."

"You sick bastard, you say it as if it doesn't matter, as if you think our son having sex with his sister is acceptable?"

"Of course, I don't but there's no point in shutting the fucking stable door after the horse has bolted no is there?"

"What about the baby, it might have all kinds of

deformities."

"I wouldn't worry too much about that. Ellie is bright and there's no way she will let that kid be born, she'll make Beth have an abortion."

Sue poured herself another stiff drink and as the alcohol started to take effect she calmed down slightly.

"They've gone Ritchie, Daniel and Beth have disappeared and they've taken their passports so they could be anywhere. The shame this will bring on us will be horrific, incest for God's sake! Someone as upstanding as me in this community and her son is in an incestuous relationship with his sister? Ellie said that Michael was calm and wanted to think about it all before he decided what to do."

"He always was a soft cunt, got no fucking balls that brother of mine. Well it's about time he fucking grew a pair"

"Is that why you raped his wife; because he was soft? Was I not good enough for you or were you just jealous of what your brother had?"

"Of course you fucking weren't good enough, I can't stand you Sue and if I'm being honest I never could. You were there for me to shag and you weren't that good at it either but then you got yourself up the duff and I was tied. You know I have a woman?"

The hurt expression was clear but as pools of tears welled up in her eyes Ritchie just continued with his vengeful words and when he mentioned his mistress the tears fell and Sue could only nod her head. As years of resentment finally escaped from his mouth, he was enjoying the pain he was causing her.

"Hilary is a hundred times more of a woman than you

are or ever will be and she doesn't ask me for anything, unlike you, a greedy bitch who is out for all she can fucking get. I stayed with you because of Danny but you know what? All this fucking aggro has given me my freedom. You can keep the house but try and come after me for anything else and it will be the last fucking thing you do. There's a few grand in the safe which will see you through but from now on my bitch of a wife, you'll have to go out and earn your keep like the rest of the fucking world."

"But what about all the money you have, you're rich."

"Yes I am and that's the way it's staying. I've been funnelling my cash into offshore accounts for years, just in case this day ever came and you won't be able to touch a fucking penny."

With that, Ritchie stood up, made his way upstairs and packed. Within twenty minutes he was on his way to London to make Hillary's birthday the best she had ever had. Alone in the kitchen, Sue looked around at her beautiful home and then began to sob. It would all have to be sold if she wanted to survive. Tomorrow she would start making plans, tell her friends that they were moving to the south of France or somewhere even more exotic just to keep face. Maybe it was time to find her family, her mum would never turn her away and when the money from the house sale came through she could leave again. Once again there was no thought for her son's needs; all Sue could think of was herself.

CHAPTER TWENTY-FIVE
One week later

Ellie felt like she'd been walking on eggshells for the past seven days and she was just about at breaking point. Michael had been friendly enough but that was it, he'd just been friendly whereas he was usually loving, always cuddling and kissing her but since the revelation, any kind of intimacy had abruptly stopped. She knew he wasn't about to let things lie and as they still hadn't heard from Beth he would be even more determined to get revenge. Michael was a planner down to the last detail and whatever he had in mind would end with his brother's death, she was sure of that.

On Sunday morning Ellie cooked breakfast as usual and while Michael ate, she sat down opposite him.
"Molly I can't take much more of this."
"Of what babe?"
"You being distant, I knew this was how you would react that's why I kept quiet for all of those years but now, well now if our marriage is over then I just want you to tell me. I'm too old to continue living with a man who no longer wants or loves me."
He was out of his seat in seconds and kneeling in front of her he took his wife's hands in his.
"Sweetheart I'm sorry, I never meant to shut you out but I'm seething and need that cunt to pay for what he did. Love you? Of course, I love you with everything I have and no, our marriage is fine and as strong as it's always been but just cut me a bit of slack, let me deal with this in my own way and then we can get

back to some normality."

When Ellie started to cry he took her in his arms and held her tightly, that bastard Ritchie had done so much damage and if they hadn't been so strong as a unit it could have completely wrecked their lives. For the rest of the afternoon, the couple lay upstairs in each other's arms but when it was time to open up the bar again Michael said he would like some time alone. Telling Ellie to take the night off, she didn't argue, the last few weeks had taken their toll on her and tired was an understatement regarding how she was feeling. Sundays were always quiet and if things panned out, he had business to discuss that he didn't want her to hear. Old Stan had just arrived but after telling him that he wasn't needed, Michael gave him a score for his work earlier, knowing fine well that the old boy had been drinking for free on his earlier shift. Holding the front door open he said goodnight and then glancing up at the overcast sky, he closed the door again. Michael took a seat at the bar and prayed that a particular customer would come in but the weather outside was now atrocious and the rain was lashing down so hard that he wasn't holding out much hope. By nine o'clock there wasn't a single customer and Michael was about to close up. Walking towards the door to pull the bolt over he was stopped when the door opened and Tommy Makenzie walked in, Michael quietly breathed a sigh of relief.

"Evening landlord, pint of your finest please."

Michael didn't reply and his normal friendly demeanour was nowhere to be seen. Tommy had come to like the man and something was obviously bothering him.

"You okay Michael?"

Handing Tommy a drink, Michael then sat down and slowly shook his head.

"Anything I can help with squire?"

"If only it were that easy."

"Well, we'll never know unless you tell me, a problem shared and all that."

Things were going to plan, at least at the moment and standing up again he walked over to the front door and pulled the bolt over. Tommy didn't know what was about to be shared but whatever it was it wasn't for anyone else's ears. When Michael was once again in his seat he could only stare at Tommy Makenzie, almost as if he was afraid to speak, fearful that once he started he wouldn't stop and his brother's fate would be sealed.

"Cat got your tongue or what?"

"You married Tommy?"

"Nah, never met the right one and don't suppose I ever will now."

"Kids?"

"No, I'm old fashioned that way Michael, wife then kids and as I never found the first well…"

"You know I am? I also have a beautiful daughter, except I don't really."

"You been at the spirits Michael, you know I've met Ellie so you ain't making any fucking sense mate."

"Of course you have. Sorry, my head is all over the place."

"Can I tell you a story Tommy; it might take a while though."

Tommy Makenzie pointed towards the front door.

"Take as long as you want pal, I ain't going anywhere

in this weather."

Michael began slowly, he told his customer all about his childhood, about his parents, about Ritchie and Mavis and Burt. When he got to the part about Ellie he stopped for a moment and smiled. It was a smile, a feeling, that Tommy had never experienced himself but the look on the landlord's face made him wish he had. Strangely even though the landlord was long-winded in getting to the point and Tommy knew there obviously was a point, he was enjoying hearing about someone else's life. Michael continued, told of his marriage and about having Beth but then he stopped again.

"What's up?"

"Well, this is where it all goes wrong. I've just found out that my brother raped my wife on the eve of our wedding. My Ellie was too afraid to tell me and has kept it a secret for all of these years."

"What a cunt!"

"That's not the worst of it Tommy. Seems my daughter ain't my daughter but my brothers. Ellie has only just found out, well actually a while back when Beth first applied to go to university. She says she didn't tell me as it would have broken my heart and she was fucking right. Then she dropped another bombshell, my, our, her daughter is only seeing my brother's son and he's got her pregnant. Of course, it goes without saying that she didn't know he was her brother when they met."

"Fuck me, what a pile of shit you're going through."

"They've run away because she thinks they will take the baby away from her. I want my brother to pay Tommy but I don't know how. Ritchie has always

273

been far stronger than me at least physically he has. His bitch of a wife ain't much better, she's treated my Ellie like shit over the years and now she doesn't want anything to do with sorting it out in case it damages her snobby reputation."

"They sound like a lovely couple Michael. You want me to sort it for you, you only have to say the word and the fucker is toast."

"Would you do that for me, really?"

"Certainly."

"Yeah but then I'd end up owing you and I've been in the game long enough to know that it don't bode well owing favours, especially to a man like you, no offence."

"None taken."

The two men were quiet for a while, both deep in their thoughts as they sipped at their drinks. Strangely it was Tommy who was the first to speak again.

"Tell you what; I'll do this favour for free. How's that sound?"

This was exactly what Michael had been hoping for and now he went in with the icing on the cake that would see an end to his brother. There was no guilt, no feeling sorry for Ritchie, any love he still had for his brother had died the day he found out about the rape, about Beth and then the baby. Of course, he didn't have to tell Tommy but something deep inside was pushing him on and he couldn't stop it.

"It sounds great but there's something else I want to share with you and it could backfire, you could end up making me pay as well. If you do then I can't blame you."

Tommy's eyes narrowed and his brow creased, he

didn't like where this was going.

"What's that then?"

"Remember twenty years back when someone ripped off a shipment of your drugs?"

Now Tommy was more than interested and he could feel the palms of his hands start to sweat as he waited in anticipation for what was coming next.

"It was my brother. Back then we ran a small firm and I was there as well. The driver and his mate had nothing to do with it so I hope you didn't make them pay for something that wasn't their fault."

For a few moments Tommy was struck dumb, he'd waited years for this and if he was honest didn't think he would ever find out. Wondering if the landlord was just saying it to sweeten the deal, after all, every man and his wife had known about it at the time and Tommy had felt like a fucking idiot for a while. He had to be sure and decided to delve a little further.

"If you're just telling me that to make sure I take my revenge then there's no need Michael."

"I'm not I swear. There was a white transit van and it took place just off Binfield Road. There was a mixture of coke, H and plenty of weed. In all, I think it could have netted close to two mill give or take but don't hold me to that as it was a long time ago. The driver had a mate with him but neither was involved so I hope you didn't make them suffer.

Again Tommy didn't reply to the last question regarding the driver.

"What do you mean 'would have netted'?

Michael couldn't help but smile as he slowly shook his head.

"Ironically, we got robbed; some cunt came into our

unit and helped himself. That's the reason me and
Ritchie initially fell out but somehow all that I've
learned lately is far worse. My brother and his wife
are driven by greed so you could say money came
between us."

"I suppose that's some kind of a result and I thank you
for your honesty Michael and as for making you pay?
I think what you've recently been through, are going
through, is torture enough but when it comes to that
brother of yours, I'm going to make him suffer like
you wouldn't believe."

"Can I ask how?"

Tommy stared at the landlord and for a second
Michael thought he'd asked one question too many
but after a while of just silently looking at each other,
Tommy Makenzie smiled but never said a word. With
that Tommy finished his drink, said goodnight and
left Michael standing there thinking about all he'd just
revealed. Did he feel guilty? Not on his life, he was
just sorry he wouldn't be there when Ritchie's life
ended as Michael was in no doubt that was exactly
what was going to happen. He poured himself another
drink before pondering over whether to tell Ellie what
had occurred.

Back in Lambeth, Tommy spent the rest of the
evening planning his revenge and it was getting him
so excited that he hardly got any sleep that night. In
the morning he was up with the larks and was already
waiting at the unit in little Portugal before any of his
men or even Jock, who was usually the first one in,
had arrived. When Jock came into the unit and
walked into the office he had the fright of his life.

"Fuck me! You nearly gave me a fucking heart attack

Tom, everything alright?"

"Alright? Its fucking fantastic bro. I've only found out who robbed us all those years ago."

Jock rolled his eyes upwards as he took off his jacket. "Not that fucking shit again, when are you ever going to let it go?"

"Jock, didn't you hear me? I know who it was."

Jock stopped dead in his tracks and studied his brother's face.

"You sure?"

"Without a doubt, I got it straight from the slags brother. With or without you I ain't letting this go, Jock."

Jock slowly nodded his head. Normally he would have been chaffing at the bit for revenge but his mind was occupied with other things. The previous night he had used the services of a well-known tom and had messed her up badly, so bad in fact that she had needed to go to the hospital and Jock wasn't convinced she would keep her trap shut.

"Okay, how do you want to tackle it?"

"Tell Spud to do some digging, find out all he can about a bloke called Ritchie Spies. I want to know where he lives, his daily routine, anything that might help us when it's time. Tell him to take Terry along, he's always up for a bit of aggro but I want them to hold off until I say, this has to be planned out meticulously. I don't want any mistakes."

It took several days for his men to get back to him but when they did, they had everything Tommy would need to put his plan into action. Spud had been the most fruitful in the information he had gathered.

He informed Tommy about the wife and big house in Hitchin and then went on to explain that the couple had now separated and the geezer was shacked up with some old bird in a flat on Jamestown Road over in Camden."

"What about you Terry, anything to add?"

"I do indeed Boss. Seems the bloke runs a small firm but its activity has declined a lot over the years. They still carry out the odd robbery but the top bloke, Ritchie Spires now makes his living trading foreign currency and by all accounts, he's fucking good at it."

"You've both done well. Now, I have one more little job for you, find out about the wife, where she goes, friends and the like and if she has a set daily routine. Take your time, a week should be enough and when we have that I can make a plan. Well, fuck off then!"

Terry and Spud turned and walked out of the unit with no bad feelings, they were used to Tommy and Jock talking to them as if they were shit on their shoes. In the early days, it had bothered them and the rest of the men that made up the fifteen-strong crew but Tommy also paid extremely well so a bit of abuse now and then could easily be swallowed. Jock, who was now seated behind one of the desks and had been silent throughout, studied his brother's face as he spoke.

"So, what's this really about, cause the fucking lengths you're going to and the info you want isn't your usual kind of payback."

Tommy wasn't about to share all of Michael's business, even with his brother but he also knew that without something, Jock wouldn't let the matter drop.

"This one feels more than a bit fucking personal and I want to pay back the robbing cunt and anyone who profited from my drugs, in a way they will never forget! If we go in all guns blazing as usual it won't take the Old Bill long to realise it's our MO. No, this has to be done differently so they won't suspect us and will be looking for someone else entirely."

CHAPTER TWENTY-SIX

Terry Nelson hadn't dared breathe a word to anyone in the firm that the target was in fact his brother-in-law. He hadn't set eyes on Ritchie for years but he still remembered the dislike he'd had for the wide boy who seemed to take over his family whenever he came to visit which wasn't that often but often enough in the early days to dislike him. His old mum and dad seemed to be cap in hand whenever Ritchie was around as if he was some kind of king and Terry had hated it. He remembered back to one incident when his brother Gary had been a bit lippy and Ritchie had shoved him so hard that Gary had fallen and hit his head and no one said a word. There and then he had vowed to get his own back when he was an adult but until now hadn't imagined it would ever happen or as the years had passed even given much thought to the man. His brother Gary had died five years ago in Afghanistan and it had hurt Terry deeply, now when he thought of Richie Spires the rage he'd felt as a child seemed to burn stronger than ever. Terry hadn't seen his sister in years and he was certain the couple would have divorced by now, it was obvious, Spires always thought he was too good for her but in any case Terry had no feelings left for his sister either. When she had turned her back on the family he had cut her from his heart and mind. Terry knew she had money but Sue had left it up to her brothers to care for their parents and it hadn't been easy, especially when Gary joined the army and everything had fallen on to Terry's shoulders. Work was thin on the ground and with each passing month Terry's anger had grown. Through his frustration he was continually fighting and getting arrested so it was a natural path to follow the life of a villain. When his mum had passed and then when his old man was forced to go into a care home, Terry needed to earn money and a lot of it if he wanted the old boy to be looked after well and not end up in a council run home. For the last few years he had worked for the Makenzie's and was a valued member of the team because he would do whatever was asked of him to whomever they wanted without argument. When this new job had arisen he was no different and was now looking forward to carrying out his boss's orders.

Terry had been watching the house in Hitchin, completely unaware that the woman he was spying on from a distance was in fact his sister. It had been years since he'd seen her and Sue, with the help of fillers and Botox had significantly changed in that time so he had assumed wrongly that it was Ritchie's second wife. Terry knew that the woman always went out for a boozy lunch on Wednesdays with her rich girlfriends and as soon as she left the house and drove off he made his way around to the back and with expert skill, he picked the lock and was inside in seconds. Walking from room to room and although he was told to get in and out quickly, Terry couldn't help himself, he wanted to see just how far Ritchie had come and how much money he had made. The items in people's homes always showed someone's wealth and careful not to touch too many things even though he was wearing gloves, he couldn't resist when it came to the photographs. The one in pride of place was a large silver expensive looking frame that contained a photograph of a young boy. So, Ritchie Spires had a son did he? That was never a good sign; kids always wanted their revenge when they got older just as he did now. This gaff must have cost a fortune and it was done so tastefully that Terry imagined it must have been down to the woman of the house. Making his way upstairs Terry went from room to room, again the furnishings and decorations were elaborate, what he wouldn't give to live in a gaff like this. Walking back down he realised that he had wasted enough time so made his way into the kitchen. Terry was looking for keys, all houses like these had a key rack, and he'd carried out enough burglaries in the past to know that. Sure enough he found it inside one of the wall cabinets hidden behind some tinned food. Removing what he thought was the backdoor key; he tried it in the lock just to be sure. Bingo, it fitted and after relocking the door he pulled a small tin from his pocket and pressed the key into the putty like substance inside. Replacing the original key back into the cabinet he closed the unit door and made sure nothing was disturbed and everything in the room was as he'd found it. The front door was a Yale lock so it was easy to get out and once on the outside he walked to the rear of the house and retried the back door for a final time. When he was happy that all was secure, he left and headed back to London with a smile on his face.

At the unit, Tommy was waiting and as soon as Terry returned he handed over the key mould. Tommy then took it over to Acer Cohen who ran 'Good as New', a shoe repair and key cutting service on the High Street. Acer knew how to keep his mouth shut and would deal with anyone and cut any key for a price. He didn't ask any questions and just accepted that the Makenzie firm was probably planning to blag one of the posh houses up West. Giving Acer ten minutes to cut the key, Tommy went for a cuppa at the small café two doors down and wondered if this was where all the other villains who used Acer's service would wait for their items to be copied. Mo Tanner had run the café for the last fifteen years and she fancied Tommy like mad though you never would have known it. Mo had a raspy voice due to the twenty-a-day Benson she smoked and would shout out the orders as they came through from the kitchen. When she saw him enter she smiled to herself and took his drink over to the table personally.

"Hi there Tom, how's tricks?"

"Pretty good thanks Mo, how are you?"

Mo could feel her cheeks redden and she felt like a fool as she giggled like a schoolgirl.

"Couldn't be better thanks, especially since I booted out that cunt Graham."

Tommy knew how she felt about him, it was obvious even though she thought she was doing a good job in hiding her feelings but Tommy Makenzie wasn't interested in women and even if he had been it most certainly wouldn't have been with the likes of Mo Tanner.

"Good to hear."

Saved by the bell, a new order came out and Mo, much to Tommy's relief was called back to the counter. Not wanting to be caught out he quickly drank his tea and made a mental note to give the place a wide berth from now on. Entering Good as New, he was pleased to see that Acer had finished the cutting.

"There you go Tommy and if I do say so myself it's a good job."

After inspecting the item, Tommy smiled as he handed over the agreed ton. He reminded the old Jew not to share his business with anyone else or there would be a price to pay and it wouldn't be a good one.

"Goes without saying Mr Makenzie, my livelihood depends on it."

Tommy moved on to the next task on his list, it was time to collect the most important item he would need. Driving to Margate Road in Clapham Tommy called at the home of Warren Kahill. Warren was the man to go to when you wanted a gun and this one had to be untraceable and never used for violence before. After a lengthy wait, the door was at last opened by Linda Kahill, Warren's wife. Rotund and complete with a frilly edged apron, Linda was the epitome of a housewife and certainly not someone you would associate with an arms dealer. Linda smiled and spoke in a broad Norfolk accent.

"Hello my lovely, come to see my Warren have you?"

Tommy nodded and when the woman turned he followed her inside. The house was heavily clad and cottagey on the outside and nothing like the other dwellings on the street. The inside was no different with bold floral wallpaper covering every wall and the carpets were the same but clashed as they didn't match. Walking into the front room Tommy was greeted by the sight of Warren Kahill sitting in an armchair in his pants. His shirt was unbuttoned to his waist revealing a vest and he had an oxygen mask strapped to his face. As he removed the mask Warren pointed to a seat beside him for Tommy to sit.

"Can I get you lovelies a nice cup of tea?"

Warren only nodded and Tommy smiled but neither spoke until they were alone.

"Right Tommy I take it this ain't a social visit?"

"Correct. I'm after a handgun and silencer but it has to be clean and I mean squeaky clean as the Old Bill will be getting hold of it in the not-too-distant future."

"It'll cost you; most of my stuff has been used before. There's no serial numbers of course but still probably traceable if some dick head detective cared to look hard enough."

"Not a problem Warren. So, what do you have?"

Reaching down beside his chair Warren flipped the lid of a wooden box and pulled out a Glock 17.

"Believe it or not this little beauty was originally a police issue; of course, the numbers have gone so no link back and it was never actively used. Now it comes with a suppressor and not a silencer."

"What's the difference?"

"A man in your position and you don't know?"

"Never had the need for one before."

Just then the door opened and Linda entered carrying a tray of tea and biscuits. Warren momentarily stopped talking. Of course, Linda knew what was going on but he never talked about his business in front of her. If he was ever collared then she could plead ignorance and it would be the truth.

"Thanks, sweetheart."

Warren only continued with the conversation after his

wife had left the room and the door was once again closed.

"Unlike in the movies, a silencer makes the shot almost unheard but not totally. They are known amongst the gun fraternity as suppressors. As its name states it only supresses so your man will still need to be on his toes as anyone around will still wonder what the noise was and if you get someone who knows their stuff then the Old Bill will no doubt be called. If you're prepared to wait I could probably get my hands on a PSS silent pistol. They are double-action handguns used by the Soviet secret police and Special Forces. They have a special cartridge with an internal piston thus achieving a sound level of only around 122dB but it will be several weeks as they're hard to get a hold of."

Tommy thought for a moment, he didn't want to wait as his desire for revenge was growing by the day and besides, it would most probably be Jock who would carry out the murder and he was always out like a flash.

"Thanks, Warren but I think I'll take this one, so how much do I owe you?"

"Let's call it a monkey."

Tommy nodded and removing a roll of cash from his pocket, pulled off five hundred pounds.

"Appreciated, Linda will see you out. Linda!!! Obviously there is no need for the usual 'Keep your trap shut' because if you get your collar felt, I will have no knowledge of our transaction'

Tommy had carried out a lot of business with Warren over the years and the code of silence went without saying. Warren then replaced the oxygen mask over his face and reclined his chair, for all of his dealings and money, he was well aware that his life on this mortal coil would soon be at an end. A few minutes later Linda appeared and smiling, led Tommy to the front door. Now the planning could start in earnest and Tommy had already decided that he would keep the group small. Spud had originally followed Ritchie and given Tommy information but that would be the sum total of his involvement. The fewer people involved the safer it would be so for now it was just Tommy, Jock and Terry. When he arrived back at the unit the best part of the day had gone so he told his men, all except Terry to have an early one. Jock and Terry made their way into the office and the next hour would be spent making a water-tight plan.

CHAPTER TWENTY-SEVEN

Since leaving Sue, Ritchie had been living the high life. Hillary was everything he wanted in a woman; she was a good cook, easy on the eye and unlike Sue, was happy to have sex whenever Ritchie wanted. Recently he had all but closed the firm down after handing the reigns over to Willie Downes, on the understanding that any jobs carried out didn't bear the name of Spires and he would receive a ten percent cut of any money taken. Willie had been with Ritchie almost since day one and he knew better than to try and rip Ritchie off. That said, he couldn't have been happier and having a firm of his own had been a lifelong dream but he was still unsure what had prompted the move by his boss. The foreign currency business was going from strength to strength but Ritchie had given up his office and now traded from the spare bedroom so that he could be closer to Hilary. He didn't venture out much unless it was to take Hill's to dinner or to go shopping so he hadn't noticed the two men lurking on the other side of the street but when things are going good, something or someone always comes along to fuck it all up. Hilary's birthday was that night and Ritchie had arranged for them to go to The Ivy Asian in Mayfair. Tommy had decided that Jock should carry out the hit; his brother was brutal and had no qualms when it came down to making sure he got his target. Terry Nelson would drive Jock to the flat, park up a short distance away and wait for Jock to come back out. Tommy stayed in Little Portugal and to say he was nervous was an understatement and it had nothing to do with getting caught. He had waited years for this and didn't want anything to go wrong. At just after eleven and sitting alone in the dark, he willed for some news to come through.

Ritchie and Hilary had enjoyed a fantastic evening celebrating her birthday and after parking the Aston in the underground car park they headed up to the flat, unaware that Jock Makenzie was hiding on the lower landing. Hearing the couple exit the lift Jock made his way up to the next level and after pulling on a pair of latex gloves, tapped gently on the front door of flat 4C. From inside Ritchie could be heard laughing as he made his way along the hall to answer the door. When he opened up and came face to face with Jock pointing a gun at him he suddenly froze. Jock didn't speak and motioned with the gun for Ritchie to step back.

"What the fuck is all this about, do you know who I am?"

Once inside Jock pushed the door closed with the sole of his foot and only then did he speak.

"Sure I do. I'm one of the Makenzie brothers. Remember us, remember the shipment you robbed?"

The colour instantly drained from Ritchie's face.

"Look pal, that was fucking years ago now, surely we can come to a compromise can't we?"

"Move or that bitch will be meeting her maker as well."

Ritchie did as he was told, if his life was over there was nothing he could do about it but he would agree and promise anything if it meant saving the woman he loved more than anything else in the world.

"Who was it darling at this time.........."

As the two men entered the front room Hilary saw the gun and was about to scream but immediately stopped when Ritchie held his hand up.

"Don't worry sweetheart, me and this gentleman have a bit of business to sort out. Why don't you go to bed now?"

"She stays! Sit fucking down, both of you!"

Jock barked the order which wasn't a request and Ritchie knew it. Taking Hilary's arm, Ritchie could feel her whole body as it began to shake, this wasn't going to end well. Leading her over to the sofa and taking a seat next to her he puffed out his cheeks as he spoke.

"What is it you want, money? I have plenty though it might take a few days to get it all together."

"Shut your trap!"

"Please, I can get you whatever you want, just name it?"

Ritchie had never begged in his life but that now instantly changed. He would do anything to keep Hilary safe but the knot in his stomach was telling him it was futile.

"This ain't about fucking money you cunt! My brother has spent the last twenty years trying to find out who robbed him, this is about payback and you are going to pay the ultimate price."

Jock moved forward and pulling a roll of duct tape from his pocket he proceeded to bind Ritchie's wrists and ankles. Next, he slapped tape over his victim's mouth and then pulling Hilary to her feet, bound her hands behind her back before throwing her to the floor. At the thought of what he was about to do Jock could feel the first stirring of an erection. Lifting Hilary's dress he roughly pulled down her knickers and when Ritchie realised what was going to happen he cried out from behind the plastic gag but it was useless. He thrashed about on the sofa but there was no chance of release and he was now forced to watch events unfold. Hilary now also had tape over her mouth and tears streamed down her face as Jock unzipped his trousers, released his rock-hard penis and then put on a condom. Kneeling on the floor he forced her leg open and then roughly pushed himself inside her. The pain was evident and the look of agony on her face made Ritchie try again to get free but his assailant knew what he was doing and had a lot of experience at securing victims. Just as he did with the Toms he used, Jock began to punch Hilary in the face and when she thought the attack was almost over, he flipped her and pushed her knees under so that she was bent over. With one savage thrust, he forced himself into her rectum and then climaxed. Jock removed Hilary's ties and then told her to sit beside Ritchie on the sofa. As she looked at her lover his heart broke, she didn't say a word but her tear-stained and pained face spoke volumes. Jock then removed the tape from Ritchie's legs; unbeknown to the victims he was doing as much as he could to ensure a speedy getaway. Ritchie's hands which were still tied but resting in his lap would be left until last so that he couldn't fight in any way. Raising the gun Jock coldly shot Hilary in the forehead, blood and brains sprayed from the back of her head and hit Ritchie's face as he tried to scream out.

"Before I finish I have a message for you. This is

from your brother, you cunt!"

Finally, Jock repeated the shot on Ritchie and then quickly removed the tape from his victim's mouth and wrists. Removing a cotton wool ball and a small bag from his inside jacket pocket Jock wiped the trickle of blood from Ritchie's forehead and then placed it into the bag. Checking round to make sure he had left no evidence, he pulled a baseball cap from his pocket and then quietly left the flat, keeping his head low just in case anyone was watching. When Terry saw him exit the building he started the engine. Jock didn't get in but threw the gun and the small plastic bag through the open window and then continued to walk away. It was now down to Terry to carry out the last part of the plan. Pulling on a pair of gloves he placed the gun under his seat. He then began his journey over to Hitchin, all the time praying that he wouldn't get a pull from the Old Bill. A mile from his destination he pulled up and turned off the headlights. Removing the gun he meticulously cleaned the hand grip and trigger for any prints Jock might have accidently left but hopefully leaving enough of the victims DNA to convince a jury of its previous use. Dressed in black, Terry was almost invisible to any passing traffic as he tucked the gun into his waistband and then made his way along the main road.

Tommy was still waiting when his brother got back to the unit in Little Portugal and the look of relief when he saw Jock was evident.

"You okay Tom, only you're as white as a fucking sheet?"

"Just concerned about you, did it all go to plan?"

"Like a dream Tom and so long as Terry gets his end

done I'd say It's been a success all around."

Tommy Makenzie smiled and then walking over to the filing cabinet, lifted two glasses and a bottle of scotch from the top. Pouring a liberal amount into each tumbler he was champing at the bit to hear every last detail.

"So? Come on then, what did the cunt have to say?"

"Pleaded like a baby, especially for the bird he had with him."

"Bird? What bird?"

"The one he's shacked up with but I made her pay as well. Had a bit of fun with her right in front of him. That cunt went to his grave knowing that his bit of stuff had it up the arse."

For a moment Tommy just stared at his brother. What had gone down hadn't been planned and as much as he wanted his revenge, killing someone who had nothing to do with any of this bothered him.

"You are a sick bastard Jock, what the fuck made you do that."

"Leave it out Tom, I was horny alright and it ain't as if I could leave the tart alive now is it?"

Tommy rubbed his forehead with the palm of his hand. Recently he had come to loathe his brother and the sick fantasies that he acted out. This wasn't a one-off; recently he'd had numerous complaints from pimps that Jock had roughed up some girl or another. Well, there was nothing he could do for the poor woman now, whoever she was but it still bothered him more than he would admit.

"You going home, Tom?"

"I can't, not until Terry gets back and I know all is well. You can get off though and go straight home; I

don't want any extra fucking aggro tonight."
By now Sue was tucked up in bed and snoring softly.
It had been an evening of tears and wine and by the
time she had climbed into bed her head was woozy
and she was desperate for sleep. Since Ritchie had left
it had become a nightly ritual and she knew she had
to get a grip but it was so hard. Now that she lived
alone none of her so-called friends really wanted to
know her. She hadn't heard a word from Danny and
she was desperate to talk to someone, anyone that
would feel sorry for her but there was no one. Sue
thought about phoning Ellie but if her old friend
wasn't forgiving and sorry for her plight, she didn't
think she could take it. Instead, she took two
Zopiclone she'd got from the doctor months ago when
Ritchie was being cruel and lying back on the pillow,
prayed for sleep to come.

Taking his time to walk up the drive, Terry was on
full alert as he looked for anything that could tie him
to the crime he was about to commit. Sure that there
was nothing, he let himself in with the copy key
Tommy had supplied. The house was deathly quiet
and in complete darkness but with foresight, Terry
had thought to bring along a Velcro headlamp.
Slowly walking through the house he listened intently
for any sound and there was nothing until he reached
the bottom of the stairs when he heard Sue snoring
her head off. Slipping his shoes off he made his way
upstairs and slowly going from room to room he
finally found her bedroom. Spying the half glass of
wine and pills on the bedside table Terry knew she
was out for the count. He studied her face which in

294

sleep was now relaxed and now he recognised her. About to gasp, Terry was able to stop himself just in time. It was Sue but his sister had changed dramatically and for just a second but only that, he doubted what he was about to do. If he didn't see this through to the letter then he would have to leave London because the punishment he would receive from Jock and Tommy didn't bare thinking about. Under his breath, he whispered 'Fuck her!' The door to her dressing room was open and walking inside he looked around for a place to hide the gun. There was a pile of four shoe boxes on the floor and lifting off the top three he removed the bottom lid. Next, he removed the gun from his waistband and the plastic bag from his pocket. There was a hairbrush on the dressing table and after daubing the wet blood onto the gun's handle and barrel, Terry pulled a couple of strands of hair from the brush and laid them onto the blood so that they would stick before it dried. Placing the gun in the box and then restacking the others on top he quickly made his exit from the house.

CHAPTER TWENTY-EIGHT

Late that night and after Terry had returned to the unit, Tommy did his part. Using a voice-changing machine and a burner phone, he called the emergency services and reported a possible crime.

"Emergency services, how can I help?"

"Well I'm not sure you can but I was walking past Haversham house in Camden tonight and I saw something strange. A woman was at a window in the corner flat, I would say on the fourth floor and she looked distressed. I then heard a strange noise, it could have been a gun and the woman dropped out of sight. I'm sure I also saw a woman running away from the scene."

"Can I have your name caller?"

Tommy immediately hung up knowing there was no way the police wouldn't investigate. Three hours later and wrapped in each other's arms, Michael and Ellie were deep in sleep when Michael woke up startled. He could hear a loud banging on the pub's back door and at this hour it was never a good thing.

"What is it Molly, what's wrong?"

"Go back to sleep babe, someone's at the door, it's probably just a drunk."

Pulling on his dressing gown, Michael padded down the stairs to the back door and peered through the spy hole. Seeing the uniforms he instantly opened up.

"Good evening Sir. I'm sorry to bother you but we're looking for a Michael Spires?"

"That's me, Officer. What can I do for you? Oh, excuse my manners, please come inside."

PC Fred Warren and WPC Sharon Monroe stepped into the kitchen as Michael closed the door.

"So, what can I do for you at the ungodly hour?" The sarcasm wasn't responded to and after Michael had offered tea which was declined, he took a seat at the table and waited to find out what on earth was going on.

"I'm sorry to inform you that earlier this evening the remains of two bodies were located at a flat in Camden. We believe one of them to be that of your brother Richard."

Ellie was standing in the doorway just as the news was revealed.

"Oh my God!"

Michael was out of his seat in seconds and making his way over to his wife, he stared deeply into her eyes. It was a silent signal telling her not to say another word.

"Mr Spires, we need someone to identify the deceased. Would it be possible for you to accompany us to St Pancras Hospital?"

"What now? Can't it wait until later?"

"Unfortunately not. The death was not through natural causes so we are now in the midst of a murder investigation and the first twelve hours are always crucial."

Michael nodded as he took Ellie's hand and led her back upstairs.

"Oh Michael, what on earth has happened?"

"I know as much as you do darling. Go back to bed and I'll come up as soon as I get back."

A few minutes later he reappeared dressed and eager to finish this. It took just under ten minutes to cover the two-and-a-half-mile journey to the hospital and

Michael was starting to feel sick at the thought of seeing his brother's body. Luckily when they arrived at the mortuary they were shown straight through to a viewing area. When the curtain was drawn back Michael gasped and at the same time silently kept saying to himself 'I'm sorry, I'm sorry'. A few minutes later he was informed by Detective Steve Lemon that it was now a double murder and the second victim was assumed to be Ritchie's girlfriend. Knowing it was only a formality, Michael gave a statement of his whereabouts that night but as he ran a pub and there were numerous witnesses he wasn't questioned further. When he walked through the back door to the pub Ellie was seated at the table and her eyes silently asked a million questions when he entered.

"Yes babe, it was him."

"Did you have a hand in it?"

Taking a seat his expression was pained and for a few moments, she regretted her words until he spoke.

"Not physically but yes, I do know about it."

"Why? Why, would you do such a terrible thing, Molly!?"

Michael didn't reply straight away, he couldn't work out why she was upset and then his brow furrowed as he became angry.

"You ask me fucking why! Because he raped my wife, he fathered my only child and because of that she has gone away and we'll never see her again. How the fuck can you ask me why!?"

Ellie leaned over the table and took his hands as the tears flowed freely down her cheeks.

"Because, it's a life Molly and no matter what he did, you had no right to take it."

Michael didn't elaborate further about the second body. He knew it would come out eventually but for now, he wanted to let the dust settle before causing any more upset.

In Hitchin, Sue had just woken and was coming down the stairs when there was a loud bang on the front door. Checking her appearance in the hall mirror she sighed heavily at her reflection. Black circles encased her eyes, her hair was a mess and she was still in her nightclothes as she opened the door.
"Yes?"
The two plain-clothes detectives gave little away but then Sue spied a patrol car further down the drive which was parked in such a way that no one could get in or out. As they showed their warrant cards a million scenarios flashed through her mind.
"Mrs Susan Spires?"
"Yes, what's happened? Is my Daniel okay?"
"I'm Detective Lemon and this is Detective Kinder. Could we come inside?"
Sue opened the door fully and then made her way along the hall to the kitchen. Steve and Brian followed her but not before Brian motioned for the two uniformed officers, who were now standing beside the car, to come inside.
"What's this about Detectives?"
Sue had placed the kettle on to boil and was now sitting at the breakfast bar hoping that whatever this was all about, it would soon be dealt with.
"I'm sorry to inform you but there was an incident late last night in Camden. A person, who we now know to be your husband, was involved in a shooting."

"Ritchie? He may well be a complete bastard Detective but I can assure you he would never shoot anyone."

"He was the victim Mrs Spires and sadly he didn't make it."

"No, you're wrong!"

The colour instantly drained from Sue's face and her feelings were genuine as the tears began to fall.

Within seconds her mood changed as she realised that she would most probably now inherit everything.

"You mean he's dead!? How do you know it was my Ritchie?"

"His body was identified by his brother earlier this morning."

"Oh, that long steak of piss would say anything. He and that bitch of a wife will do anything to hurt my family."

"I'm sorry to ask you this at such a delicate time, but could you tell us where you have been over the last twenty-four hours?"

Sue couldn't believe what she was hearing and for several seconds her mouth remained open in stunned silence.

"You think I had something to do with it? I swear I didn't, I was here all night."

"Can anyone corroborate that?"

"Well no, I was on my own but I can assure you I was definitely here."

Steve Lemon nodded to the officers who were now standing in the hallway and they began to climb the stairs. After the anonymous call and the mention of a woman being seen leaving the property, he had arranged for a search warrant to be issued before they arrived in Hitchin.

"Where the fuck are they going? Oi! You two, get out of my house and you two can sling your hooks as well."

"I'm Sorry Mrs Spires but we have a search warrant, now if as you say, you had nothing to do with the shooting, then there isn't anything to hide. We will be as quick as possible and I regret having to cause you further grief but we have to follow procedure and it is imperative in a murder case that we act as quickly as possible."

The silence in the kitchen was uncomfortable but a few minutes later when a uniformed officer appeared at the bottom of the stairs and held up a handgun contained in an evidence bag, Sue began to scream.

"Mrs Susan Spires, I am arresting you on suspicion of murder. You have the right to remain silent, you do not have to say anything but it may harm your defence if you do not mention when questioned something which you later rely on in court. Do you understand your rights?"

Sue could only nod her head and at the same time, she started to sob.

"Officer, please place the lady in cuffs. "

When Sue was safely in the patrol car Steve Lemon secured the house and then followed the other vehicle back to the city.

Sue was processed and her fingerprints and DNA were taken but the interview didn't begin for over three hours as it took that long for Draper Hayes, Ritchie's solicitor, to arrive. Given thirty minutes in a private room with Sue, he asked the crucial question.

"Did you do it, Mrs Spires?"

"Of course, I didn't, someone is setting me up."
"Forgive me but I have to ask before we go any further, do you have the appropriate funds to engage my services?"
Sue thought for a moment. She had about thirty grand in the bank but that was about it. If she got off then there would be more than enough to pay his bill, if not, well that wouldn't matter, would it?
"Yes."
"Good, now let's get down to business. Tell me what little you know."
The interview didn't last very long as Draper advised his client to answer no comment to anything asked of her, at least until it was known what evidence they had. Sue was remanded until the following Monday and then at her hearing luck was on her side due to her previous good character and that she was not deemed a flight risk. Draper had worked hard to show Sue in an impeccable light and she was given bail but with strict conditions. The main one was that she had to hand in her passport, was electronically tagged with a curfew set for seven pm until eight am and she had to check in once a day at her local police station. On the steps of the court and although she felt relieved, what bothered Sue more was the possibility of being seen by anyone who knew her.
"When will this come to court, Draper?"
"Hopefully, it won't but until we find out what they have, it's anyone's guess. Do you need a lift home?"
Sue's lip began to quiver as she nodded her head. The drive back was taken in silence but when they reached the house, she was about to get out of the car when he touched her hand.

"Don't go anywhere as they will be here pretty soon to put the tag on. I will pop by in a few days so we can start to plan our defence strategy, earlier if I hear anything regarding evidence, though that is unlikely at this stage."

Again, Sue could only nod as she climbed out of the car and let herself into the house she had thought of as a palace but now held nothing but bad memories. Within an hour of her getting home, there was a knock at the door and the ankle tag was swiftly fitted. Limping through to the kitchen, though the tag was in no way heavy, Sue poured herself a large glass of wine. She was about to get blind drunk in an attempt to forget this horrific mess, if only for a few hours, when she suddenly had a better thought. Changing into trousers so that the tag couldn't be seen she checked the time. There were eight hours left until her seven pm curfew began, more than enough time to get her there and back with time to spare for talking. The one-hour journey to London went without event and pulling up outside the Lamb public house she wondered for a moment if she was doing the right thing. Still, there was no one else she could turn to and if she had to beg Ellie for forgiveness then that's exactly what she was prepared to do. So much water had passed under the bridge and when she thought back to how close they had once been she could feel the tears as they dropped down onto her cheeks. Checking her reflection in the mirror Sue tried to tidy her face, her eyes were red but she couldn't do anything about that. Taking some time to gather her thoughts and calm down a bit, she sat in the car for a further ten minutes until her nerves got so bad that she knew it was now or never, or she would end up driving back home.

CHAPTER TWENTY-NINE

Since receiving the news, Michael and Ellie had been in complete shock, though more on her part than his. Opening the pub was not on the cards, for Ellie, it was down to the fact that it was what the locals would expect and the murder had truly rocked her but for Michael, he was worried that Tommy Makenzie might just stop by and having to explain the situation in detail to his wife would be difficult. Sitting at the kitchen table there was little conversation between the two. They hadn't yet been informed of Sue's arrest or release or when the funeral would be arranged and they both felt lost. It was a momentary happy release when the knock came at the back door but when Michael opened up he was speechless when he saw who was standing there.

"Not going to invite me in?"

Michael didn't speak but held the door open so Sue could enter.

"Hello, Ellie."

Ellie was straight up out of her chair and hugged her old friend to her.

"I'm so sorry to hear about Ritchie, come and sit down."

As if he didn't already know, in that instant Michael saw how loving and compassionate his wife was. After all she had been through and how Sue had treated her in the past, she still had empathy for the woman. Doing as she was asked, Sue took a seat and while Ellie joined her Michael put the kettle on to boil. All the while he was wracking his brain trying to

think of something positive to say and feeling extreme guilt knowing exactly who was to blame.
"So, do they have any idea who did it?"
Sue looked over to where her brother-in-law stood and her brow furrowed for a moment.
"You mean you don't know? They haven't told you both?"
Ellie took hold of her friend's hand and stared deeply into the eyes of a woman who looked like she was carrying the weight of the world on her shoulders.
"Told us what?"
"That I've been charged with Ritchie's murder and that of the whore he was shacked up with."
Raising her leg Sue lifted the bottom of her trousers to reveal the tag.
"What the fuck are they on about, I know you and my brother had a strange marriage but murder him? Never!"
"I just hope a jury sees it like that. They took a gun away from the house but I swear it wasn't mine. I think someone is trying to set me up, well not trying, has succeeded by all accounts."
"You must come and stay with us sweetheart, there's no way my oldest friend is staying in that house on her own."
Sue's tears rapidly began to fall at the show of kindness, the kindness she knew she didn't deserve.
"I can't' Ellie, I have to live at the house, I'm on a curfew and have to report daily to the police station but I thank you from the bottom of my heart for the offer. Have you heard from the kids, only Daniel doesn't know and I have no way of contacting him?"
Ellie slowly shook her head, there had been no word

and she had no idea how to get in touch.

"If we hear anything, I promise I will tell you and also let him know about his dad."

Michael was grateful that she hadn't included Beth in her last sentence because he wouldn't have been able to handle it. Sue slowly drank her tea but within the hour had said her goodbyes and was making her way home. In the pub's kitchen, Ellie repeatedly tapped her index finger on the table top. It was something she had done for years whenever there was something on her mind. Michael knew the sign and was dreading what she would ask or even how he would answer.

"What's up love?"

Sighing heavily, she stared across the table as she spoke and her eyes never left his.

"How much were you involved in all of this?"

"Excuse me?!"

"Don't you dare Molly? It's no coincidence that you find out about the rape and about Beth not being yours and....."

"And?"

"Well, you've already said you knew something about it, so how exactly are you tangled up in it all?"

Ellie stopped mid-sentence when she saw the hurt look her words had caused and she was sorry but not sorry enough to stop questioning him.

"Suddenly Ritchie gets killed, though I don't have the faintest idea why Sue had to be involved and you don't think I should want to know what part you played in it all?"

"You're being stupid Ell."

Standing up she slammed the flat of her hand down onto the table.

"If you don't tell me then this marriage is over!" Storming off, she made her way up the stairs and took a seat on the bed. Everything was falling apart and she didn't have a clue how to stop it. It was a few hours before the bedroom door slowly opened and walking inside, Michael took a seat beside his wife who by now had fallen asleep.

"Ellie, you awake?"

"Depends if you're ready to tell me everything or not?"

"Okay, I'll tell you but you won't like it."

Ellie just looked at him and Michael knew he had to tell her and be honest about the details or that would be it.

"Remember when Beth was born and we'd just robbed that large haul of drugs? What we didn't realise was who we robbed them from. I know it's irrelevant as we then got robbed ourselves but it turned out they were the property of another London firm, the Frazier's. Anyway, a couple of years ago this bloke started drinking here, about once a month it was and he seemed like a decent geezer, a quiet, kept himself to himself kind of bloke. After a while, I found out it was Tommy Frazier, head of that firm we robbed. Over time we got friendly, not besties or anything but we'd watch the odd match together on a quiet night and he seemed okay."

Michael stopped for a moment, scared about what he was about to say but Ellie digging him the ribs forced him to continue.

"Seems this Tommy geezer has always been desperate to find out who stole his drugs and even all these years later he still wanted revenge. When I found out about what Ritchie had done to you and then when you told me about Beth well, I kind of fucking lost the plot, Ell. I ended up spilling my guts to Frazier one night when I'd had a few too many jars."

Michael bent over and placed his head in his hands.
"I swear I didn't know it would go this far babe."
"Just tell me the rest will you."
"Well, I told him our story and he offered to sort Ritchie out. At that moment I wanted him dead Ellie and then I told Tommy about the robbery. Maybe I hoped he'd kill me as well. I was in so much fucking pain and if I'm honest, I didn't want to live and I know that's selfish and I wasn't thinking about you but you wanted the truth. Strangely Tommy said I'd suffered enough and he had no plans for me but Ritchie was a different kettle of fish."
"So how did Sue get involved in all of this?"
"When we were talking, I told him what a cunt she had been, how she had whispered in Ritchie's lug about us and it was probably the real reason we split. I didn't think any more about it but obviously after tonight's little revelation we know who has set her up. I can't do anything, can't say anything without incriminating myself. You probably think I should, that I deserve it but you don't know these people, sweetheart. I wouldn't last five minutes on the inside and then they would come after you and this place. I'm not trying to justify things but before tonight, we both hated her and just because she's been charged with murder nothing should change our feelings. Remember what a cunt she was to you, Ellie!"
"I know but there's no way she should be made to

suffer for something you've done."

Michael stood up and crossing his hands he put them on the top of his head as he began to pace the floor. "So what should I do? It's me or her Ellie and you won't be able to visit me as I'll be six foot under." The conversation stopped there, Ellie was drained and climbing into bed she turned off the lamp leaving her husband standing in the dark.

Several weeks later but to Sue it felt like a lifetime had passed since she'd been charged, she had begun to rebuild her life again but it was nothing like before. She now did her own cleaning as Ritchie's bank accounts had been frozen so she was living on what money she had and needed to make it last. There was still no word from Danny, he didn't even know that his father had died but there was nothing she could do about that. The funeral had been allowed to go ahead on a Friday, two months after the murders but it was a sad affair. Supported by Ellie and Michael, the members of Ritchie's firm all sneered at her as she walked to the front of the church to take her seat. Michael leaned over and whispered in Ellie's ear 'So much for innocent until proven guilty'. The look she gave him was one of disgust, he immediately looked away and at the same time regretted his choice of words. The case date was set and proceedings were to begin on the Monday after, Sue was just glad that she had at least been able to bury her husband.

Scheduled to last for six days, the case was long and drawn out as Sue was determined to plead not guilty. Ellie had sat in the court every day and listened intently to the damning evidence. Even some of Sue's so-called friends had put the boot in by testifying against her. They told stories of her excessive spending and bragging which gave the prosecution even more reason to state that she was angry at losing access to her husband's money. When Sue got on the stand they tore her to pieces and her barrister did little better. The final nail in her coffin came when she was asked about Hilary Parker. Sue was honest and said that they had come to an agreement and that as long as Ritchie stayed married, Sue was happy to turn a blind eye. The look on some of the juror's faces spoke volumes and even before their deliberation, they had found her guilty. Out for just twenty minutes, when the twelve returned Sue stared at her barrister desperate for him to smile but his face was solemn and set in stone. The foreman was asked to stand and when asked for the verdict the man loudly announced 'Guilty Your Honour'.

Ellie, who was sitting in the gallery, felt her heart drop and as she looked across the room to her friend, Sue's tears were flowing freely. An adjournment had been expected and for the court to resume at a later date for sentencing but the Judge concluded it wasn't necessary. Sue was told to stand when the judge addressed her.

"Susan Anne Spires, you have been found guilty of murder and the heinous crime was made worse by the fact that it was carried out in rage against a man who was your husband and father of your child. You then continued to take the life of an innocent woman. This court can find no pity and you will be incarcerated at Her Majesty's pleasure for life. Furthermore I am making a recommendation that you should serve a term of no less than twenty years. Officer, take her down."

Before the court officers could reach her, Sue fainted. Ellie screamed out and the judge banged his gavel for order. Ellie felt sick, guilty and somewhat responsible but what could she do?

When she reached the Lamb and let herself into the back kitchen she could hear all the noise and revelry coming from the bar. It sounded busy but she did not attempt to go through and help her husband. It was a good thirty minutes before Michael came into the kitchen and found her sitting at the table with a large glass of brandy clasped in her hands. He'd heard her when she'd first come in but the place was so busy that he hadn't had a minute to spare.

"Well?"

"Fucking well! How dare you, that poor cow got life with a minimum of twenty years and it's all your fault!"

Michael grabbed her hands forcing her to release the glass as he pulled her to her feet.

"What did you want me to do Ellie? To confess would mean the death of me, I told you that. I know it's terrible but at least Sue is still alive and maybe in the future they will find a way to get her out. I'm gutted over this but there's nothing I can do."

The following few weeks were tense between the couple but over time things, to some extent, started to get back to normal but Ellie could never look at Michael in the same light. The deep love and trust she felt for him had died but she had no alternative than to stay. Her only child was gone and her poor old mum's health was going downhill fast so she had little left in life but to continue serving drinks and smiling to punters, punters who were completely unaware of how heartbroken their landlady was.

THE END

EPILOGUE

Ellie and Michael continued running the pub and shortly after Ritchie's funeral, Ellie's mum Eileen moved into Beth's old room. Diagnosed with early onset dementia, it didn't take too long, much to Ellie and Michael's relief, for her to stop asking where her granddaughter was. Sadly they only heard from Beth and Danny once over the following year. A small photograph of a chubby baby and a short note with no return address stated that a beautiful baby boy had been born a few months earlier. They had named him Joey and he was perfectly healthy. At the end of that year and after Sue's trial, Michael had instructed a private investigator to find the couple but every avenue had drawn a blank. Danny still didn't know that his father was dead and that he had inherited a vast sum of money and property, in British Law a person cannot gain from murder so Sue was now penniless. The house in Hitchin would remain empty for many years and would eventually fall into disrepair.

Sue Spires was incarcerated at HMP Bronzefield on the outskirts of Ashford in Surrey. Purpose-built, it was actually the largest female prison in Europe. Known for its lax regime, sadly that wasn't the case for Sue, due to her 'restricted status' as a murderer she was watched more closely than many of the other prisoners. She didn't take part in any educational courses on offer nor did she socialise with the other inmates. Instead, she spent all of her time alone in her cell. Her only visitor and it was more out of a sense of duty than love, was Ellie. Thankfully there was a regular train service from London but the visits were still only fortnightly. Every time the women met the first thing Sue would ask was if there had been any news from Daniel but the answer was and would always remain a heart-breaking 'no'. Recently Ellie had noticed a change in her old friend, Sue seemed to repeat herself a lot, would stop talking mid-sentence and gaze across the room as if she was momentarily in another place, another life even. There wasn't anything Ellie could do to help her and she just hoped that wherever Sue's mind had wandered to, it was a happy place and at least brought her some peace.

Tommy Makenzie continued to run his violent firm but he never ventured into the Lamb again. He would reign as head of the villains for a further three years but eventually, his luck ran out. After an anonymous tip-off was received, a raid was carried out on the unit in Little Portugal and both he and Jock were in attendance so they were caught red-handed with enough cocaine and heroin to service the whole of London. Both of them were given a thirty-year sentence and much to the happiness of the local residents, would probably never see freedom again. It finally left Brian Makenzie able to live his life how he chose and with whom he chose without the fear of his brothers finding out.

As for Danny, Beth and baby Joey, they lived in a small cottage in a remote part of northern France and hoped to remain there for the rest of their lives. They had both learned to speak basic French and had become valued members of the local community. Danny worked as a farm labourer and Ellie cleaned part-time at a large chateau. Financially they just about managed but money or the lack of it never seemed to bother them. After much deliberation, they had decided not to reveal the truth to Joey regarding his parentage, not unless it was absolutely necessary for some medical reason, to do so would only bring him heartbreak. Danny and Beth accepted that their lives were a lie but the love they had was too strong and no matter what, the forbidden fruit they shared was too valuable to ever let go of.

Printed in Great Britain
by Amazon

57464326R00185